I0603342

FREE

The *Luminous* Pearl

A R I A N A
K E D D I E

Free – The Luminous Pearl.

Book 3 (Bound by Infidelity trilogy)

Published by Ilomilo Press

Copyright © 2020 Ariana Keddie

All rights reserved.

ISBN: 9780648836759 (eBook Edition)

ISBN: 9780648836735 (Paperback Edition)

Ariana Keddie asserts her right to be identified as the author.

This book is a work of fiction derived from the imagination of the author. For the sake of realism certain locales, business names, events and places have been used, but have been done so in a fictitious manner. Any resemblance to a true event or business is purely coincidental. Any character or name resembling a person, alive or dead, is also purely coincidental.

The contents here within are explicit and adult in nature. Some scenes or themes may affect sensitive readers. Reader discretion is advised.

No part of this publication may be reproduced, distributed, or transmitted in any form or by any means, including photocopying, recording, or other electronic or mechanical methods, without the prior written permission of the author and or publisher, except in the case of brief quotations embodied in critical reviews and certain other non-commercial uses permitted by copyright law.

Draft edit – Chelsea Kuhel MS Editing Services

Final edit – Marni MacRae and Julia Davies

Final proof read – Amber Kleesh and Joanne Thompson

Cover design by David Prendergast @ Reedsy. Photo complements of Pixabay

ALSO BY ARIANA KEDDIE

(Bound by Infidelity Trilogy)

LURED - The Unrivaled Serpent

BOUND - The Catalytic Rose

FREE - The Luminous Pearl

For my children.
Thanks for believing in me.

1

HIGH ENOUGH

I've never been to a sex club before, so I'm surprised when the taxi weaves its way around an industrial estate then pulls up outside a plain concrete building. The entrance looks like a warehouse office, but unless staff are allowed impromptu parties, the red hue emanating from inside and the slight pulse of music are a dead giveaway as to what's really going on. There are no signs to say what the club is called, and I don't bother to ask Rebecca, who has been laughing and joking with Alex the whole hour it's taken to get us here, because I have no intention of ever returning.

I'd remained quiet for the most part. Opting to watch the world whirl by while we passed through suburbs then hit the highway en route to Hollywood—apparently.

It was a sobering experience, and the longer I sat in silence listening to Rebecca during the ride in, the more foolish I felt. I have no business going clubbing when my husband is out of town, let alone with another man and his *ex-girlfriend.*

Rebecca has spent the entire time reminding Alex about their past, people they once knew, and reminiscing about their school days. She tried to include me in on their conversation, but I had nothing to contribute. My life seems so trite and uneventful in comparison. She'd ended their witty bantering with a list of things she swore to do before she dies. All of which sounded exciting and so out of my reach. Me being stuck in matrimonial bliss and all. To say I'm feeling a little envious would be an understatement.

Shifting off my tender butt cheek, to relieve the pressure on the raised flesh from where Gerard's belt had made contact last night, I retrieve my purse from beside me and get ready to exit the car. I must be a closet thrill-seeker really. What if there's someone inside that I know? But Rebecca's excitement is contagious. She giggles and flirts as she hands over her credit card to the taxi driver and pays. Suddenly, I'm feeling elated and a bunch of butterflies wreak havoc. Inside that building is a whole world of taboo that I'm just dying to see now.

Outside the taxi, I shiver and grab hold of my pant legs to keep them from soaking up the rain puddles, then dash through the drizzle before Alex is pulling open the reflective glass doors for Rebecca and me to enter. Just as I'm passing him, he grabs my arm.

"If you don't want to go in, you can wait here. I'll just hook Rebecca up with her friend. Then we can go." Alex gestures toward a leather couch in front of a red-painted brick wall covered in a variety of framed notices explaining the club's etiquette and some pop art depicting sex symbols through the ages. Ranging from the late 30s, there's a picture of Marilyn Monroe, Grace Kelly, Brigitte Bardot, and Jayne Mansfield, with Ursula Andress being the most recent. I think. All amazing likenesses, and with their names scrawled across the background it confirms I'm right in guessing who they are.

"Paige?" Alex jolts me to attention, just in time to notice

Rebecca disappearing through a large black door to our left. I glance at the couch then back to Alex. Now that we're here, it's too tempting not to take look for myself.

"No, I'll come along."

Once through the door, the dull sound of music comes from behind another closed door next to a desk. This reception room is also painted red and hosts a row of lockers against one wall.

Rebecca confirms our invitation with a bald-headed guy covered in tattoos. He sizes up both Alex and me before holding out his hand for ID and asking all of us to sign some sort of waiver. When I hesitate, Alex squeezes my hand.

"We can still leave."

"No, you're not. Come on, you guys. Hang with us. It'll be fun. Besides, Paige is curious. Aren't you, Paige?" Rebecca chimes in.

I give a small shrug and look up at Alex, who has raised an eyebrow in questioning. From the look on his face, he's not bothered either way, but that just piques my interest more. Is this suddenly something he doesn't want me to see?

Without a debate, Rebecca snatches hold of my hand to tug me along as she pushes through the door and into a scene straight out of Beyoncé's music-clip, 'Haunted.' There are long red drapes hanging at intervals on either side of floor-to-ceiling wooden wall panels, around the large room. Framed mirrors are everywhere, but when my eyes settle on the one closest to me, I realize it's not a mirror but a window that looks down a hallway. I swivel my head, trying to make sense of it. But before I can grasp the illusion fully, Alex is pulling me close and blocking my view.

The club isn't loud. I expected music to be thumping, to see couples drinking, dancing wildly, and sex taking place. The only thing that meets my expectations is the dim lighting and what some guests are wearing. It feels more like an intimate costume party than a nightclub filled with strangers.

Wedged between them, I make Alex and Rebecca walk painfully slow so I can assess the scene. I imagine I must look like a meerkat because I'm twisting my head in all directions and drawing attention. But as curious as I am, I'm starting to have second thoughts about hanging around. Everyone is so uninhibited, it's scary.

Rebecca grips my hand and leans into me, momentarily resting her chin on my shoulder. "It's okay. Nobody will bite. That is unless, you want them to." She must smile because her chin digs in against my bone. I twist and catch the naughty glint in her eyes before she gives me a big grin and tugs me onward.

Everything looks opulent, but dominating the room are two skilled dancers who hold my immediate attention. Their lithe bodies look magnetized to poles anchored to both the floor and the sky-high black ceiling. Lining a backlit bar are stools that look polished and shine like expensive Italian leather. Some are vacant and others nest bums. There's only one bartender, and it seems all he is doing, is filling water jugs with ice. Ultraviolet lighting has turned everything white, bright and the seductive clothing everyone is wearing is quite captivating. Silk gowns, crisp white shirts with loose-laid ties. Stilettos and thigh-high boots seem to be the favor. There are sequins and lace and ladies wearing their hair braided or in sleek ponytails. Pleather corsets, skin-tight underwear, chains, cuffs, and latex is everywhere. Rebecca fits right in.

Alex presses his hand to the small of my back. "Just tell me when you want to leave." He reaches around further to take hold of my waist in reassurance.

"It's okay. But look what they're wearing. I think we need

to go home and change," I whisper, my attention still held by a nightlife I've been selectively ignorant to.

"You don't have to dress up, but like I said the other day, I think you'd look good in latex," Alex murmurs close to my ear, letting his hand slide until he is playing with my ass.

"I see Kaitlyn. I'll get drinks," Rebecca announces, letting go off my hand and heading to the bar.

"Is this the type of place you mean when you say you go clubbing, Alex?" I ask, scared now that the haze of lust surrounding me when it comes to Alex might be similar to why I fell for Gerard. My flaw being—I fall in love with the thought of a person without seeing who they really are.

"Sometimes. Let's find a seat," he suggests, taking my hand. I'm not sure if I'm disappointed or intrigued by this new level of knowledge. I mean, it's obvious the man has experience, but the thought of Alex decked out in leather, chains, and whips just doesn't seem to gel, and I can't stop ogling everyone as he leads the way.

The people we come across blatantly size Alex and me up. Their salacious smiles turning into lustful pouts as we pass. I've never seen such a display of eroticism. Couples and groups are freely caressing each other as they talk amongst themselves, and there is a steady stream of people heading down a flight of stairs that intrigues me. Before I know it, my palm is sweating in Alex's hand. I grip him tighter and I don't let go until he slides into a vacant booth. He pulls me in and draws me close. The warmth of his body and deep steady breathing is reassuring, and then I'm aware of the effects the drug I took earlier is having on me. All my senses are heightened. Even my face feels fuzzy.

I look up from under Alex's chin then down at my hand resting on his thigh. It feels like I'm melting into his flesh and I let out a giggle from the strangeness of it all.

"Rebecca gave me Molly before we left your place. I hope I don't do anything crazy."

"Jesus, you don't need that shit."

"I know. But this is the best I've felt in months, maybe even years, or even ever. I had no idea drugs felt this good."

"Yeah, well, Rebecca shouldn't have given it to you."

"She said you'd like me high on it."

Alex rolls his eyes, then turns his attention to the crowd until he settles on Rebecca and her friend. Kaitlyn is the shorter of the two, with tanned skin and on the voluptuous side compared to Rebecca. I glance up at Alex again. He can't seem to take his eyes off them.

"Look at her. She's so fucking out there." He shakes his head. "Sometimes I think she just does it for attention."

Kaitlyn is standing on her toes, trying to reach for something over the bar, and Rebecca is using the opportunity to slide a hand along the back of Kaitlyn's thigh and push her short skirt higher to reveal a round, meaty butt cheek. Kaitlyn, unfazed, wiggles on her toes as if encouraging Rebecca. I can't tear my eyes away. Heat travels not only to my face, but everywhere.

"Are you jealous or something?" I ask, pulling away from him so I can study his expression, praying I'm not going to regret being here. It would be my worst nightmare come true —Alex crushing on someone else.

"Not at all. I just can't believe it's the same chick I grew up with. She was always straight. Not that I give a fuck. She can do whatever she wants. I just worry where she's headed."

"Oh. Well, maybe she's just putting on a show for you. Is she still in love with you, do you think?"

Alex's head snaps around, and he frowns. "No romance there, Princess. We're just friends. Nah, I think she's putting on a show for you, actually."

"Me?" I gasp, taking her in again, then flush in

embarrassment when Rebecca looks our way. I quickly divert my attention back to Alex, but I'm sure she caught me gawking.

"Was Rebecca who you went to visit when we were in the city together?"

Alex nods.

I need to make a conscious effort to relax my mouth. It's not because I'm annoyed, but for some reason, I can't stop clenching my jaw, and my mouth is so parched, my tongue feels like a piece of beef jerky.

"God, I feel feverish," I comment, gripping onto the table to pull myself upright again so I can fan my jumpsuit.

Alex chuckles. "That will teach you for taking drugs."

I give him a nudge in the stomach before my attention returns to Rebecca and her friend, wondering if Alex is serious about her showing off for me. Suddenly, I'm panicked that Gerard may have tried calling. I reach into my purse for my phone to check. He hasn't called, but the guilt that I'm out with Alex makes me feel sick, and I stare absently at the screen. I'm such an untrustworthy hypocrite.

Suddenly, there's a man standing beside us. "No phones," he snaps, drawing Alex's attention to me holding my phone.

"Sorry I was…"

"No phones. Lock it and leave it in your purse. Any calls are to be taken or made out in the foyer."

"Okay, okay." I slip my phone back into my purse. It's only when I've snapped it shut and put it on the far side of the table does the security guy leave.

"Christ, that's a bit over the top. What is this place?"

"Photos can be used against someone. *Especially* in a place like this," Alex explains.

"Well, I wasn't going to take photos. I was just seeing if Gerard tried to call."

My admission puts the scowl back on Alex's face. He

stiffens before his attention goes back to the girls at the bar, and the hand I place back on his thick thigh doesn't seem to register my apology because he snaps out,

"Wish she'd hurry up with those fucking drinks."

We sit quietly for some time, taking in the music which seems to meld with the scene that's at the bar. Rebecca is still caressing Kaitlyn's ass, making large circles on her bare flesh and with one boot heel poised on a barstool footrest, she sways to the music, daring and enticing Rebecca to do more. Rebecca looks our way again. I feel my embarrassment for only a split second before it gives way to a heady erotic feeling and I'm imagining myself in Kaitlyn's place, Rebecca stroking and caressing my ass. I'm there at the bar, and Alex is watching me with her. Is that something Alex would like to see? Me with another girl.

"Kiss me, Alex," I murmur, pulling myself onto his lap. "I need to feel your lips. I miss them."

"Is that right?" Uncertainty lingers in his squinting gaze, but he shifts in his seat to accommodate me. Then he's laughing. "You're high."

Relieved by the shift in tension, my mouth meets his and I let myself get lost on his lips until they're tingling and melt, and I can't discern the difference between his lips and mine. I forget everything. It's just me and Alex, our uniform breathing and the music. When he pulls back, I'm left breathless and giddy. I open my eyes slowly. Alex is watching me, searching my eyes and drinking me in.

"I love it when you do that, Alex. When you search inside for my soul."

"Is that what I'm doing, is it?"

I nod dreamily and stroke his face without an ounce of inhibition.

"You're just rolling."

"Is that what they call it? God, I'm so high, it feels

amazing. I want to know everything about you, Alex. Tell me everything. I just want to hear your voice. I love the sound of your voice. Do you know how often you're on my mind?"

Alex shakes his head, still amused by me.

"All the time. Every day, even when I'm asleep, I hear your voice. I honestly can't get you out of my head. What you said earlier about how I feel around Gerard, you're right, and I don't care if you're a player. I only care that you want me around."

"I'm a player, am I?" His mouth curves downward, his head nodding slightly as though in mock agreement.

"Gerard's words, not mine." I squirm on his lap, desperate to get closer. Alex wraps his arms around me tightly to still me, then plants a kiss on my forehead.

Lingering there, he whispers against my skin. "Well, don't believe everything you hear. Anyway, I should get our drinks. Rebecca doesn't seem to be in any hurry." He sounds a little curt, like I've hurt his feelings. Not knowing what to say, I slide off his lap and stand. I look toward the bar.

Rebecca now has Kaitlyn's skirt around her waist, her ass exposed, and my eyes dart around to see if anyone else is watching. I'm siding with Alex—Rebecca seems to love the attention she's getting because she's teasing two men sitting at the bar who seem to be enjoying the salacious act.

I look at Alex again, take in his eyes, his nose, his delectable lips. I brush the back of my fingers along his stubble then weave my fingers through his hair and give his head a tug.

"Do you enjoy watching girls get it on, Alex?"

"Doesn't every guy?" My breath hitches when his hand is suddenly between my legs, feeling me. I know I must be hot to the touch because he smirks and presses harder.

"I don't know." I glance back at Rebecca and her friend.

"But I suppose it looks erotic enough." I turn back and face Alex. "I've never been with a girl."

"No shock there, Princess. But it sounds like I shouldn't have brought you here. I'll turn you wicked."

"Maybe I enjoy being wicked around you, Alex," I tease, pressing against his hand still between my thighs. "This is—interesting," I say, looking around again.

"You think so?" He pulls his hand away and slaps my butt. "I think I need to get you out of here to keep you pure."

"Pfft. Bit late for that. No, I want to stay awhile. As long as I'm here with you, I feel safe."

"I'm right here, Paige." Alex reaches for me again and pulls me closer, his chin resting on my belly. "You know, you look pretty fucking sexy tonight." He drops a kiss between the opening of my jumpsuit, right below my necklace, then pulls back to take the piece of jewelry between his fingers to study it.

I could honestly push him back on the booth seat and throw myself at him right now. It's crazy how relaxed I feel around him, and all I want to do, is make him happy. I glance toward the bar again. Kaitlyn's skirt has returned to its rightful place, and both she and Rebecca are sitting on barstools talking.

"How about I go get the drinks?" I suggest, grabbing my purse and stepping away. Snatching me back, Alex pulls me onto his lap before his mouth dives onto my neck, kissing and nibbling me hungrily then cupping a hand to my breast with a growl. I giggle and look around the room, suddenly conscious that people could be watching us.

"No, I think I should take you back to the beach house and fuck you," he whispers into my ear. "But all right. We'll have one drink, then go."

I stay there in his arms for a moment, enjoying the closeness, the eagerness of him because the drug in my system seems to turn reality into a fantasy that eludes to no consequences. I know I shouldn't be behaving so uninhibited in public with him. There could be people here who know me and Gerard. Everyone is so dressed up, I'm certain I wouldn't recognize anyone, even up close. For a brief second I feel anxious and paranoid that I don't know what I'm doing, but then my feet seem to have a will of their own, and soon, I'm drifting toward the girls at the bar, faking confidence I don't own.

I'm only halfway across the length of the room before a man and woman approach me, halting me in my path. The woman tucks her fine silver blonde hair behind an ear and smiles, then starts fiddling with the top button of her short silk dress that looks authentically Asian. She nudges her partner who is bald, middle-aged, and reminds me of Vin Diesel, though not as robust. I notice the way he is holding his glass tumbler, looking slightly on the feminine side. When he speaks, it confirms my suspicions.

"Well, hello, sweetie," he playfully oozes the noun. "My name is Howie." He runs a hand down my left arm as he makes the introduction then tilts his glass toward his companion. "And this here is Carol."

"Hello." I feel awkward and throw a look back at Alex. To my horror, he is no longer sitting at the booth. I scan around quickly, trying to locate him, and as if people are becoming aware of my presence, they stop talking and look at me for a moment before resuming with their conversations.

"This must be your first time here? Because we..." Ignoring Howie for a moment, I look ahead at the bar for reassurance and see Rebecca and Kaitlyn still seated. I calm myself and draw in a deep breath then turn my attention back to Howie.

"... and we've been watching you over there with your boyfriend and just couldn't tear our eyes away. You're just gorgeous, sweetie," Vin Diesel's doppelganger says, running a finger along the edge of his glass then reaching out to touch my hair.

"Ahh, thanks, I guess."

"What he means to say is, would you'd like to join us in one of the back rooms?" Carol asks, getting straight to the point.

When my eyes go wide, Howie slaps her arm playfully and scolds, "You're meant to ease into questions like that, Carol. God," he says on an exhale. "Now look at her, she's scared."

"What? Oh, sorry, no. I'm just here with friends. I don't do…" I pull a tight apologetic smile. "Stuff—like this."

"You can bring your boyfriend along if you like," Carol suggests, looking around, I assume for Alex, and I'm betting it's the real reason they're inviting me to join them.

"I don't think so. Sorry, I should go. I'm on drink duty."

"Well, if you change your mind, just come looking for us," Howie says, taking a sip from his straw and eyeing me seductively.

Ignoring them, I wander over to Rebecca and when I reach the girls, they are already studying my expression.

"Oh, my God. Did you see that couple trying to hit on me?" I laugh, then take a seat next to Rebecca.

"Well, duh, that's why we're all here," Kaitlyn says, cutting me down sarcastically.

Rebecca slaps her thigh. "Get down bitch, be humble." Rebecca turns back to me, an apologetic grimace clouding her features. "Don't mind Kaitlyn here, she's possessed by the devil himself."

"Ha, she should hook up with Gerard," I mumble under my breath, putting my purse down and looking for the bartender.

"However." Rebecca keeps speaking. "Paige, Kaitlyn. Kaitlyn, Paige."

"Hello. Nice to meet you." I hold out my hand for Kaitlyn. She takes it then pulls firmly so I'm stretched out over the bar in front of Rebecca, then puts her lips around one of my fingers. I snatch my hand back and fall onto my stool. Rebecca laughs, then slaps Kaitlyn again.

"Stop it, you're frightening her."

In an instant, beads of sweat are dampening my brow and I'm swiveling on my stool looking for Alex. Thankfully, he has returned and is watching us from the shadows of the booth. I give him a little wave. He gestures in return by rocking his wrist in front of his face, encouraging me to get our drinks.

"Kaitlyn is just playing around. Aren't you, babe?"

"I am. It's nice to meet you, Paige," Kaitlyn says. I reward her with a friendlier smile. "Bec tells me you've only just met."

"We had dinner. Rebecca cooked. And—it was excellent."

Rebecca growls and rolls her eyes. "Call me Bec."

"Sorry, Bec it is."

"Bartender," Kaitlyn hollers, clicking her fingers to get the bare-chested male attendant's attention. "We ladies are getting a little dry over here, sir."

Waltzing over as he polishes a glass, the guy looks like he stepped off the edge of a calendar page. "Well, there's two ways I can fix that, ladies," he suggests, winking then placing the glass and towel on the bar. "One, I could serve you drinks, or two, I could take each one of you out the back and fuck you until you come."

We all burst out laughing. Me from shock.

"You know I'm serious." He elbows the wooden surface the drills his eyes into Rebecca.

Kaitlyn rises on her stool and leans over the bar,

intercepting his gaze. He twists his head attempting to stare her down.

"Maybe we don't like cock," she says coyly.

Rebecca twists her stool slightly, so she has access to Kaitlyn's ass again, and I watch in disbelief as she runs her hand between her friend's thighs.

"Girlfriend," she says sweetly, catching the bartender's eye. "You're not dry at all." With Rebecca's hand hidden under her friend's skirt and Kaitlyn gyrating her hips, I can only imagine what Rebecca is doing under there. I'm embarrassed to admit it's all very arousing.

"Well then, I guess I only need to service your mouths then." The bartender concludes standing straight. "What'll you have?"

We order our drinks sending the bartender on his way. Then I'm reaching for the pitcher of iced water to pour a glass then drink it down in one go. "I'm so thirsty, it ridiculous."

Rebecca leans into me. "That's the Molly," she whispers, placing a hand on my thigh. "What do you think of the place, is it how you imagined?" She licks her lips, drawing my attention to the shape of her pretty face.

"A little. I can see I've lived a slightly sheltered life though. At least… the latter part." I glance around the room, letting my voice trail off. Rebecca squeezes my leg. She has lost her smile, and her eyes cloud over.

She nods knowingly. "Tough childhood?"

I pull an awkward smile because I really don't want to get into it. Not here, not now. In fact, not ever if I can help it.

"Me too. But we can't let that shit weigh us down." Rebecca lifts a shoulder and tilts her chin, exuding confidence that's hard not to admire. "Just party harder, is my motto."

I cover her hand with mine and squeeze, but when

Kaitlyn notices my gesture, she hisses. Abruptly, I remove my hand. Rebecca's quick to respond by slapping Kaitlyn forcefully on the thigh.

"Stop being a bitch, it's not funny anymore. I'll need to punish you if you keep it up." She giggles and makes a joke, which lightens the mood somewhat. At least I think she's joking.

"Promises, promises," Kaitlyn says, dispelling the doubt which has my mind going in all directions.

"I'm going to look downstairs. Want to come with me, Paige? It's interesting," Rebecca asks, taking hold of the drink the bartender places down in front of us.

"No. I'll stay with Alex." I stand, then pick up the Budweiser I ordered for Alex. "Do you want to come to sit with us, Kaitlyn?" I offer hesitantly, knowing I'm not winning her over because Rebecca seems to pay me way too much attention.

"No, I'm good. I like it at the bar." She takes hold of her glass, but she seems to be sulking. I'm about to turn away when Rebecca presses herself behind me, pushing me up against the bar. Kaitlyn looks out the corner of her eyes and rolls her shoulders over her drink.

"I like you, Paige. You're cute but way too innocent," Rebecca whispers, her breath tickling my ear. I sense Kaitlyn's not happy about Rebecca's flirtatious remark by the way she's squeezing her glass.

"I—should go. Alex is waiting."

"Alex is waiting all right, but it's not for his drink," Rebecca purrs, sliding her hands around my waist, her mouth coming closer to my ear again. "You know, he can't stop talking about you, Paige?"

"Really?" I pull back and stare at her, then glance at Alex again.

"But you know what you're doing to him is cruel, right?"

Her remarks hit its target. Suddenly I'm finding something interesting about the floor and rubbing my forehead.

"Hey!" Rebecca lifts my chin with a finger. "I'm just saying. Alex is one of the good ones, you know. He's like a brother to me, and I don't want to see him get hurt. I know you care about him and everything. But I mean, what's with this guy you're married to? Is he an asshole or what?"

"What do you mean?"

Rebecca gives me a look that tells me she's not naïve about what's going on.

I glance over at Alex, who seems to watch us intently, wondering if he asked Rebecca to have a word with me, why he asked me to come out.

Rebecca shrugs and takes another sip, then smiles at Kaitlyn. "Let me guess something?" she says, turning her attention back to me, her eyes roaming over my face, her head tilting from side to side like she's trying to figure something out. "I bet you're a Gemini."

"Libra."

"Hah, so is Kaitlyn. I wonder if you kiss the same." Taking a finger and thumb, she pinches my chin and licks her fiery lips. I can feel Kaitlyn watching and try to look, but Rebecca keeps my face directed at her, gently swiveling me so my back is to Kaitlyn, and I'm now looking at Alex instead. He's watching intently but flicks his gaze across the room. Rebecca taps my chin to get my attention back.

I don't know if it's because I'm rolling, as Alex put it, but I find Rebecca both alluring and intoxicating. She's mysterious yet transparent. Calm but exciting. She's like Alex. A contradiction. The longer she gazes at me, the heavier I'm breathing.

"Let me take you on a tour of this place."

"What?" I murmur in a daze.

"I want to show you what you've been missing since you've been tangled up in matrimonial bullshit."

Then her lips are coming closer, and I do nothing to stop her. When her lips reach mine, she teases, nipping gently, then runs a tongue between my lips. I pull back, shocked by her forward gesture.

"You taste like coconut," she whispers. "I like it. What could you taste?" She searches my eyes.

"Um… Bubble—gum. I think." I'm shocked that I let her kiss me. I stare at her lips, mesmerized by the memory. How they tasted and how soft they felt.

Rebecca is a canvas of lust. Licking then rubbing her lips, satisfied. I look nervously in Alex's direction. Even though Rebecca made the advance, it feels like a betrayal, nevertheless. I twist around and catch Kaitlyn chuckling and wonder what's so funny.

"Sorry," Rebecca apologizes. "It's the Molly. It makes me just love everybody." She rubs my arms. "Kaitlyn, can you take Paige's purse and our drinks to the table, please? I'm taking her on a tour of the place. Can you let Alex know where we're going?"

"What—fucking—ever. Maybe I'll suck his cock while we're waiting."

I hope she's not serious. Would Alex let her? Not giving me a chance to see if Kaitlyn even goes over to Alex, Rebecca takes my hand firmly and leads me away. When we're out of earshot she says, "Seriously, that woman drives me crazy sometimes. We aren't even dating, and she's possessive as all hell."

I don't comment, and I'm sure I look like the newbie I am as I'm taken along a darkened hallway and past the toilet block, because everyone we pass smiles and wiggles their eyebrows. Then we're turning left onto some stairs.

"Now. Don't freak out. We are just looking, okay?"

Rebecca says over her shoulder.

"O—kay."

"You've got to keep in mind, people come here willingly," she says, navigating down the stairs in her heeled boots and gripping her spare hand on the rail.

The walls, painted a deep pink musk color, are dotted with framed black and white erotic photos of people clad in leather and chains, bound and gagged. Holy crap, this place is totally a bondage and discipline club. I jerk on Rebecca's hand.

"Ah… Bec. I really don't think this is my thing."

"I'm not saying it is. I just want to show you something. I promise I won't let anything happen to you." She pulls me a few reluctant steps down. I'm feeling ill. What the heck am I even doing here? Is she trying to tell me Alex is into this kinky stuff? Maybe Gerard knew and has been trying to protect me from this, always insisting Alex is a player. Is this what he means? I come to an abrupt halt and jerk my hand out of Rebecca's.

"Come on, don't be such a baby. Everyone here is a consenting adult." Rebecca grabs my hand again. When she sees my concerned face, she lets go. "What's wrong?"

"Does—Alex do this kind of thing? I mean, was this the kind of thing him and you were into when you were dating?"

"Dating? We've never dated. More like fuck buddies, and I don't know. Maybe you need to ask him. You can go back upstairs, but I'm going to see what's happening in the viewing rooms."

Viewing rooms? Christ, maybe Gerard does come here.

Rebecca moves on without me. Interested to know about Alex and viewing rooms and people jumping bones with strangers, and now that the pressure is off, I follow her slowly down the stairs until we're standing in another long hallway. The passageway itself is dimly lit, illuminated solely by a series of windows to the left. Along the right wall are nothing but doors and more artwork. If that's what you can call it. Old iron chains and things that look like ancient torture devices, and more erotic photos adorn black walls. Thinking of Oliver, I try to spot a signature but don't find one. But I'm certain these are the type of photos he'd shoot.

The closest window to us is only a few feet away. Rebecca marches toward it and peers in. I assume there is nothing going on behind the glass because she quickly moves onto the next window. and then the next. Finally, she stops at the last window and coaxes me to join her.

I want to look, but I don't want to see. Once I've seen it, I know I cannot unsee it. I'm terrified that it will taint how I regard Alex. But with curiosity getting the better of me, I step forward, my eyes focusing on Rebecca as she stares longingly in the window. She checks to make sure I'm coming, and as I pass the first window, I glance in expecting it to be empty, but it's not.

Stopping dead in my tracks, I'm embarrassed that I've caught a couple in the throes of lovemaking. Afraid they have seen me, I retrace my steps, my stomach doing a flip-flop. What if I see someone I know? I'll never be able to look at them again. I should turnaround, go back upstairs and ask Alex to take me home, but I'm too intrigued now, especially when Rebecca turns with a big grin plastered across her face.

"They can't see or hear you, Paige, go ahead, watch."

After a moment of hesitation, I move in front of the window again and see a masked gentleman with his partner lying face down on the bed. Her ass is in the air and he's fucking into her. His eyes are locked on his reflection in a large mirror on the right-hand wall, and the woman is gripping the bedsheets as though for dear life. When the man pulls out of her, I can understand why. His appendage is massive. My face contorts. Can she really be enjoying that?

Intrigued and slightly aroused, I stay to watch when he rounds the bed, his companion waiting for his next move. She's still on all fours, her fists still knotted. Slowly, the man kneels on the bed in front of her. Then a door next to the mirror opens and I guess it's someone who may have been in the next room watching through the mirror. This man is not wearing a mask. He is bigger in stature but his cock not as ridiculously large. The two men exchange words that I can't hear, but the woman on the bed looks up and smiles at the intruder. Still in position, the woman looks ahead and reaches for the first man's erection. He feeds himself into her mouth before the second man moves around to the other side of the bed and takes hold of her ankles. The first man quickly removes his cock just in time, so the woman doesn't scrape him with her teeth as the second man flips her over and jerks her roughly toward his awaiting penis.

Even though he's so rough and demanding, I'm shocked by how my body reacts. Anxiousness and excitement coalesce and then I'm tingling everywhere. I can't imagine why Rebecca moved on past them—this alone is enough, my racing heart and damp panties being a clear indicator.

Not quite as intimidated now, I skim past the other rooms, barely looking in. Rebecca turns as I approach, a broad, lush smile still on her face. Her eyes are wide with fervor, her pupils large and hungry to see more by the way she turns back in an instant, leaving me to sidle up shyly beside her. I peer into the room. What's going on behind the glass is so confronting, I gasp. Then in an almost infantile manner, I reach for Rebecca's hand and grip tightly, then move until I'm standing slightly behind her, as though for protection.

"I know, right," she says, twisting her face to look at me. "How dirty, hot is that?"

2

BLOOD IN THE CUT

"Why are only some of them wearing masks?" I ask, at the expense of sounding naïve.

"Some people don't mind being recognized, I guess."

"Have you done something like this?"

"Not here. But I want to. And I'd like to be the dominatrix."

"You do?"

"Wouldn't you like to be one of them?" She nods toward the window.

"No."

"Bummer." Rebecca pauses for a long moment, maybe waiting for me to question her, but I'm too shocked by what I'm looking at to reply. "Kaitlyn only pretends to be innocent when we play. But you *are* innocent, aren't you? Have you even watched like full-on porn?"

I shake my head, still looking straight ahead. "No. Not the real dirty stuff."

"Wow. You really are sheltered."

Inside the room where we're staring, there are six people sitting on chairs. Some wearing masks, but all of them blindfolded. Their chairs are arranged in a line facing us, and they're scantily dressed. I count four males and two females. Each one of them has their hands secured behind their backs and their ankles bound by leather cuffs linked to the legs of the chair, clearly exposing their sex for all to see. I shudder at the thought of being so vulnerable and on show.

Walking in amongst them is a dominatrix dressed in the whole kit and caboodle. Her exposed breasts are heavy, and her black panties are riding up her ass. She looks extremely sexy and although her face is covered in a Catwoman mask, I guess her to be in her mid-thirties. She drags her hair, that's tied into a low-set ponytail, through her hand like it's a tail. Twirling and stroking it as she weaves in and out between the chairs, then drags a whip she has curled up in her hand over the half-naked bodies around her. Some of them throw their head back and speak. From the smirk on her face, it seems she enjoys playing her role. I keep getting drawn to the blindfolds everyone is wearing, battling a rising fear of not being able to see, but I don't understand why.

"I think they've only just started," Rebecca says.

"How do you know?"

"Because none of them are begging yet." Rebecca moves closer to the window, then feels for something along its edge. Suddenly we can hear what's being said inside the room.

"… think you can take it, but you'll be wrong. I'll have you weeping before you're satisfied." After a pause she asks, "Who is Sia?"

"Me." A young brunette answers, her voice aimed at the floor. The domme's heels clack loudly within the room until she is standing in front of the girl.

"So, you requested I go easy on you. Is that right?"

"Yes," she replies meekly.

The woman acts powerful and trails a fingernail along a

slender shoulder, making the object of her attention shudder. "So, this your first time then?"

Sia nods.

Circling the young woman, the Catwoman's mask lifts along with a smirk. "Lucky me." She positions herself between the young woman's legs and bends forward slightly, slapping the curled-up whip left and right between the young lady's thighs. "This means open your legs wider, little slut. And FYI. I don't know how to do—easy." We hear a whimper, but the young woman's nipples pucker when she arches, tilting her beasts in the air before opening her legs a little wider. "That's right, kitten. Open your legs for me. I want to feel my way inside you," the domme says seductively. "Are you willing?"

Everyone in the room has their faces turned to the direction of her voice, and cocks are twitching in anticipation.

The young lady squirms in her seat. "Yes. I think so."

I can't tear my eyes away. It's like I'm watching an erotic horror movie. My mind's not able to figure out if I like or hate what I'm witnessing. Like I'm trying to turn something disturbing into something I'm aroused by. I think the ecstasy is sending me off-kilter, my mind wants to leave, but my body wants to stay.

The dominatrix marches away and retrieves something off the wall.

"What in the world is that?" I whisper, thinking they can hear me.

"A spread-bar."

I feel so naïve. What the hell is a spread-bar?

As soon as the domme touches the bar on Sia's thighs, the young woman draws her knees together. "Uh-uh. Don't you dare close your legs." The domme slaps the side of the woman's thigh. We hear the others suck in their breaths.

When the woman doesn't respond, the domme pushes the curled-up whip between cinched legs, pressing hard against her pussy. Finally, she gets the message and opens her legs again.

"Good girl, but you see, now I *know*, I'm going to need this spreader." Putting down her whip, the Catwoman crouches in front of the expectant young lady, attaches the bar between her legs and uses the leather cuffs to fasten it in place, positioning it just above the lady's knees. Sia is now spread wide, with no chance of closing her legs whatsoever.

"There! That's so you can't change your mind on me, little kitten," she torments, in a condescending tone. "I want your legs fixed open while I finger you."

Sia's mouth falls open.

"Jesus Christ," I gasp.

The girl quickly snaps her mouth shut.

"Shit, did she just hear me?"

Rebecca laughs. "No way. Not through that thick glass. But shh, I want to listen." She presses a finger to her lips, her hazel eyes still locked onto the scene in front of us.

"And then, if you're a good girl, I will lap my wickedly fast tongue, like your pussy is a bowl of warm milk just for me."

The domme is giving such a good running commentary, the blind witnesses are moaning, their imagination no doubt running wild.

"Mmm your skin is so soft, Sia," she purrs, running her hand along the inside of her target's thighs. "You're so young and soft and… Ooooh, so lovely and wet," she wails, inserting fingers inside the quivering Sia.

The young lady vocalizes her pleasure and slides her ass down the chair, raising herself as much as her bound hands will allow to gain more penetration. Suddenly, the domme withdraws her fingers that are glistening from Sia's arousal and steps to the right to take hold of the cock that's prancing beside her.

"Holy fuck," the man sings out, startled. I'm imagining he'll lose his erection from fright, but the more the domme pumps him, the more vocal he becomes. "Oh, fuck yeah, you bitch. You do your thing."

The Catwoman stops immediately. "What did you just call me?" She snatches a hand full of his hair with her left hand and jerks his head back. "Did you just call me a bitch?" When she visibly squeezes the guy's cock, his knees curl inward and he groans.

"Sorry, but hell yeah that felt good."

Releasing him, the domme marches over to her wall of wonders again and returns to hastily attach clamps to his nipples.

"No one calls me a bitch and gets away with it. You'll wear these clamps on your nipples all night."

There are a few chuckles.

"Oh, so you all think that's funny. I'll get you all whimpering soon." The room falls silent except for the guy wearing nipple clamps who's groaning softly and shifting in his seat.

"Is she really going to leave him like that all night?" I ask.

"Don't worry, his nipples will go numb, and he'll stop complaining."

"Do you do all this stuff to Kaitlyn?"

Rebecca turns to me smiling. "Wouldn't you like to know?"

A rush of embarrassment hits my face. I can't believe I asked such a personal question. What's wrong with me and why am I even curious?

"Where was I? That's right. I was finger fucking Sia, wasn't I? Getting her all hot and wet and ready for my tongue."

I hold my breath, waiting to see what, with sexy prowess, the domme will do next. When down the corridor near the staircase a door opens, and a gentleman in a suit wearing a mask comes out. Although I can't be sure, I think it's the man from the first room that I was watching. He pauses and looks at me for the longest time. Trying to ignore him, I turn back to the window.

The dominant is untying the girl's restraints and encourages her to her feet. "I need you standing and bent over, kitten." She positions the girl to her liking. "Yes, that's better, sweetie. Now I can see your beautiful, wet snatch." The dominatrix slaps at Sia's ass but clearly aims for her slick folds. Everyone moans, including me when my pussy constricts from being so aroused. I've never witnessed anything like this, and the fact it is turning me on is super confronting. Does enjoying this mean I'm lesbian? I mean, only minutes ago, I was letting Rebecca kiss me. Surely, it's like Rebecca said, it's the Molly having a strange effect on me too.

Suddenly, the Catwoman's head snaps up when a door clicks open and another leather-clad dominant enters the room. A male. A big, scary looking man.

"Oh goodie," the domme drawls seductively. "Hard-core Harry is here. Hello, Harry."

Harry grunts then slaps a riding crop he's holding against his leather-clad thighs.

"Which of these little soft cocks is going to take my cock up his ass?" he demands to know.

My eyes grow wide. I'm shocked that I'm still standing here watching, and then out of the corner of my eye, I notice the masked gentleman in the hall meander toward Rebecca and me. Instinct has me slipping to the right side of Rebecca, putting her between me and the gentleman. There's something about the way he keeps watching us, taking his time to walk our way. He grins. I think it's because of my nervous maneuver. Men like him probably like women like me, scared and vulnerable. He sure seemed to like pounding that poor woman in the first room. I take hold of Rebecca's hand for security. When I do, I see him smile again. My brow creases, and I jerk on Rebecca's hand. She looks in his direction briefly but goes straight back to watching the action, unperturbed even when the man sidles up to her. But having someone else watch us watching the room full of people makes me unsettled. It's no longer our private thing.

"Let's go," I whisper to Rebecca.

"Just wait one more minute. I want to see what they do."

With my eyes focused ahead but my peripheral vision monitoring the masked gentleman, I keep watching the sex show before us.

Sia is bent forward, resting her hands on the seat of the chair now. She still has the spread-bar between her legs, and all the domme's focus is on the pussy she is thrusting her fingers in and out of. Moans of pleasure are erupting from Sia, who is now frantically bending her knees up and down, trying to help her own climax along.

"Greedy Sia, your pussy is almost biting my fingers, you wicked girl." She slaps the wanton woman's ass.

Then the dom starts walking around the group, slapping his crop on unsuspecting backs, hips, and breasts. There is a chorus of yelps that have everyone's head swiveling blindly around, trying to guess what's going on.

The male dom picks out his prey by gripping one man's shoulder until he yields, and his shoulder falls away. "Do you want to suck my cock before I fuck you? Or should I fuck you dry?" he asks, his voice harsh as a seasoned smoker.

"It's quite entertaining, isn't it?" the masked gentleman beside us asks. We don't answer him, but I give him a tight smile and squeeze Rebecca's hand with a tug. The gentleman is creeping me out. I want to leave.

"Just wait, Paige. I'm dying to see the domme go down on her."

At the mention of my name, our gentleman friend snaps his head around, and a knowing expression ignites his face. "Yes *poppet*, stay and watch," he drawls with a widening grin.

I feel the blood drain from my face, and I grip Rebecca's hand even tighter.

"Hey, dude. Mind your own business," Rebecca snaps.

"I have to go." I yank my hand away from Rebecca and all but sprint along the corridor and pelt up the stairs.

"Paige, wait," Rebecca calls after me.

I don't stop, and I don't look back. Fuck, fuck, fuck. How could I be so stupid?

When I'm at the top of the stairs, I search for Alex. Thankfully, he's still seated at the booth with Kaitlyn. I'm almost tripping over my jumpsuit pants as I scurry toward them, breathless and checking behind me.

"Alex, we need to go."

Alex reaches for my hand. I snatch it away and pick up my purse then repeat myself.

"We need to go now. Shit, shit, shit. I'm such an idiot." I look around nervously.

"What's the matter?" Alex climbs out of the booth and wraps his arms around me. Just then, I feel another set of hands on me. I spin around, frightened, then catch Alex throwing Rebecca an accusing scowl.

"What? Don't look at me. Some creepy fucker came up behind us and started whispering in her ear," Rebecca says. "Are you all right, Paige? What happened?" She reaches out to stroke my arm.

Alex looks back at me.

"It's Jamison. He's here." My mouth is suddenly so

parched, I take hold of the first drink my hand lands on and drink it down.

"No way?"

"Yes way." I slam the empty glass down and look around again. "Christ. He's probably calling Gerard. Alex, we need to leave before he sees you."

Alex nods. "Sure."

Rebecca slips into the booth next to Kaitlyn. Alex and I are just about to leave when we spot Jamison coming toward us.

"Quick let's just go," I beg, pulling on his hand.

"Don't let that fucker scare you, Paige. Fuck him."

"Alex, I know he'll tell Gerard." I snatch my hand out of Alex's before Jamison gets close enough to notice. He has removed his mask, and he's smiling as though we are long-lost friends.

"Hello again, Paige, and… Alex, right?" Jamison points a finger.

Alex thrusts his chin at Jamison. "What's going on?"

"Oh, just this and that." He smiles smugly having used my own line from Jenna and Nadal's dinner party to intimidate me.

"Hello." Jamison turns to Rebecca and Kaitlyn. "I don't think I caught your names."

"We didn't offer them, asshole," Kaitlyn replies, picking up on the angst she realizes we must feel toward him.

"Touchy—touchy. Be careful, lovely. I have friends in high places. Don't I Paige?"

I'm guessing he's referring to Gerard. But who knows, I'm starting to think I was right at Jenna's party, implying he was a human trafficker.

"Ooh, how scary." Kaitlyn fakes a quiver and reaches for her glass totally unperturbed by Jamison. Despite my anxiousness, I need to stifle a giggle. God, I wish I had her spine.

"Well, you certainly surround yourself with live ones, don't you, Alex? So, where is my old friend, Gerard, tonight? I might like to have a drink with him." Jamison looks around the room in mock curiosity before his gaze lands on me.

"He's away on business."

"Oh. How convenient, perhaps you'd like my company then? You know the saying, 'While the cats away.' But in your case, I'd have to say, while Limp Dick's away, his little tiger likes to play."

As horrible as it sounds, it's reassuring he berates Gerard. Obviously, there's no loyalty between them.

"Fuck off, Jamison." Alex steps in front of me.

"Oh, I see. Gardener turned boyfriend, turned bodyguard. My, my, I never took Gerard for the type to let his wife out and about with other men, *without him*. How do I get in on that action, I wonder?"

"Christ, you're a piece of work." Alex shakes his head. "I think you need to learn some respect, old man."

"What? Why, I haven't done anything wrong. But now, you on the other hand, Mrs. Whitmyer. I dare say you've been very naughty, or is that still on the cards?"

"That's none of your business." I look toward the exit and notice almost everyone is staring. I'm just grateful the music is loud enough to cover what's being said.

"Oh, but I think I'd like to make it my business, *poppet*. I did so enjoy our little game the other week. You certainly put a spin on things with your little temper tantrum. I wonder what else I can get you to do."

"What's he talking about?" Rebecca asks, looking between the three of us. I just shake my head and roll my eyes, knowing I've now given her more to frown upon.

I feel my skin crawl.

"Jesus, just fuck off already." Kaitlyn screws up her face.

Jamison eyes both Rebecca and Kaitlyn for a split second before lunging and taking Kaitlyn by the throat. Her hands whip up to loosen Jamison's grip, but he holds fast, his mouth contorting with his effort to choke her out. Rebecca screams, then leaps to her feet.

"What the hell?" Alex yells, taking a handful of Jamison's suit jacket, trying to pull him back and readying his fist. I spin in a circle, not knowing what to do, or who to call out for.

Spotting security, I'm relieved when they come rushing over. Two men jerk Jamison back by his arms. He lets go, leaving Kaitlyn coughing and spluttering, trying to get air. She rubs at her throat, staring up at Jamison in wide-eyed shock, her face flushing back to color. Rebecca slides back into the booth seat to put a reassuring arm around Kaitlyn.

"Gentlemen, gentlemen." Jamison steps back, his hands raised then turns to face security. Seeming to recognize him, the two men instantly let him go.

"Sorry, sir." They step back to give Jamison room. He straightens his jacket and fixes his tie then glares at Kaitlyn.

"I suggest you watch yourself, young lady, or you might find your pretty little friend here floating in a river one day." Rebecca jerks her head away when Jamison strokes her hair.

"Now, what was I proposing? Oh yes, I'm certain I have some paperwork for Gerard. Mind if I drop it off, say, tomorrow at noon?"

"What the fuck! Who do you think you are, Jamison?" Alex growls, puffing up and shoving Jamison back with a hand to his chest. "Just stay the fuck away from Paige. You hear me?" Both Alex and Jamison match each other, size for size, and for a moment, I think a brawl will break out. The two security men flare up behind Jamison but don't move in when Jamison holds up his hand.

"Well, you are a cocky little prick, aren't you? I must mention to Gerard how gallant his little handyman is. Defending his wife and all."

"I won't even be home, Jamison, so don't bother." I butt in, hoping to defuse the situation.

"Oh. You have plans then?"

"My mother's funeral if you must know."

"Oh, how sad. My condolences. Well, best I leave it for another time then. I suppose I can keep your indiscretion to myself for now."

"Gee, how big of you, Jamison," says Alex. "But who said anything about tonight being an indiscretion?"

Jamison dusts at his jacket and gives the hem a tug. "You underestimate me, Alex. I know more about Gerard than you could ever possibly know." He smooths down his tie and throws his piercing gray eyes around.

Alex folds his beefy arms across his chest. "Is that right?"

"Anyway. I can see you are eager to leave. I'll be in touch, Paige. Ladies." Jamison nods and smiles at a very subdued Kaitlyn.

"Please don't." But my plea only serves to animate Jamison's face further before he turns on his shiny heels and leaves.

I clamp my eyes shut. God help me. I'm so in trouble now.

3

I'M IN LOVE BUT...

All the way back to the beach house, I'm shaking, and the taxi ride seems to take forever. Alex keeps stroking my leg, trying to reassure me, but it's not working. I'm so angry at myself, I feel wretched.

"Jamison is probably on the phone already to Gerard. I am so dead. Fuck!"

"I don't think he'll talk. I think he was just trying to intimidate you. But just the same, I don't think you should go home tonight. Go to a friend's or stay with me."

Slumping, I elbow my knees so I can sink my face into my hands. "Christ, I'm a wreck, look." When I hold up a shaking hand, Alex takes hold and tries to steady me, pressing my fingers against his lips, then slips his arm around me.

"So, stay tonight."

"God, Alex. What am I doing? I'm running around reckless. I don't respect my husband, and I'm getting off watching people in masks having sex. What's happened to me?" I look up and the cab driver throws a look in my direction. Groaning, I flop my head forward, hoping to retrieve the blood that is neglecting my brain. Alex rubs my back.

"I shouldn't have pressured you to go."

"It's not your fault," I mumble into my knees. "I knew what I was doing. I wanted to go because I wanted to be with you." I twist my head and look at him. "I've done it again, you know?"

"Done what?"

"Dragged you into my shit."

"Ahh, I think you're worth it."

Sitting up, I try to compose myself. "No. I'm really not. Because when Gerard finds out I was with you, he's going to make your life hell."

Alex huffs. "Can't get much worse. Anyway, I don't think he'll find out. Jamison is all piss and wind." Alex removes his arm from behind my back and rubs his thighs.

"I think Gerard suspects I'm not in love with him anymore. He's become a total control freak. He scares me."

Alex nods and takes a hold of my hand to play with my fingers. "You need to get out then. Can you stay with your friend? It's Sheree, isn't it? Use your mom's funeral to get away. I'm sure she'd help." I nod in agreement, but the possibility of that happening would mean telling Sheree everything. And the fallout could possibly do more damage to my psyche than living with Gerard's condescending nature.

"Can't you and I just run away together? Live happily ever after. Pretend there'd be no fallout." I let out a nervous chuckle, hoping he realizes I'm not kidding.

Alex looks out over my head and stares out the window, one corner of his mouth twisting up in an attempted smile. It seems like he's mulling the idea over, and for a moment, I let myself believe we could do just that.

"You know I'm not someone to rely on, don't you?" He mumbles then looks at me.

"What do you mean?"

"You get that I was locked up for six years, don't you?"

"Are you saying being with me would be like prison?"

"No. I'm saying I'm enjoying my freedom, that I don't want a serious relationship with you or anyone. Besides, what the fuck can I offer someone like you?"

"But, the other day, the times we've been together, it feels like you want to be with me, that you care," I say a little despondent. Then he delivers his punch.

"I do care, but I don't think you really know what you want."

Turning away, I clamp my eyes to get rid of the sting, then stare at the passing traffic. What was I expecting from him? That he would confess his undying love, say that he can't live without me either. That he plans on fighting Gerard for me. I feel… stupid. But hasn't it been obvious what I want?

Gerard is right, he is a player. I want to hate Alex, but I can't. I just want him more. I swipe at my face, toying with the idea of sharing him. But imagine being alone in an apartment knowing he's being intimate with Rebecca, then massaging Bronte. My mind spins. Then I see Jenna, and I can't suppress the anguish that leaves me via a groan. I pull my hand out of his tight grip and swipe at both eyes.

"I'm sorry, I just thought…" Alex says but I cut him off.

"You thought what? That this was a game for me. That somehow you and Gerard could toy with me and I wouldn't get emotionally involved. That I was just someone to use. Like all your other girlfriends."

"That's not fair, Paige. What's going on with you and Gerard is between you guys. You know what I'm about. I've fucking told you from the start, and you still came after me.

You did that yourself. In fact, I remember telling you specifically not to fall for me."

I stare at him blankly for a moment. "Not fall for you. How is that even remotely possible when you have such an effect on me? I don't love Gerard. You know that. I thought that's why you were paying me attention."

"Then leave Gerard. Stop waiting for me to give you a damn out."

"I thought you wanted me," I say, looking out the window again.

"Paige, end your shit with Gerard first because I'm not promising to take you in and have a relationship while he's still on the scene. And I mean, he needs to be long gone. It's that simple." There's a flatness to his tone that's cutting. I don't even know why I'm pushing him when it's me who has the problem.

The taxi slows, then comes to a halt. The driver flicks on his overhead light. "Card or cash, buddy," he asks over his shoulder. I fish around in my clutch for my credit card.

"I'll get it," Alex offers. But I beat him to paying, thrusting my hand out at the driver.

Alex gets out of the taxi and paces, his hand running through his hair. When the taxi drives off, I walk toward my car.

"What? So now you're leaving?"

"I need to sort myself out. I can't keep doing this to you. I've been stupid thinking I could live a double life. Gerard will find out about tonight. He'll punish you. God knows how, and as for me? Well." I huff. "Say goodbye to this stupid person." I circle my face with my pointer finger. "Because Gerard's going to lock me up and throw away his damn fucking key."

"Come inside and we'll talk about it, sort something out. And look, you're shivering." Alex gestures with his hand as if

I haven't realized. When I don't move, Alex starts walking away mumbling into the wind. "I'm going in. You can suit yourself, but I wouldn't trust Jamison. I wouldn't be surprised if he's at your place waiting for you."

"How can you just walk away from me?" I yell.

He turns abruptly. "I'm not gonna stand out here and tell you what you want to hear just to make you come inside. Not when you keep ignoring what you need to do. I'm not going to fucking save you. The truth. I'm not the guy for you. You want to fuck, we'll fuck, but don't get clingy. I just don't need that shit in my life."

Staring at his back, I watch as Alex walks off without me. I can't make myself move in either direction. I feel stuck. I stare at the highway, watching as the cars speed by, their headlights cutting through the darkness. I don't want to be anywhere anymore. I just want to disappear. Somebody stop the fucking planet because I want to get off.

The cold is wrapping itself right around, and my teeth start chattering, and yet, I still can't make myself move. I love Alex. I want to be with Alex, but I don't want to be just another one of his girlfriends, his conquests.

Suddenly his arms are all around me and he leans into my neck. "I wish I could be what you want me to be, Paige."

I relax in his arms and a tear breaks free.

"What's your favorite color, Alex"

"Orange," he mumbles in my hair, then drops a kiss there.

"And when's your birthday?"

"Second of February."

"How much did you weigh when you were born? Did you like school?"

"I don't know, yeah, sure, but... "

"What was your favorite subject? And where's your dad? You've hardly told me anything about anything." I roll out one question after another so I don't become a blubbering mess.

"Stop. What's with all these questions?"

"Because I want to know everything about you, Alex." I twist in his arms to eke out what warmth he has. To draw in his essence, pull it right into my bones.

Pressing my face onto his chest, I inhale deeply the glorious scent of him, intent on encoding it in my memory forever. The gesture of him coming back for me made the ache inside worse. I want to say more. I need the words out to ease the pain inside. I need him to know how much I've thought of the possibility of an 'us.'

"I wanted to cook you a meal, Alex. Help you dig a garden." I slip my arms under his jacket and link my fingers. "I wanted to walk down the street holding your hand. I wanted to agonize over what to get you for Christmas and your birthday. I wanted to meet all your friends and your dad. I wanted to watch movies and laugh and sing in front of you. I wanted us to get a pet. I wanted to splash in the ocean with you, go on vacations, go camping, lay on a sleeping bag and study the stars. I wanted… I wanted to have your baby." I can't stop the tears from breeching my lids. My vulnerability has my heart hammering so hard, my ribs are tightening. I've never been this candid and desperate before. "You are everything I want you to be, Alex, but I can't be with you like this. I need some kind of commitment from you. That you'll be there for me. Otherwise, all we're doing is cheating. And we deserve to be punished."

"Paige." He hugs me tighter.

"Why can't you love me like I love you?" When I look up at him, his eyes are cast toward the road.

He hugs me tighter. "I don't know. Maybe because I'm scared."

"Scared of what?"

He looks down at me. "Rebound relationships never work, Paige."

"Are you saying you can't imagine us together?"

"I'm saying." Alex steps back and holds me at arms length. "I imagine you'll break my fucking heart, Paige. It'll be fun to start, then some young educated rich prick will come along, and you'll be pining for the lifestyle you once had, and leave me."

I'm speechless.

In a not-so-direct way, he's saying, that because I cheated on Gerard with him, it's confirmation of the stupid belief. *Once a cheater, always a cheater.* I'm gutted. He's never going to commit to loving me, not ever. He'd rather keep me at a distance along with all the others he most likely has, just so he doesn't get hurt.

"Is that it? You only want me for sex?"

Alex shrugs. "Are you going back to Gerard after tonight?"

"No, I'm going to bury my mom, remember?"

"But after that," His arms fall away from me. "Are you going to stay in Ponderosa Park with Sheree?"

"Alex," I whine, taking a step closer. "You don't understand. There's no way I can just stay there and start over."

"Somewhere else then?"

I stare at him blankly then my gaze falls to the wet asphalt, and I'm shaking my head. We're just going around in circles. He's pressuring me to stand on my own and I'm passive, aggressively trying to get him to rescue me. If I stand on my own, he's not obligated to commit to anything. And if he rescues me, I'm not to blame if Gerard comes after us or if Alex learns the truth about me. And all this thinking is just giving me a damn headache. I palm my face to wipe my eyes, then nod.

"You're right. I'm going to end it. I'll ask for a divorce. I'll move out. Get my own place. Get a job. Not for you, but for me."

Alex pulls me back into a hug and plants a kiss in my hair. "That's the way. You grab that fucker by the balls and take everything you deserve." He lets go of me and heads toward my car. "Now, pop that trunk, Princess, and let's get your things inside."

Watching his back, I'm suddenly plagued with an uneasy feeling. Why does that suggestion suddenly seem to imply, that what he really wants me to do, is to take Gerard down?

4

I FOUND

Once inside, Alex rolls my suitcase toward his room. The house still smells of curry, and the music's still playing quietly in the background. "Is it okay if I shower?" I ask, following him into the bedroom.

"You should. Your lips are turning blue. How about I make us a drink? It will warm you up." He lifts my case onto the bed.

"Thanks. I know I could use one."

When he leaves, I get busy gathering my things. My movements are slow and deliberate. Not only am I freezing, but I'm mentally and physically drained. I suspect I'm also coming down off the Molly.

In the shower, I run through a dozen plausible excuses should Jamison tell Gerard about my 'outing.' I know Alex is right. I can't rely on him to get me out of this. Even Rebecca dropping hints should have penetrated my thick skull. I want it all but without the risk, looking for my next knight in shining armor to rescue me. I need to be strong. I'll sell some stuff to get money. As soon as I'm back, I'll get a new computer. I might even see if there is any work available at a convenience store or clothing shop. Maybe I can even ask at the veterinary clinic. I can scoop poop. I emerge from the shower in my nightshirt, feeling a little better.

When I come through to the living area, Alex is on the couch, looking at his phone. When he sees me approach, he clicks off the screen and places it on the coffee table in front of him. "Warm now?"

Nodding, I take a seat next to him and my hand automatically goes on his thigh.

"So…" he says, raising his eyebrows with a smile, trying to break the tension and offering me what looks to be Scotch Whiskey. "Gerard's an asshole now?"

"I don't know. Maybe I deserve his bad moods and cutting remarks. It's not like I'm throwing myself at him anymore." I take a sip of liquor, then cut straight to the chase. "Have you *ever* had a committed relationship?"

Alex leans forward. Resting his arms on his thighs, he stares at the floor then picks up a shard of wood from under the coffee table and starts picking it apart. "Only the one your asshole husband moved in on and stole away. Buying her flowers and jewelry—chocolates. You know, all that crap you girls seem to like. I couldn't compete with that. I was an apprentice mechanic paying off my bike. Anyway, she fell for him, so I was history." He turns to look at me.

"So, why not do the same to him?" I wiggle my eyebrows several times.

Alex chuckles, then goes back to whittling. "Truthfully, what I'm doing is worse, isn't it? Sounds like you're there, but not. I shouldn't have held a grudge over Jolene. I mean, can you ever really steal someone away?" He squeezes my knee and tosses the bit of wood on the coffee table, then pushes himself back into the couch and draws me closer. "Eight pounds, seven ounces."

"Pardon?"

"How much I weighed."

"Ouch. Your poor mom. Forget what I said about having your baby, okay."

Alex laughs. "And I hated school. There were no favorite subjects. I earned my smarts being hands-on." Alex scratches through his hair and gets to his feet. "And well, my dad, unfortunately, is in a psych hospital."

"Oh, Alex. I'm sorry."

"The war fucked him up. Now come on, drink up. You need sleep."

"Sleep?"

He gives me a sheepish grin.

"Can I ask you something else?" I sip from my glass before going on, screwing up my face at the bitter taste, then placing it unfinished on the table. "Tonight, with Rebecca and you at that club. Is that what you're into? Do you honestly like having sex with strangers with no attachment?"

A hesitant frown etches his forehead. "Want to know the truth?" He pulls me to my feet and leads me toward the bedroom, turning off the lights as we go. We are cast in near darkness, except for a small amount of moonlight spilling in through an undressed window which illuminates our way. "Sticking with one person scares the fuck out of me. You do that, then they leave."

"But even you must believe the saying? That it's better to have…"

"Yeah, yeah, I know it." Alex cuts me off, tugging me into the bedroom and spinning me around to face him. "But in answer to your question, no. I don't enjoy fucking just any stranger, and I don't get dressed up and shit if that's what you mean. You know what I do enjoying doing though?"

I shake my head.

"Sexing you the way you need it." He grabs my wrists and pins them behind my back, then fondles a breast before his hand is traveling down my silky nightie until he reaches the hem. My legs stay pressed together, teasing him as he tries pushing between them. His green eyes scan me, taking in every blemish, every wrinkle, every contour of my face. His mouth twitches from the thoughts that must be going through his head before he's looking straight into my eyes and his grin widens.

"God, I love the way you do that." I get heated the second Alex caresses me between my now relaxed thighs.

"What? This?" He brings his hand back up to rub a thumb over my nipple. "Or this?" His voice grows deeper, his breathing becomes heavier, as he fondles where the lust in me resides.

"That too. But no, I mean." My body surrenders to his caress, swaying slightly with his delicate touch. "It's the way you look at me. Like you're searching for me. That you know the real me is in here somewhere. Hiding." Alex stops what he's doing and frowns. With my hands still pinned behind my back, I've got nothing to use to control the sting that's suddenly burning my eyes. I clamp them shut in the same moment his lips join mine. His kiss is tender and loving. Alex could do anything to me right now, and I would let him. His desire and desperation radiates so strongly from him, he turns me into putty.

"How would you like me to fuck you, Paige?" he asks against my lips before trailing kisses up my neck. "I want to make you feel better. Is this how you like me to make you feel better?" He rubs the warm area between my thighs, making me go weak at the knees.

"Yes. But then, no. Because I feel so helpless around you." I'm trembling from his touch, his hot breath, and the light kisses he places all around my neck.

"This isn't helpless?" he murmurs straight in my ear. "But

I know what would make you totally helpless and at my mercy."

"Oh, is that so?" My lips search for his.

"Yes."

"Why? So you can do anything you want to me?"

Alex arches an eyebrow. "Do you want me to do whatever I want?" The heat in his voice alone, is almost making me come.

I nod, my skin tingling with desire, my lungs heavy from rapid breathing. I'm so ready for him, his hand between my legs must be burning up.

"Are you sure?"

"Yes," I whisper. "As long as you don't hurt me." I gasp when he catches me off guard, finally gaining access, he slides a thumb between my hot folds.

When he lets go of my hands, he's instantly on my lips with his own. He's full of heat and passion. Taking hold of my face with both hands and weaving his fingers through my hair, he holds me still so he can devour me, taking minutes before coming up for air. When he does, he's out of breath, his lips red and puffy. "Man, there's just something about you, you're so willing. Fuck, it turns me on."

I can't tear my eyes away from his. He tells me everything with his gaze. He loves me—I know he does.

"I wish we could have enjoyed the club better tonight," he says, kissing my neck again, getting close to my ear, brushing his wet lips and tongue along the sensitive edge. "I would have gotten a room and done nasty things to you while Rebecca and Kaitlyn watched. I would have made Rebecca jealous."

I pull back and stare at him. "Really? In that sleazy place."

Alex chuckles. But I can't tell whether he's serious or just making fun of my shock.

"And just how would that have made her jealous, Alex?" I ask, as he slips my nightie straps off my shoulders. The garment hovers for a few seconds before slowly sliding down my body. Instantly, Alex bends to suck my nipples causing me to suck in my breath and reach for his head, his face wallowing against my heaving chest. He grabs both breasts and pushes them together, giving me full cleavage so he can lick between the valley he's created. My hands slide to his face, bringing him upward so I can see his eyes when he answers me.

"First, I would have demanded you undress because you love me telling you what to do." He steps back, quickly peeling off his shirt.

"Do I?"

"Don't you?"

"Yes, that's true. I do like you telling me what to do." I give him a stern look. "But only in the bedroom."

Alex pulls me close again. "Oh, of course, Princess. Only in the bedroom."

"Then what would you make me do?" I ask, sliding my hands along his smooth, tanned chest.

"I would have made you bend over and spread your ass cheeks so Rebecca and Kaitlyn could see your perfect pink pussy. I imagine they would have gotten all creamy and hot just looking at you." He trails a finger down one breast, circling until he's touching the puckered skin of my nipple. He bobs and takes the peak between his lips again, sucking one and then the other.

Finding his belt buckle, I fiddle until I've finally set him free. With a quick shove, he removes his jeans and briefs.

"You know, Rebecca got excited when I told her you were coming around. I might have mentioned how sexy you are. That's probably why she came onto you tonight. I also told her you needed a good spanking for being such a prick tease."

I cringe thinking of the way Gerard took his belt to me. Erasing the thoughts away, my hand squeezes his cock. "I'm not a tease." I pout, pulling his face gently toward me with a finger under his chin so I can kiss the stubble there.

Looking into my eyes, he feels his way to my nipple again and pinches me roughly. I let out a yelp.

"Yes, you are, but that's what I like about you."

"And I…" I lick my palm and take hold of him. "Love your cock. I think I could become a worshiper." I keep pleasuring him until he is rock hard, hot, and so engorged, I can feel the veins as he throbs. Sliding to my knees, I claim his love rod with my mouth in one go. His sex is glorious, its girth thick, his skin smooth, his pre-cum sweet. I take him over and over until I hear him moaning. Pausing, I prompt him, "Keep going. Tell me what else you would have done with me tonight if we had stayed at the club."

"I would have…." his voice catches as I take him all the way down again. "Fuck! I would have—licked you and—and fucked you. Whoa. Christ, Paige. Stop, you'll make me come too soon." He grabs hold of my head to slow me down.

Helping me to my feet, he walks me backward, his hands roving all over my back until my knees hit the edge of the bed. Grabbing hold of my ass cheeks, he squeezes, and I wince. The moisture on his hand stings the horizontal welt across both cheeks.

Alex frowns. "What?"

"Nothing, it's fine." I sit down abruptly, my focus on his cock, ready to take him in my mouth again.

"Wait here." He turns and switches on a bedside lamp, lighting the room in a gentle glow, then goes over to his dresser and rummages inside before coming back.

Feeling salacious, I spread my legs then touch myself as he walks back toward me, carrying something in clenched fists, his erection raring to perform and making me so aroused I have to contain myself from lunging at him. Instead, I wait patiently as he crouches in front of me, kissing one knee then the other before letting lengths of fabric dangle from his hands. My attention darts from them to him.

"You want to tie me up?" I shift backward on the bed, my heart kicking up a notch. Alex grabs one ankle, and although he's smiling, I can't help that a small golf ball rises in my throat. Alex seems to notice I'm holding my breath.

"I promise to not hurt you. You can trust me. Completely."

I search his face, looking for a reason to not trust him, but I can't find one. Everything about Alex is true. He makes sense. There's no contradiction in what I feel to what I see. After a little nod from me, he attaches the lengths of fabric to my ankles and wrists, my heart is hammering inside my chest. I want to let him do it, but there is rising panic that I don't want to feel. I'm being reminded of what Gerard tried to do to me. And then there's the faint shadow of something else. I need to keep it in. Not let it out. Not here, not now. Not with Alex. I don't want to ruin what could be my last night with him. So, with some trepidation, I let him tie me.

When he's done, he stands and looks straight down at me. His cock, inches from my face is begging for my attention again, and to distract from the darkening thoughts, in a microsecond, I grab him, licking then sucking on his knob feverishly. I want him so badly—I lose all restraint until he slowly extracts himself with a hand on either side of my face.

"Whoa. Slow down, Princess. You'll have me blowing my load before I get to satisfy you."

"I don't care. I just want you so bad." I try taking him in my mouth again, but he jerks back.

"Then go lay in the middle of the bed for me."

Pulling back the bedspread, I position myself in the center of his bed while Alex moves to the head of the bed.

"I almost feel guilty right now, you know," he says, taking my wrist then fastening it to the metal frame. It takes all my strength not to break out in a cold sweat and remain calm.

"Why?" I ask, dubious and suspecting he's about to say something about Gerard.

He ties my other hand before answering me, and again, I resist the urge to lunge into flight mode.

"Because Rebecca would have loved to see you like this. Tied up and vulnerable."

I sigh in relief.

"I'm pretty sure she loves making women come almost as much as I do." Alex throws me a look and grins. And I realise now, that he's just using words to excite me. That he doesn't know this from firsthand experience. I hope.

But the thought of Rebecca having a fascination with me is enough to distract me from my now vulnerable position. And the more I imagine Rebecca wanting to touch me, the hotter my core gets. Squirming at the discomfort of my pussy becoming increasingly alive, it takes slightly more effort for Alex to catch my foot than it was for him to catch my hands.

"If I had you bent over in front of them at the club tonight," he adds, taking hold of the ankle he captured, jerking it roughly to the corner of the bed and making me gasp. "You could be guaranteed there would have been a crowd in the hall watching on. Did it turn you on watching other people fuck, Paige?" He ties my ankle to the frame.

"Yes. I think I can understand Gerard's fascination better now."

Alex cringes, and instantly I regret mentioning my husband's name.

"I thought it would." Alex glosses over my admission. "I told you I knew you better than you know yourself."

"Alex, my panties. Take them off," I plea when he takes hold of my other ankle.

Alex squints his eyes. "Maybe I'd like to chew my way through them."

"Alex, no. Not another pair."

"You agreed to anything," he reminds me, cocking his head, and as soon as I'm tethered, he's between my legs and feeling my crotch. "So wet, already. Were you this wet in the club tonight?"

"Yes," I pant, pressing myself against his warm palm.

Alex tugs at my panties, pulling them down until they nestle just under my ass cheeks.

"I can smell you from here you're so turned on," he murmurs, gliding a finger along my slit, making me arch, begging for his finger.

"Do you think I should call Rebecca and Kaitlyn? Invite them over to watch? Watch me make you quiver and scream?" He brings his finger to my lips. "Open your mouth."

I let my mouth fall open, enthralled by the look of lust when his gaze drops to my mouth.

"This is how good you taste," he says, swirling his finger over my tongue, his other hand exploring between my legs, making me moan around his finger inside my mouth. Then he's bringing his other hand up. Smelling me on his fingers first, then licking me away and staring at me, my mouth still latched on. "Should I invite the girls to come taste you, Paige?" he smirks.

"No," I reply, although the thought that he'd like to see me with another woman seems to arouse me more.

"No?" he challenges, tilting his head to the side. "You wouldn't like Rebecca to slide her soft tongue into your tight hole? I had the feeling you liked her." I know he's just teasing but still, I blush.

"I did. I do."

"I would make Rebecca beg to touch you. I would have made her suck my cock and beg me until I let her stick her fingers inside your gorgeous body. You know she's most likely finger fucking Kaitlyn right now imagining it's you instead."

My body feels like an inferno, and my heart is racing. Alex's suggestions are putting wicked imagery in my mind. Images I'd never conjure on my own. I can't believe how turned on I'm getting. I pull on the restraints, desperate now for contact.

"Please, Alex, you're driving me insane. I'm throbbing."

He brushes his full warm lips across mine and fondles my nipples. Kissing, licking, and nipping me all over, running his hand along the inside of one thigh until it reaches my steamy apex. One hand reaches behind my neck to lift me as his other hand glides down to cup my vulva before sliding a finger effortlessly inside. I clench myself around his digit and moan, already so close to coming undone. In seconds, I'm wiggling and squirming, so sensitive I can barely take it.

"Alex," I almost scream. He slows his pace, letting me come down gently before withdrawing his hands away from me and tasting me again. I relax back onto the pillow. My head swiveling when I hear his bedside drawer open and he withdraws a pair of scissors.

"Well, they're handy," I say, my voice sounding labored. He returns my smile but says nothing, just glides the cold metal along my neck and down my throat. I hold my breath, then take short shallow intakes as the cold steel travels between my breasts and along my stomach. He stops at my navel and pushes the tip of the scissors in. His eyes are fixed on mine, watching for my reaction, pushing harder until I flinch from the pain. He lifts the scissors away then bows his head and plunges his tongue into my navel, licking, and soothing me. He has me so transfixed on his gentle tongue that I don't even realize what he is doing with his hands until I feel the edge of the scissors slide along my wet slit.

With lighting speed, he comes up to cover my mouth just as I'm sucking in a startled breath, catching the air between us as he slides the cold steel so close to my opening. I freeze, petrified he's going slip and cut me. He wiggles the edges of the scissors from side to side lightly, just grazing the outer folds of me, his eyes never leaving mine. Then in an instant he flicks his wrist, and the scissors catch hold of the lace fabric. Making two cuts, he destroys my panties and then along with the scissors they're shoved to the floor.

"Freaking hell, Alex." I let out the rest of my breath.

He says nothing, just lowers his face until he is plunging his tongue inside me, causing me to call out his name again, only this time it's in rapture.

"See how quickly your pussy tightens at the thought of a threat," he tells me. "Now I'm gonna open you up again. Nice and slow with my fingers."

"Holy crap, Alex, you're freaking me out."

I feel myself quivering. I can't discern my emotions. I'm extremely aroused but incredibly nervous. Alex glides his hands around my now fully naked body. Over my peaked pink nipples, my abdomen, along my inner thighs.

"Christ, you're beautiful. You're flushed and spread wide. Your pussy is so wet, you're dripping. And you haven't even come yet. Would you like me to make you come?" He kisses me everywhere. Little kisses, teasing kisses along my legs and hipbone. Moving higher and higher, planting a trail of sensation. Pulling on my restraints, I try to catch his lips when he comes closer, but he keeps pulling away, teasing me until I groan. He repeats his question.

"Yes," I whisper, my focus locked on his deep green eyes.

Alex travels quickly down my body with his lips. Kissing my neck and armpits, my torso and licking between my breasts. Long lasting licks before latching onto a nipple. He sucks furiously until I'm arching and humping the air, frustration building because I'm tethered and so desperate to touch him. Then he's shifting, moving down, and in an instant, his lips latch onto my clit, and then… he sucks.

I curl, twist, and arch against the sensation. "Oh fuck," I wail, pressing my ass into the mattress trying to escape the intensity of his mouth. I'm so sensitive it feels like he's trying to suck my clit clean down his throat. Then, with his finger, he finds that magic spot inside me and rubs or pumps or presses. I don't know what he's doing, but it is sublime. Alex's small gentle sucks are relentless until I feel myself falling. My climax is coming from everywhere. I'm moaning over and over, my lower half turning to mush. He presses firmly with his spare hand, just above my pubic bone to intensify the sensation on what I now know is my G-spot. Never has anything felt so good.

I want to open myself up wider, I want—no, I *need* more. I'm climbing. The faster he rubs, the more intense the build-up, and then he has a finger in my ass. Every sensitive spot inside me is being targeted.

"Oh God, yes." I twist my restrained body, then arch again, hating yet loving that I am bound because I can't stop him from taking me over and I'm beyond ecstasy.

"Fuck yeah," Alex groans, his voice so deep now it doesn't even sound like him. I close my eyes and shudder. My need to be penetrated with something bigger is so overwhelming now, I let go completely. Moaning, I beg for his beautiful cock.

I want him to untie me. I need to touch him. I want to be the one putting that condom on him. I'm frustrated that it's him and not me holding his cock and lining it up against me. I'm desperate to feel him inside and just when I think he is about to enter me, his thumb finds my clit and he squeezes.

"Holy hell. Oh Alex, I don't think I can take another orga..." I don't get to finish what I'm saying because I become consumed by a rush of heat as he builds me up again with his finger inside me. I can't focus, and my body is shaking as he gets faster with his movements. Then Alex is pressing up inside me right up under my pubic bone, gripping and clenching. Pressing his palm firmly against my clit, digging and curling his fingers inside me, like he's milking me somehow. The sensation is beyond description. I just feel the expansion within me, like my pussy is filling up from the inside. I let go in total surrender because it feels so... orgasmic.

Then, as if that's a silent signal, Alex slows his hand for a brief second, then squeezes one last time, and I climax again. Alex dives between my legs to taste me. I sigh and moan over and over, before he resumes squeezing and clenching me until I release again. I never thought it possible to feel such serenity after climaxing. The world could blow up around me, and I wouldn't care right now. Everything is surreal, like I'm dreaming. I'm lost, devoid of any coherent thought. I barely notice when Alex unties my ankles, I just lay limp. Like there is no blood, no oxygen, and yet my heart is racing so hard I think it will burst, and just when I think I can't take anymore, Alex brings my legs up and enters me, driving his cock in deep. One violent thrust after another. I clamp my eyes closed, gasping, moaning, and singing out his name.

He is divine, beautiful, and fits me so perfectly that I melt into the mattress beneath him, reveling in the sensation that his thick cock now feels like liquid heaven inside of me. My pumped-up pussy grabs him like a vice, possessed and hell-bent on claiming him without my conscious assistance. I'm murmuring incoherently from the intense sensations around me, totally out of my mind quivering and spasming around my expert lover.

I'm so absorbed in the feeling of him. It's as though I'm drowning as he journeys in bliss, my body squeezing his unyielding cock for the longest time before I feel him peaking, his cock expanding. Then he stops and lays perfectly still—yet buried deep inside. His twitching is teasing me beyond belief. I spread my legs wider. He pushes in deeper, then holds still.

"Open your eyes," he whispers.

I spring them open, and there I am, in his eyes. We don't move, we just lay there, staring into each other. Our breath in unison comes out as short, sharp pants. I want to scream, to wail, but I clamp my lips. I want him to crawl right inside me, to fill me entirely, to become part of me.

"Paige." He breathes in and out, deep and lasting.

"Yes, Alex," I murmur in delirium.

"I'm going to come. Come with me." He remains perfectly still as he speaks. His mellow words seeming to amplify the thrumming between us. So I do. I climax again with Alex, gripping him tighter on the inside as he shudders out his orgasm within mine, making involuntary jerks together as though we have discovered a unified heartbeat within us. But I don't just feel our orgasm—I see it. It radiates back to me from his irises, causing his pupils to become a universe and, in that moment, I see everything we are. A boy, a girl. Man, woman. We are scared, lonely, joyful, hopeful, determined. I see it all and more. Things I can't explain. "Oh God, Alex," I sigh. "I can see heaven in your eyes." I'm so overwhelmed by the transparency, tears well.

I lay motionless, apart from my chest rising and falling. I'm exhausted yet utterly satisfied.

Alex swipes sweaty strands of hair away from my face. "Are you all right?" He kisses me over and over, covering my cheeks, my lips, my eyes. I can't move my arms to wipe the tears that suddenly break free. Still hovering over me he begs, "Please don't cry, Paige." He wipes at my tears. But I can't help it, he moves me like nothing I've ever known. Reaching up, Alex undoes my wrist restraints.

I struggle with the covers, pulling them over us feeling suddenly cold. "Why do I always cry when you make me orgasm?"

Alex chuckles. "You're gorgeous, and don't you ever forget it." He helps me with the blankets then lays beside me, his chest, rippled and sweaty. I glide my hand over his slippery canvas, like I'm a child discovering finger painting. I want to design, sculpt, create something on him, with him, and imprint my desires all over him. If I had a tattoo pen, I'd make it permanent. I want him to remember me.

"So are you, Alex. You're the most beautiful being on this planet," I whisper, though those words feel totally inadequate. "And I'm sorry Gerard hurt you so much that you're not prepared to love again." I stroke his back, feel him go a little rigid before he's pulling me in tighter.

"Yeah. Well, that's in the past now." He tucks my head under his chin. "The only sad thing about that now, is Grace."

"Why is she the sad part?" I ask, tracing the dark image of an eagle on his chest with my finger.

"She's been in the hospital this week. She might need full-time care now."

"What do you mean full-time care?" I lift myself onto an elbow and push tangled hair away from my face. "You mean she's like, really sick?"

Alex smooths my concerned look away and nods.

"Yeah. She's…" He shakes his head. "Let's not talk about that now. Okay?"

"But…"

"Shh." Alex grabs hold of my stunned face by the jaw. "Paige, stop. Let's not talk about them. This is our night. Okay?"

I search his shadowed face, confused by how calm he is. Why is he so calm? Then he's smiling at me. He pulls me back down to lay beside him.

"I'm glad you came out tonight. And you know, all that stuff I was saying about Rebecca and watching and shit. I didn't mean it. I was serious the other day when I said I wouldn't share you. And I wouldn't. You're the best thing that's happened to me in a long time, Paige."

Burying my face in his chest, I wrap my arms tighter around him. "You know, saying things like that will put thoughts in my head, which gives me hope for us." I bring my face up to meet his eyes, alive with a gentle smile.

"Don't worry, Princess, everything is gonna work out just fine." And Alex says it so tenderly, I almost believe it isn't a lie.

5

KARMA

It's his smell that wakes me. Strong, spicy, musky. He's all over me. I smell him on my arm, my hands, my hair, he's everywhere. I clench inside, and he is there. I press my back into him, and he is there, and then I press a hand to my now fluttering heart and even feel him there. The reality of how much I crave Alex is excruciating.

Rolling carefully so I don't wake him, I watch him as he sleeps. I memorize his face, his neck, his shoulders, his arms, his chest and his lips. His beautiful, sexy lips. So soft, so firm. Gentle, though still demanding. Thick dark lashes rest on his cheekbones, and beneath his lids, his eyes dart about witnessing something I'm not privy to and I wish I was there with him, in his dream-state, so I can stare into his eyes, see again what I experienced last night. The eyes of a soul seer.

His bow-shaped lips are slightly parted, and occasionally he lets out a small sigh. I desperately want to kiss him, to make love with him one more time. With his limp arm resting over me, I read over and over, "Love is a Battlefield" tattooed along his underarm, and for some reason, the words make me angry. I'm annoyed at him now for giving me so much, because without him in my life, and that's where this is going, the loss will be insurmountable. He's left a yearning inside me that I know will never be satisfied by anyone else. He was made for me, we're the perfect fit. And yet, he's still not prepared to let down his guard for me.

I need to go. I don't even want to process what happened last night anymore. He is too gorgeous, too perfect, and too dangerous. He will break my heart and leave me a mess. I can't bear that Gerard is right. Scared now because of how desperate I am to belong to Alex and no one else, I suddenly realize why he is afraid to love. Love like this is too painful and letting go is already traumatizing me.

Sliding out of bed, I gather my things and pile them into my suitcase. The zipper closing cuts through the silence and stirs Alex. I wait until he rolls over and his steady breathing resumes, then tiptoe out of the room. I freshen up in the bathroom then move to the living room where I get dressed. I put on jeans and a casual top, plait my hair, and then pile everything back into my suitcase. I take one last look around to make sure I haven't left anything behind, then notice a pen and notepad on the makeshift entrance table that consists of two step ladders and a plank. Grabbing them, I scribble a quick note.

I get it now, Alex. When it's real, it's just too painful. Forever in my heart, Paige x,

I cry non-stop along the esplanade. I cry the whole time I'm on the freeway, and even when I pull up at my first restroom stop. Sobbing uncontrollably into the dirty stainless steel sink as I splash chilling water on my face. Then, I stop. Finally falling numb, I become robotic. Fill my car with fuel. Grab a coffee. Fasten the seat belt. Get back on the road, get back to reality. But I'm a confused wreck who can't figure out what I want. Alex makes me feel vulnerable on a whole different level. There's so much he doesn't know about me.

I start thinking about my night with Oliver. Eww. What would Alex think if he knew about that? Then there's Jamison. And what's with the way he grabbed Kaitlyn's throat and his threat to kill Rebecca? He was in a room screwing a stranger and he knows the security guys. Why, Gerard would acquaint himself with a man like Jamison. Who the hell is he anyway? And how can he think he knows Gerard better than Alex?

My heart starts racing again at the prospect of Jamison calling Gerard and I'm so caught up in thoughts, I miss my exit to the airport and need to go the long way around. Then, I only just make my flight because it takes forever to find long-term parking and check-in became a nightmare. It's nearing one when we land at Denver, and I'm thankful that I managed to get some sleep on the flight.

I wait for the luggage to turn up on the carousel then rent a car. It's around two when I settle in the compact Ford Fiesta and prepare myself for the hour-long drive to Ponderosa Park. But when I reach the parking lot boom gates, I remember I still have my phone set on airplane mode. Quickly, because there's a line-up of cars behind me, I enable my cell, then toss it on the passenger seat and finally get going.

Just when I'm entering the freeway, my phone rings. Annoyed that I didn't take the time to pair it to Bluetooth, I swipe without looking and press it to my ear. It's most likely Sheree just checking I've arrived.

"Hi, I'm on my way."

"You could have said goodbye."

I pause until my stomach rights itself and the cringe leaves my face. "I didn't want to wake you."

"It would have been nice to see you before you left." Alex says, making me smile. "And what's with the note?"

I inhale audibly. "I don't know."

"You don't know?"

"I think we... No, you... Shit, Alex. What do you want from me? You keep telling me to leave Gerard, but at the same time you say you don't want me. How can I just leave him and float around until you've had your fill of screwing other people?"

"So… What? You think I'm gonna stop being a man with urges and wait for you when you've made no attempt to leave Gerard? What are you fucking waiting for?"

"I'm not waiting for anything. But you're trying to damn well save Jolene. How come she's worth rescuing and I'm not? You keep saying I don't know what I want, but I do. I want you. But the reason I can't just up, and leave is because he threatened you. I'm trying to protect you, damn it. When the police came the other month about the robbery, Gerard implied you were responsible. He used your name as a threat. If I just up and leave Gerard, he will hurt you to get back at me. That's what he does. That's why I stay.

"Paige."

"No. Stop being so loving and confusing me. Have your carefree life with all the woman you can screw. It just hurts loving you." I pause to catch my breath and lower my voice. "Gerard's probably right anyway. You'd just break my heart and I'd be left with nothing. Maybe that was your plan? Turn me into a wreck so Gerard ends up with some shell of a wife. Because it worked. I'm fucking dead inside. I'll always be dead inside because loving you kills me a little more every day, but for you, I'm just some sex on the side."

"You think that's all you are to me, a quick screw?"

"Well why do you keep letting me back in if you're only going to push me away?"

"Because you need to be free to be yourself. You asked me a thousand questions last night. My turn. Who are you, Paige? What do you want that doesn't include a man? Do you want to become famous for your art? Have you ever wanted to travel? What about that chick in the shop? She said you wanted to go to Bali. Why haven't you gone? Do you need to do everything with Gerard? You deserve to live your life. Not the life Gerard has planned for you. Or should I say, himself, which includes you? Take his money and fucking run."

"So that's what this is really about, isn't it? You're setting me up so you can get your hands on his money somehow?"

The silence that follows is nauseating. I can almost imagine him crushing the phone in his hand. I've said too much. Meant none of it. Hurt him beyond repair.

"Fuck you, Princess on Solsbury Hill," he finally spits out.

"What does that even mean?" I yell.

"Google it."

Frustrated, I disconnect.

My tears and anger turn into a wail. How can he not understand how hard this is for me? It's not as if I don't want to be with him, and he knows it. It's him who doesn't want me, he'd rather screw everything else in a damn skirt. Set myself free. Free to do what if it's not something with him?

My phone springs to life and jars me out of my rage. I don't even pause, just swipe the screen, ready with an apology.

"I'm so sorry. I didn't…"

"You should be, you selfish fucking rapacious bitch. I hope you realize what you've done?"

Instantly, my tears evaporate and I'm shaking.

"Seriously, how do you even sleep at night? Haven't I given you everything you've ever wanted? I forgave you. I trusted you, and the second I go out of town you're with him."

"Stop yelling at me, Gerard, I'm driving, and you're scaring me."

"You should be terrified—and ashamed. You fucking cheater."

"Ashamed? Going out doesn't mean I'm cheating, Gerard." I reply, believing Jamison has spoken with him.

"Oh. So you don't think it's cheating, being tied to a bed and fucked by a man who isn't your husband?"

I feel the life drain from me.

"What?" I breathe out slowly, my foot easing off the accelerator. Tears rise to the surface. Alex outed me.

"You really must think I'm an idiot. Boy, don't you have some groveling to do? Let's see. There's been... The dry hump on the couch. Then you sucked him off. Oh, and the fuck on the table, not to mention the marathon in his bedroom last night while I was out of town. What sort of lowly wife are you? Tsk, fucking tsk. And throughout this whole time, you've been holding out on me because of Oliver, which you seemed to enjoy—by the fucking way!"

Pulling over onto the side of the road, I can hardly breathe.

"Alex told you?" I ask, needing the confirmation.

"Did you think I was joking when I said I have friends in high places, Paige? I will have that bastard sent back to prison quicker than he seems to make you come. Where else have you two been screwing around? I'm keeping score, and right now you owe me. Didn't you catch on when I said an eye for an eye?"

"What, nowhere, I didn't. We didn't." I answer between tears, praying to God he's just bluffing, guessing. But he's too accurate. Alex must have told him but no, why would he describe those details? It's as if Gerard was there in the house. And then it hits me.

"Oh my God, Gerard. No, no, no. You have cameras in Alex's house. Why?" I exhale heavily within a sob.

"It's my fucking house," he screams, sending me into another fit of tears. "I should kill the son of a bitch. How dare he try stealing my wife when I've helped him out, not to mention you! You! Words can't even describe what you've become. You don't deserve me. I thought I might catch you visiting him once maybe, but no, you've been going at it like goddamn rabbits. You disgust me. Who the hell are you, and where is your decorum?"

Gerard's bellowing is so loud, my ear is ringing and snot is running down my face so fast, I have trouble wiping it away quick enough. I'm hot and scared out of my mind.

"Please, stop. I'm sorry. Gerard. I'm sorry. I promise it's over with Alex, just stop yelling at me. I'll leave. I'll pack my things when I get home. You're right I don't deserve you."

"You're not leaving me, Paige." Suddenly, he is calm again and my stomach drops. "I'm invested in what we have. You're mine. I could have had anyone, but I chose you. We took vows. You said you loved me. I thought if you were bored with our sex life, I could spruce it up. In the motel room, before Alex, it was you who said it needed to be a 'we' thing. So why have you shut me out? I was including you. I had plans for us to explore things together."

I can't stop crying. I'm wrecked to the bone and the calm way he's speaking is making me feel even sicker.

"I know I said that, and it was true." Shame inflames my face. "But you're different now. I don't know who you are anymore."

"I've become different?" He sounds bewildered. "You're not serious, are you? You're the one changing; into a trollop. I had sex with someone else to teach you a lesson. That you can't hold out on me and not expect me to get it elsewhere." Gerard is so calm; my sobbing seems uncalled for. "I've been extremely tolerant of both yours and Alex's behavior. Like I warned, I could have him back in prison in a heartbeat. You've been playing a treacherous, deceitful game, don't you think?"

"You have been tolerant, Gerard, and I'm sorry. Please, don't do anything to Alex. I take full responsibly."

"Oh, I could see that. Don't you have any class? You've become a cheap slut, throwing yourself at him, even letting him tie you up like that. Who's the one with a fetish, Paige? I can't believe you let him do that after what happened to you. Makes me question if you were telling the truth about Carlos. You're a dirty, disgusting harlot for letting Alex do that, aren't you?"

I've stayed silent as he berates me, my hand swiping at my face as every beautiful moment I had with Alex gets stripped away by Gerard's repulsion from what he's witnessed.

"Aren't you?" he yells again, forcing me to admit it.

"Yes," I whisper.

"For now, given you are about to bury your mother, I will allow you to continue using the credit card. But if you use it to get away from me. I will hunt you down and bring you home because that's where you belong. Are we clear?"

"Yes."

Abruptly, he ends our call, leaving me shattered and staring at my cell. Never in my entire life have I felt so scared, ashamed, alone, and completely sick inside.

Over the next hour, I drive in a daze. Twice, I pull over and vomit. My head is pounding so relentlessly that I just can't think anymore.

The pine forest five miles before Ponderosa Park is an indication I've almost arrived. From what I can tell, nothing much has changed, and any earlier plans I'd had about revisiting my old stomping grounds, are abolished. After my heated call from Gerard, my mind is literally numb. The most I was capable of doing following his call, was to concentrate on the road. In places, the road was still a little icy, and I nearly lost it several times around the bends. Although only an hour, it was the longest drive of my life, and contrary to telling Gerard I would stay at the Caledonian, I'm so exhausted, I pull into the first hotel I come across.

By the state I'm in, I'm not surprised the hotel owner wastes no time showing me to a room.

Sitting slumped on the end of the bed, I try to make my mind work. I need to let Alex know about the cameras. I search for my phone and scroll my contacts but there are none. Only Gerard's remains. Confused to what has happened to my contact list, I search apps on my home screen thinking they've moved, then it dawns on me. Gerard. He deleted them. My entire contact list is gone, and the only other number I know by memory, apart from Gerard's, is Sheree's. I re-enter it then text her letting her know I've arrived.

Sheree texts back, suggesting dinner with her mom, but I text back and decline, telling her I'm shattered from a late night and rough flight. The only thing I want is sleep. I curl up in a self-indulgent ball, wiping away more stupid tears. Both Alex and Gerard have fractured me in so many ways, I'm unsure who's right and who's wrong. What's definitely wrong though, is Gerard having cameras on Alex. I sit up quickly and reach for my phone. I press the recent calls list. Gerard's number is there, and…Where is Alex's number? No. No, no, no. Of all the things in the world for Alex to have, why oh, why does he have an unlisted number? I toss the useless phone to the floor, then my eyes dart around the room that looks hauntingly like the hotel room Gerard and I shared with Oliver. Then I spot the bottle of wine amongst the minibar. Screwing off the top, it takes me less than an hour to drink the entire bottle before passing out in my clothes, my feet still hanging over the edge of the bed.

~

I'm shaken.

"Mrs. Whitmyer."

I'm shaken again.

"Mrs. Whitmyer."

"What?" I groan, rolling because my lower back hurts like hell.

"Mrs. Whitmyer. I'm sorry to come in but I've been knocking, and you didn't respond."

"What?" I'm so groggy I can't even comprehend where I am.

"Mrs. Whitmyer, the police are here."

Abruptly, I pull myself into a sitting position, my vision spinning erratically. The hotel manager takes a step back and glances at the open doorway of my room. My gaze follows hers to two uniformed policemen looking somber until they glance at the empty bottle of wine at my feet, then scowl.

"Thank you. That's all we'll be needing from you." One officer says to the lady who woke me. I notice she is in her dressing gown, and I glance at the clock radio on the wooden shelve next to the bed. It's nine thirty-eight.

I wipe the sleep from my eyes and stand. "Has something happened?" I look from one person to the other. The police give nothing away, but the manager looks concerned.

"If you need anything, just come and see me, love," she says with a tight smile then leaves. Both policemen watch as she walks away, and I sneak the opportunity to grab the complimentary bottled water. My movements cause their attention to dart back to me, making me feel like they have caught me shoplifting.

"We need you to come with us, Mrs. Whitmyer."

"Why, what's happened?" I leave the bottle where it is and steadying myself against the cabinet instead. I'm so light-headed, I think I'm still drunk. "I've only just arrived in town. It this about my mother?"

"Please. Could you gather your things and come with us? We've had a call from your husband. You are Mrs. Paige Whitmyer, are you not?" the younger of the officers asks.

"Yes." Gingerly, I sidestep back to the bed and take a seat, my eyes scanning the floor where I spot my phone. The same officer reaches for my device then hands it to me.

"Thanks. Why did he call you?" Tapping my phone, I see I have six missed calls from Gerard.

"Your whereabouts were of a concern. Were you aware you have a booking at the Caledonia hotel?"

"Oh that. Yeah, I just… Well, when I got to town, I was so tired I pulled in here. It's fine. Thanks for checking on me though. I'll call him and let him know you found me," I say, getting to my feet and moving toward the still open door.

"I'm sorry. I'm afraid your husband has requested we escort… That we see you safely to the Caledonian. Can you please collect your belongings? Officer Munroe will follow behind with your rental car as it's apparent you've been drinking. We can't allow you to drive, I'm afraid."

"Ma'am, is this your only bag?" The older officer, apparently Munroe, asks, picking up my suitcase.

"Yes, but you don't understand. I don't want to stay at the Caledonian. I'm fine right here. I'm sure once I call my husband, and he knows I'm fine, it won't matter where I stay."

They give each other a look before Munroe makes his

way into the bathroom and checks for any more belongings, I assume. The younger officer leaves the room to speak on his radio that's calling out for all available patrol, under a code I have no clue to its meaning. My heart is racing so hard I need to sit down again. What is this? I can't help shaking. I lunge up and grab the bottle of water then quickly drink it down.

"Ma'am. Please. Can you let us assist you? If you'll just hand over your car keys and leave the room key behind." He points to the small round table near the window.

"I don't think you understand."

The other officer comes back inside, and from the look they give me, it's apparent, they're not at all interested in negotiating. Are these guys 'those' people in high places Gerard is always threatening me with, or are they legitimately concerned for my well-being? Is this even allowed? Being forced out of the motel against my will? Are they real officers or someone paid by Gerard to dress up, like the fake Jolene?

"Ma'am."

I draw in a deep breath. "I'd like to see some identification before I leave with you." I hold out my shaking hand, which I'm sure they both notice. Taking impatient turns, they hand over their ID, and I pretend to know what I'm looking for. I wouldn't be able to spot a fake if it jumped out to slap me in the face. I study their photos and then their faces. The younger officer is Beret by name, and he keeps his hand outstretched. "Do you know my husband personally?" I ask, handing back his leather badge wallet.

"We're not at liberty to discuss who and how we are acquainted with persons in the legal system. We are simply here to escort you to where your husband has been assured is a safe house."

"A safe house? What's the threat? Why am I in danger?"

"I'm afraid your husband has concerns that your life could be in danger."

"From who?" I snap.

Officer Beret takes me by the arm and hands me my handbag without answering.

"Keys please, Mrs. Whitmyer."

Oh my God! Is Gerard for real? He'll seriously go to these lengths. I'm shocked into silence and let them lead me away, no longer caring if these men mean to harm or help me. And as I'm driven away in the back seat of a police car like a criminal, the larger part of me hopes they do put a bullet in my head and leave me to die. My life has turned into a living nightmare where there are villains no matter where I go, and everywhere my thoughts go, it seems it's all downhill from here. I've screwed up big time, and now I'll spend the rest of my life in purgatory.

6

WHEN THE PARTY'S OVER

From somewhere, there's an irritating rapping sound that stops and starts, getting louder and louder until it's knocking right inside my skull, surely making the meningeal lining swell past its capacity, and why I'm groaning as I become fully conscious.

"Housekeeping."

There's a grating noise that sends shock waves along my teeth and into my jawbone, making me groan louder. My eyes peel slowly open, then clamp shut the moment bolts of sunlight pierce my pupils, shooting pain straight to the center of my brain.

"Ah! Perdoname. Volveré. I come back, Perdon, Perdon."

The room falls dark again.

～

"Zzzzz, zzzzz, zzzzz."

Silence.

"Zzzzz, zzzzz, zzzzz."

Silence.

"Hola, housekeeping. Es hora de ir a la señorita. Con permiso. It is past check-out time now."

"Argh. Whatever happened to late check-out? Please leave me alone. I'm sick," I whine out to the stranger.

"Okay, bien, fifteen minutes. Volveré más tarde," says the woman. My head's throbbing so badly I can't even open my lids to lay eyes on her when I thank her. I'm wishing now more than ever the police from last night had put a bullet in me.

After seeing me checked into the Caledonia, the most prestigious hotel in Ponderosa Park, the police left me in the lobby. I stood staring at the concierge for the longest time with my key card and suitcase clutched in my hand. When the young man asked if I was all right, I asked for a taxi to take me to a doctor. The doctor barely battered an eyelid when I requested sleeping pills. I'd gathered it was because I looked a mess. Promising him I would not mix them with alcohol, I returned to the Caledonian.

After showering and slipping into the hotel's bathrobe, I popped the pills and drank almost everything alcoholic that was stocked in the room, then crawled into bed.

Sadly, I'm still here to tell the tale.

With a splitting headache that I rightfully deserve for being so incredibly cruel to myself, I pack my belongings, put the key card on the table, the 'Do Not Disturb' sign on the door handle, then pull the door shut behind me.

Fuck you, Gerard, and that shiny horse you damn well rode in on because—I shelter my eyes until I recover my sunglasses and look about the parking lot for my rental—I'm going to Sheree's whether you like it or not. Hopefully, he doesn't even know where Darby lives or even his last name. Even if he did, surely he'd never send anyone around anyway. There would be too many questions, and I'm not prepared to lie anymore.

I get comfortable in the rental car, check the directions Sheree gave, noting the property is only a half hour drive. But I'm having trouble seeing straight, let alone driving twenty odd miles out of town.

Looking around the small interior, I find the half empty bottle of water I purchased the day before and gulp it down. It's only then I think of the Tylenol I have in my bag.

"Damn it, you idiot." I stare down at the pill packet and then the empty bottle of water before looking out at the deserted hotel parking lot hoping to spot a vending machine. I don't.

"Shit," I cuss, dry retching twice before flinging open the car door and vomiting onto the asphalt.

"Christ." I let my head fall back onto the headrest. I can't function. I need something to eat, to drink, but the thought of food makes me feel ill. Then I'm remembering my call from Gerard yesterday, and I feel worse. I need to pull myself together. Get organized, get my damn mother's shit sorted and get home. I need to pretend like the last few months never happened. I'm not going to Sheree's. I need to keep her out of it and do as my husband says. I need to run, to eat healthy and to get back to my normal life. *My normal life.* What the hell is a normal life?

I grip the steering wheel, draw in a few deep breaths trying to right my mind, then I start the engine and head farther into town to collect my mother's belongings.

The waiting room is small and hot, and there are bums in every available chair, including mine. Christ! Was there a damn death spree on while I wasn't looking? I'm surprised to see so many people can be waiting in a coroner's office at one time. I fixate on the poster of the Rocky Mountains, trying to recall the names of the peaks, anything just to get my mind working again. But, after several minutes I realize I'm just staring at the same nameless peak, nursing an empty, flimsy, plastic cup. And although my mouth feels like I've consumed chalk for breakfast, I can't will my legs to move the mere three steps to the water cooler. I'm questioning whether I've had a breakdown of some sort. I'm completely numb and shockingly hungover.

"Eleven," calls out a clerk. I look around the somber group.

"Number eleven." The clerk looks straight at me.

My brain engages. I look down at my ticket. "Yes —that's me."

In the next moment, I'm standing at the counter trying not to hurl vomit every time I catch the garlic breath of the man in front of me. I deserve this punishment. I'm a scheming and ungrateful bitch. No wonder Alex doesn't want me. Who wants to commit to someone who is a known cheater?

"I don't blame him," I mumble to myself while staring vaguely at the clerk's head as I have my epiphany.

"Excuse me?" The clerk pops his head up.

"Nothing."

"Well, if you will just sign here, and here, and one more over the page." The clerk pushes his glasses up his nose, then slides me a pen. It aches just to move. Even the pen scratching on the paper is making my head throb, including my face. I'm barely holding on to the vomit that keeps threatening, and I can't believe I've had to wait in the small stinking coroner's office for more than an hour so I can collect the belongings my mother allegedly had on her at the time of her death. Having been homeless, I can't even imagine what those possessions would be. Aside from a packet of cigarettes and a bottle of alcohol.

"If you'll just take a seat again, I'll have someone bring her possessions."

"Seriously?" I let out a noisy sigh. Finalizing my mother's affairs is getting beyond excruciating. Stealing a deep breath and slumping, I turn away, only to discover my seat has been taking by some whiny kid with a runny nose. Could my life get any worse? I wander across the room and lean against a wall then stare at the carpet.

Finally, after minutes of waiting, my name is called.

Still in a daze, I look up at a female attendant with a transparent plastic bag containing my mother's life, swinging in her hand like it's a pendulum. A splash of blue and coins, maybe a watch and something made of fabric. There's barely anything there. I've waited all this time for that! I can't help but picture my mom smirking at me. I purse my lips to stop the quiver, but I can't stop my eyes from glazing over. I want a mother. A real living mother, someone who I can run to. Someone who will help me. I want to be looked after, nursed back to health, but there's no nurturer for me because my mother is dead, and Gerard hates me now.

"Mrs. Whitmyer," the attendant snaps, her eyes fixated on me. Pushing myself off the wall, I walk the short distance to the counter again.

"Thank you." I take the bag then head out the door where the icy air wraps around my face. Bitter and wet. I stand there, letting it burn my skin. Almost welcoming it until I feel a rush of heat and then my blood seems to drain away, my wicked hangover taking root again. The pounding in my head is so severe, white light pulses and burns behind my eyeballs. And then it comes. Without warning. Vomit. Straight up and out from where I stand, in the main street of Ponderosa Park, and spraying across the hood of my rental car.

"What the hell?" I hear someone call out. "Are you deranged?"

Turning toward the voice, there's white noise, and the building in front of me sways and becomes fuzzy. A shadowy figure emerges from inside the coroner's office when the door opens. My sight goes black before someone rushes forward and grabs me around the shoulders. I'm shaking, giddy and hot. As I fall, the lady coming to my aid staggers to bear my dead weight when my knees buckle.

"Oh my God, are you all right?"

"What's happenin…" I slur. And in the bat of an eyelid…

"Someone call for an ambulance."

… I black out.

It's the sound of my breathing that enters my consciousness first. Then a familiar smell. It's subtle and earthy. I struggle to place it. My eyelids are heavy, and they stick when I try to open them. When I clear my throat, it burns, but then warm hands surround one of mine. I fight with my lids again, then give up. It's too much effort so I let myself slide back into the warmth of nothingness.

"Come on Paige, please wake up." Someone is caressing my forehead, soothing and nice, and I smell a cleanliness around me. What is that smell?

Again, my hand is squeezed. "That's it, wake up, we've got some catching up to do."

I try clearing my throat again, then I'm drifting. Dreaming about Gerard and me on opposite sides of a small lake. Every time he walks to the left or right, I follow his moves so he has no idea how to reach me. He coos my name at first, but the more I play the game, the more frustrated he's getting. Finally, he snaps out my name, and instantly he is beside me.

"Paige."

I startle, and my eyes spring open, wide but dazed until they settle on a pair of familiar eyes that come into focus. I gasp and jerk back, setting my heart racing.

"Hi there, stranger. It's been way too long. How are you feeling?" Sheree's blue eyes are misty, and she's still as gorgeous as ever. She leans in to hug me. When she pulls away, I can't help staring at her almost in disbelief. She's so beautiful, so familiar. Then I feel the crushing in my chest, and tears wring out.

"Oh, sweet pea, no. It's okay—you're fine, you're in the hospital."

"God, I never realized how much I've missed you, Sheree. So, so much." I squeeze her hand in return.

"I know. I've missed you too. Five years is way too long for sisters-from-another-mother." She smiles.

Her endearing words, as nice as they are, just add pressure to my already tight chest. And my face feels to be draining of blood.

"I'm going to get a nurse." Sheree tries to pull her hand away, but I hold on fiercely, shaking my head.

"At least I kept in contact, right?" I ask, needing confirmation that I'm not all selfish and bad.

"Not nearly enough. I can't believe how little you're on Facebook, you're practically an enigma since you left."

"I've messed everything up, Sheree. It's bad, so bad. My life is a wreck."

"Oh, Paige, don't, don't upset yourself. Everything is fine. Let me get the nurse for you."

Sheree tries to pull away, but I hold tight.

"Please tell me you didn't call anyone."

Sheree frowns. "Not yet. The doctors said you'd most

likely just fainted. I've been waiting for you to wake up before I did anything."

"Thank God." I let go of her hand, and instead of leaving, she pulls in the chair she'd been using and studies me.

"What's going on, Paige?"

"Can I have water, please?" I pull myself up into a sitting position. It's only then I notice the drip in my left arm. "How long have I been out?" I look around, taking in my surroundings, and then look for my handbag. Sheree pours out a cup of water from the plastic jug on the bed table.

"The hospital called about an hour ago." She hands me the glass. "So, I guess a little more than that. They brought you in an ambulance." As though reading my mind, she bends and picks up my handbag and places it on the bed.

"Is everything all right with you and Gerard?" She sits on the edge of the bed this time, looking concerned. "Is that why they called me and not him?"

Still taking a long gulp from the cup, I shake my head. I can't believe how dry my mouth is.

"No, I've got you listed in case of emergency on my phone. I hope you don't mind. I listed you as my sister." I smile.

"Ahh." She nods as though it answers a question I wasn't privy to. "No, of course not."

She reaches for the pitcher again and refills my glass. "So… You don't want me to call Gerard for you?"

Downing the last of the water in my cup, I hand it back to her. "No, I don't. What I really want is to get out of here. I hate hospitals." I look at the cannula embedded in my arm. Sheree frowns as I grope around the bed for the buzzer. I growl when I don't find one.

"Paige, slow down. What are you looking for?"

"Where's the stupid buzzer, fuck it?"

Sheree reaches for my hand. "Paige, stop. What's going on?"

I can't bear to look at her now. Even though I've kept Sheree in the dark, I'm afraid she will see through me, and get angry at my stupidity and deceit. She grabs my arms and gently shakes me, which seems to dislodge the waterfall waiting to spill. I know I must look pitiful. I'm worrying her all over again. But I just don't know where to start.

Just then, the curtain is whisked back, and a male doctor interrupts us. I quickly wipe my eyes and Sheree rises from the bed and steps out of the way.

"Hello, Paige, I'm Doctor Fulwood. How are you feeling now?" He flicks over the first page of the chart he is holding.

"Better, thanks."

"That's no surprise. When you were admitted, your blood pressure was low. How about I give it another check?" He smiles warmly then moves about the room with purpose until he has gizmos attached to take my vitals.

"How's your diet at the moment, Paige? Have you been taking in enough calories?"

Nodding, I think about what I've eaten lately. I'd skipped breakfast and then last night's meal was sedatives and alcohol. It has calories. Come to think of it, the last time I ate was Rebecca's curry. The only thing since then was the coffee at the roadhouse.

"To be honest, I guess not. I've been a little stressed over the past weeks, and no, I haven't been eating very well."

Sheree throws me a scowl and shakes her head. then looks on, concerned, as the doctor continues with his diagnosis.

"I'm afraid you're also extremely dehydrated. We've ran some blood tests to determine if there are any underlying factors that would cause you to faint, but I'm confident it's a matter of not looking after yourself correctly."

When he mentions blood tests, my heart flutters, wondering if they'll be able to detect the Molly.

"I'm sure I don't need to remind you that you should drink at least six to eight glasses of water a day." He removes the pressure cuff and oxygen clamp from my finger. Wheeling the stand away, he addresses Sheree.

"If you don't mind, I need to examine Paige in private? A nurse will join me in a moment. If you can just wait in the hall, we'll let you know when we're done."

"Is something wrong? Did the blood test show up something?" Sheree questions.

"No, there's nothing wrong. I'd just like to do a quick exam." He pulls the curtain back, encouraging Sheree to leave, and a nurse is heading our way.

"I'll be fine." I smile weakly at Sheree when she seems reluctant to leave.

When she's gone, the nurse pulls the curtain back around to give us some privacy. She introduces herself then stands idle as the doctor pulls back my blanket and lifts my top.

"Sorry," he says, when I flinch from his cool hands that now probe my lower abdomen.

I watch as he applies pressure gently just above my pubic bone. He turns to gauge my reaction then asks if it hurts anywhere.

"No. Should it?"

He shakes his head. "Not necessarily. I'm just asking if you feel any pain." Satisfied, he fixes my top and blanket until I'm covered again.

"Just another bag of fluids please, Karen, and then Mrs. Whitmyer can be discharged," he instructs the nurse, who touches my leg then leaves the room. The doctor gets comfortable at the end of the bed and eyes me. I shift and pull myself straighter, readying myself for what he has to say.

"Paige, are you aware you're pregnant?"

Too busy analyzing the possibilities that I don't speak for the longest time.

"But that's not possible. I'm on the pill. I take it every day. Every day. I've never missed one, ever."

"Have you recently had antibiotics or any other medication that could interfere with it?"

"No. Seriously, nothing," I say, shaking my head, expecting any second now he'll say that he must be mistaken. But he doesn't.

I'm suddenly sweaty all over. It's not possible, I've been so careful. Then I feel faint again.

"Is the baby all right? I mean I drank a bottle of wine and took sleeping pills and the other night… Christ, I…" I catch myself before I say too much. "Shit. I've probably killed it. That's why I feel like crap." I let out a groan and I'm tempted to pull back the blankets to see if I'm suddenly bleeding.

"So, you didn't know?"

"No. Are you sure? Did you run it a few times? I mean those tests can muck up, can't they? And maybe all the drinking and the sleeping pills gave a false positive."

"Generally, blood tests don't lie. That's why I wanted to do a physical examination to be certain. Although only just pregnant, I can feel a slight enlargement of your uterus. At a guess, you're about eight to ten weeks along. I suggest we do an ultrasound. We can get a better understanding of the baby's condition that way."

"No. No, I can't. You don't understand, my husband won't …" My face heats. "I need to go. I really need to get out of here. I have my mother's funeral tomorrow."

I pick at the tape that holds my cannula in place. The doctor halts my hand.

"You really need more fluids, Paige. For the sake of the baby. And I suggest you have it before you leave here. I'd also like to see you eat something."

I fall back against the pillows. "I just don't know how my life could get any worse." I shake my head. "I can't do this anymore."

Looking concerned, the doctor rises from the bed just as the nurse returns with a bag of fluids. She fusses about attaching the bag and discards the drained one.

"I'd like Mrs. Whitmyer to eat something as soon as possible. When this bag is done, she may be discharged. Unless you feel you'd like to talk with someone, Paige?" He adjusts the dial on the drip, throwing me a raised eyebrow, obviously worried about my mental health now. But I'm just hoping he's setting the drip to hyperdrive so I can get out of here, and gauging by the noise outside my cubical, it sounds as though they could use my bed anyway.

"No. I'll talk with my friend, she's as good as it gets, probably better."

The nurse smiles knowingly at me, then leaves the room, reassuring me she will return with some sandwiches.

"I recommend you see your local doctor as soon as possible. I can give you the name of an obstetrician in Los Angeles if you'd prefer to see a specialist. And I urge you to eat, young lady. It's not only important for you, but also the baby. Do you have any questions?"

Even though I have hundreds of them, I shake my head. One being, how do I get through the rest of my life now that it's falling apart?

"I'll send your friend back in then." He pulls the curtain closed in his wake.

Sheree and the sandwiches arrive at the same time. I don't even feel like eating, but my heart is racing, and I know that's not a good sign.

"What did he say?" Sheree asks, handing me the small plate with white triangles that look sad. Sheree sits on the bed again, facing me.

"Nothing good."

Sheree's face pales slightly, and she wraps a hand around my ankle.

"No, it's nothing life-threatening. Well, at least not if I keep it to myself."

"Paige, stop being so damn cryptic," she scolds softly, then looks around, perhaps feeling uncomfortable because I know she hates to cuss.

Unwrapping the plate of sandwiches, I pull back the top layer of bread and wince at the sight of the contents. "Really!" With just a shred of meat and slivers of tomato, the sandwich barely constitutes a soggy snack.

"Eat."

"I'll most likely end up right back here tonight if I do. It looks gross. Christ, can you get rid of it?" I shove the plate at her in disgust. "Just looking at it makes me want to puke again. Honestly, I think I'm cursed." I look up at the bag of saline. "Do you think if we squeeze the bag it will go faster?"

"Oh my God, Paige. What's with you? You're stalling and being bitchy, this is not you. Honestly, you look like shit. I can't believe how much weight you've lost, and it's not like you can afford to. What did the doctor say?"

"He said I'm a stupid idiot who has shit for brains."

She places the plate on the trolley then looks at me deadpan. "Stop it."

"I'm pregnant." It just slips out, and now that it's out, I know the rest will follow. All of it.

Sheree comes to life. I watch her whole demeanor swell. Even her cheeks flush and her eyes sparkle. It's enough to push me over, and I can't hold back the tidal wave.

"Why aren't you happy? A baby. You're going to have a baby," she gushes, almost squealing.

"No. I'm not," I snap. "I agreed to no children before getting married, and with the shit that I've been getting up to lately, I'll be lucky if I've got a home to go back to. In fact, I'm not sure if I even want to go home." Sheree's eyebrows become fixed at saluting the ceiling.

"I know. I've fucked up big time, you have no idea! I've been living a lie for the last five years, and I know when I tell you everything, you'll be disgusted and hate me forever. I just know it. But I couldn't help it, Sheree. It was love, and I would have done anything for him."

Sheree stares at me, dumbfounded, my anguish has tears brimming her lids. "Um. I think I need to get you to my place, pronto. Sweet pea, you have some serious unburdening to do."

7

EMPTY NOTE

It's well past two by the time I'm discharged from the hospital, and although it was a pain in the ass, I admit, I'm feeling much better. After seeing the discarded plate of sandwiches, a nurse offered me homemade pasta she'd brought in for lunch, which I happily devoured. I had a vague sense I knew her from school, but I'd kept quiet. Truth is, I'm ashamed to be remembered. After dropping me off at my rental car, which mercifully someone had washed the vomit from, Sheree left to do a quick grocery shop. Not before some serious pleading, which had me agreeing to make my way to her place, instead of sticking to my plan and returning without spending time with her.

Sliding into my rental, I toss my handbag across the front seat of the car causing the contents to spill out. Suddenly I'm confronted with my mother's meager belongings which I had totally forgotten about. Picking up the plastic bag, I study what's inside. I'm saddened all over again by how little she possessed.

I'd been right about the watch. It's broken. The glass is

cracked and no longer ticking. I'm surprised she kept it at all. It seems the fabric I'd noted was a small piece from what I assume was a blanket because of the slightly, frayed satin ribbon along one edge. Why on earth would she carrying that around? It seems strange and out of place, there, amongst the collection.

There are some coins and a five-dollar bill. Hair clips and a pair of fingernail cutters, a comb, and lastly, a key, which I assume is a relic from the house we once lived in, which would be well and truly redundant now. Certainly anyone living there now, would have long since changed the locks, if not burned the thing to the ground.

When I turn over the blue tag attached, I'm expecting to be reminded of my childhood address, but it has a stamp on it, telling me it belongs to a storage facility. Surely she didn't have a storage container and yet nowhere to live? Curious, I Google the yard to see if it even exists. When I find that it does, right here in Ponderosa Park, I decide to check it out.

After punching the directions into the GPS, the budget car and I are soon rattling along a gravel road until Siri announces we have arrived at 'Samuel's Storage,' in her billion-dollar monotone.

Pulling over, I study the ominous yard full of old shipping containers, lockable sheds, and car wrecks crammed together in random places. The yard is graveled with road-base, not concreted like I was expecting, me being accustomed to seeing the neater looking facilities dotted around Malibu.

I look down at the key in my hand and note the storage container number. Given the obvious cheap storage, I figure there is a possibility my mother has belongings hidden away in there. I call Sheree to let her know what's going on, then turn my car off the road and go through the rusty chain-link gates.

When I pull up outside a converted shipping container serving as an office, an overweight, balding man steps out. His mouth is full of his lunch, and he uses his shoulder to wipe the saucy-food smears from his pudgy lips when I move closer to meet him.

"What can I do ya for, miss?"

Stepping forward, I extend my hand and show him the key. "This belonged to my mother, Mavis Guthrie. I'm assuming she has or had a container here. She passed away recently. I've come to town to finalize things." He looks at me long and hard with a finger tapping over his mouth.

"Mavis's daughter, hey?"

I shift my weight in my heeled boots and fold my arms over my chest, then nod.

"Hey, Rocket, get out here. There's a blast from the past standing in front of me," he hollers over his shoulder.

Uncomfortable with the sudden attention, I swivel around and take in the yard, hoping not to catch someone lurking with ill intent. Then something in me jolts. Rocket, I know that name. I'm not left wondering where from, for long, before Roger Pilkington comes into view.

"Well, you've got to be shitting me?" he blurts, wiping his hands on the front of his jeans, before crossing them over his chest. "Paige Guthrie." He checks me out from head to toe. I can't help but return his warm smile. "Hell, you look different. Je-sus, I never expected to see you in this neck of the woods again. You appear to be doin' all right for yourself now?" he says, still nodding as though in approval.

Roger is thinner than I remembered him from school. But then, that was years ago. His dirty-blond hair falls over eyes that look a little haunted if not slightly sunken in their sockets.

He was once not bad looking, but it's obvious he's been doing heavy drugs over the years. Although we grew up in the same neighborhood, we had a different circle of friends. I always understood him to be a bit of a badass. Forever the prankster at parties. He did crazy stuff like setting off exploding Molotov cocktails and rolling drunk friends stuffed in rusty forty-four-gallon drums down the levy bank by the old drive-in movie. I can honestly say he looks happier to see me than I him.

"I didn't know you worked here," I comment, having nothing better to say, because how would I know anyway. It's not like I ever asked Sheree about him. Looking around again, I suddenly notice the guard dogs barely on all fours because they're straining at their chains, trying to get a sniff of me from a distance.

"Ahh, me old man, Sammy here manages this place." Roger cocks his head in his father's direction. I acknowledge him again with a smile. "He used to own it, didn't ya Pa? That's his name on the gate, but he sold it off a few years back now. I just hang around when I got nothin' better to do. I work at Wrecks & Wrenches, mostly," he informs me. I nod, recalling the motor mechanical workshop in the heart of town.

"Rocket, you help Paige out. I got things to do. That all right, Paige?" Mr. Pilkington asks.

"Sure. I mean, that's if this key still owns a container."

"It sure do, all right. Ya ma came here once in a while after she stuffed all her things in there. I can't imagine what kind of condition it's in though. Gee, she must have dumped that stuff off, gosh, maybe that would have to be at least seven or eight years ago now. We don't get paid to keep rodents and shit out, but she had herself a shipping container, so nothing much gets in those things." He lifts his cap and scratches through his sparse hair. "It's the one on the left, Rocket, next to Old Man Tully's shed," he instructs.

"Yep, I'll find it," says Roger, leading the way, dodging dog shit and mud puddles as we make our way down the aisle between tall rows of shipping containers with the odd fixed shed in between. I can only imagine what's rotting away in there.

My mother's container is the third from the end in the row of perhaps sixteen. When we stop, Roger holds out his hand, gesturing for the key.

"So how long you in town?" he asks, taking hold of the lock and working the key.

"Only two days."

"You want to go out for a drink?"

"Sorry. I plan on catching up with Sheree."

"Uh-huh, figures. Yeah, I see her now and then around town. She married, got kids? What about you? You got kids, married?" he rushes on.

"I'm married. No kids," I reply quickly, hating that he just reminded me of my predicament. "Sheree's got a man but no kids. Yet." I add, figuring her elation earlier about my pregnancy means she'd definitely like one.

It takes Roger some effort to pull open the rusted doors, but when he does, we're greeted with a dank smell that reminds me of the equipment shed in high school. When my eyes adjust, I find hundreds of mummified frogs, shriveled up against boxes along the edge of the container. "Gross."

"I'll bring back a broom and give it a bit of a sweep," Roger offers.

I study the contents. "Don't bother. I won't be here long."

There's mostly furniture inside. Some boxes and an old push bike. I see a stack of magazines piled on a coffee table with mugs. It strikes me as odd. In fact, the closer I look, the more it appears she tried to set it up like a room. My mother's antique dressing table is laden with perfume bottles and a hairbrush. The recliner chair has a cushion on it, a footstool in reach and a blanket. And a cooler. No surprise there. It looks homely, in a sad way.

"I wonder why she's set it up like this?"

"Aww, people do that sometimes, you know get comfortable to go through their shit."

I nod. "I guess." I think again about how my mother was homeless, and yet here are her things, dry and warm, protected from the elements. As if reading my mind, Roger speaks up.

"Where is she? You know, ya Ma?"

"Dead." I shoot him a quick look. "It's the only reason I'm here." I state coldly.

"Sorry. Didn't know." Roger widens his eyes then nods. "Guess I won't be seeing her at the bar no mores, then. She was there a lot," he says, by way of condolence. I think.

"So Sheree tells me," I murmur. Not wanting to discuss my mother, I step into the container, carefully placing my feet so I don't stumble. There's so much stuff, I don't know where to look.

"What do you do these days? I suppose you're one of those fancy businesswomen now?"

"Nope, not really. I'm a photographer."

"Married money then?"

"Excuse me?" I snap my head around and glare at him.

"You know what I mean? Artsy people don't dress like you, all Gucci and shit."

I don't really want to have this conversation with Roger, so I ignore his rude question and inch myself farther into the container, my eyes adjusting to the lack of lighting as I familiarize myself with my mother's things.

"I guess I'm just going to go through some stuff. See if there's anything important in there. What's the chances your dad can get rid of what I don't want? He can sell it for all I care."

Roger pulls a cigarette out of his pocket and lights it. "I'll go ask. He usually auctions it off, you know when people stop paying or they die."

When he sees me flinch, he apologizes "Sorry, didn't mean to sound heartless. I'll get that broom, might help with the smell," he says over his shoulder walking away.

"I said to not bother," I remind him, but he waves me off over his shoulder.

Taking tentative steps, I move between boxes and furniture, trying to take stock of everything. It's the same furniture I remember when I left. A tall standing lamp, its shade skewed. Bags of clothing, some items I recognize, most I don't. There's an old two-door wardrobe with a mirror in the middle. I have a memory of my mom standing in front of it in a flowery fitted dress and my dad standing in the doorway, watching her and smiling. I don't remember how old I was, but I remember I was sitting on the bed watching them and playing with something. I think they were happy back then.

Pulling some cardboard boxes out of the way, I unlock the doors to the wardrobe and peer in. More boxes. Fancy ones, like hatboxes. Most are square except one round one. Covered in floral fabric, I assume they have more personal things in them than what seems to be strewn around in plain sight. The first box contains some old costume jewelry, clutch purses, hairbrushes, and clips. It appears that when packing, Mom just threw random things in. The second box holds more of the same, including stiletto heels and some hair accessories that I assume she once wore to the races or maybe a wedding. Nothing jolts my memory though.

The third and last box inside the wardrobe is heavy as I pull it out. Pushing boxes, I make room on the floor and take off the lid. On top are photo frames, then some books and some folded fabric underneath. I pull out the photo frames one by one and set them up around me on the boxes so I can get a good look. They're familiar to me. They'd been on the dresser in our home. One is of my mother's parents. An old black and white, and they are dressed in formal clothes. My pop is wearing a hat. He's a very attractive man, and my grandmother is short and plump. She looks young compared to him. I'd never noted that before now. I think of my marriage to Gerard. And again, I'm reminded of the apple and tree saying.

There are two photographs of me. One when I was a small child, the other a snapshot from school days wearing a blue and gray checked uniform. I pick it up and study my own eyes. It was taken after Dad left, I recall, so I must have been around twelve. It makes me uncomfortable looking at it. It was too close to the time my mother went spiraling downward into hell. Dragging me along with her. Oddly, she has a framed photo of a dog, a pet, because it's sitting on her lap.

Digging deeper into the box, I find some loose photos and some old letters. Curious, I pull out a hand-written letter. I recognize my mother's handwriting with the long loopy curls on her y's and g's.

Dear Chris, I hope you don't mind that I'm writing you. After you left, I started thinking about what you said, and I realize I was being unrealistic. So, in answer to your question, yes, I'm happy to just be friends. I hope you're enjoying Yountville...

I scan the page that mentions her day-to-day life until I reach the end.

The truth is, everything is boring with you gone, especially Lorry. Last week...

My eyes suddenly dart about the page looking for a date. I thought it was a long-ago boyfriend or something, but she mentions Lorry, my dad. I flip the pages over and over in my hand. Soon, I'm pulling out letter after letter, scanning for more clues.

Hello, Mavis. I'm not much good at letter writing, sorry. But I suppose at least I'm writing. I've...

Whoever this Chris guy was, he'd been writing my mother that he was happy and earning good money and might be back one day.

Rummaging around the box, I search for more letters, then come across a pile of loose photographs. Bundling them altogether, I sort through them. Mostly, they are of my mother as a teen. There are some of her holding me, and then some with my father in the frame. There's no stranger who could be Chris. Near the bottom of the box and sitting on some folded fabric that looks like a lightweight baby blanket, I find a notebook and my stomach flutters. Could it be a journal of hers? An opportunity for me to know my mother better. I'm disappointed when I open the front cover and discover it's a book full of drawings. Little sketches of dresses and blouses. Evening gowns and jackets, all quite detailed and shaded in pastel colors. It's a book I've never seen before, and if it weren't for the fact that my mother seemed to have signed each illustration, I would never have believed her capable of such talent. Page after page, although outdated, the designs are amazing. Her scribbled time stamp suggests she drew them in her late teens. I'm wondering now if she studied fashion before she become a mother. I continue to admire her work, and when I'm almost to the end, I come across another photo of her holding me. Well, at least I think it's me because I'm swaddled in a blanket.

The photo depicts my mother breastfeeding a small baby. She is smiling down in adoration; she looks beyond happy. She looks… in love. I smile then frown, wondering why I was wrapped in blue. Flipping the photo over, I expect to see my name and a date.

'Quintin October 1989.'

What? I was born in ninety-four. I turn it over again and study it harder, looking for something familiar, the window, the couch, anything to suggest that she was in the house I remember growing up in, but there's nothing. I keep looking back at the blue blanket and the baby's face.

"Holy shit!" I begin putting everything back into the box, deciding to go through it more thoroughly at Sheree's. My mother had another baby before me. I stand, still staring at the photo, shaking my head in disbelief, then look about the container again when I spot a large cardboard box with my name on it.

Stepping over more boxes until I'm in front of it, I bend, then peel back the flaps and rummage around, pulling back old schoolbooks, a few stuffed toys, my ballerina jewelry box. Then I see the familiar burgundy fabric. I jerk upright as if it had bitten me. Everything falls back on top of it, but I keep staring into the box with my heart palpitating. It's Sheree's Broncos jersey. A rush of memories overwhelm me, sending a shiver down my spine.

"Thought you might come snooping," comes a gruff, deep voice.

My head whips around to the entrance of the container and my heart freezes mid-beat. I catch my breath as my mind reels. Suddenly I'm embellishing the possibility of a secret exit to slip through. A hole, a vent, anything to get away from the ominous form that just spoke. But when my feet refuse to move, seemingly glued in place, I understand I'm cornered. Then I'm locking onto the shiny tan-leather shoes stepping into the container. First one, then the other.

My heart leaps into action again, thumping wildly inside my rib cage that suddenly feels too small. I shuffle around, my feet finally getting blood. I search the space again, wondering if there is a narrow escape past boxes or the wardrobe, anything to help me get past Carlos Mendez who is now dominating the entrance of my mother's storage container and my only way out.

8

MIDDLE FINGER

I'm certain I now understand what's going on. Somehow, I've slipped into an alternate universe where my life has become a soap opera. Where anything that could happen, will happen. To me. In quick succession, so I barely have time to keep up with the plot. Because right now, I'm trapped in a re-run scene with a man, nightmares are born from.

Every one of my five senses have become heightened, and for a moment, my brain is using every single one of them. If it wasn't so ludicrous, I swear I've been cast as the main character in *Limitless*, who is mentally trying to utilise everyday objects as weapons, and weighing up every possible scenario and outcome.

"Stay away from me," I hiss when Carlos takes another step inside the container. Cringing, I can suddenly feel him, smell him, taste him. I rub at my mouth where his mustache imprinted my soul. Groaning, I roll my shoulders and cross my arms to grip on to my collarbones, covering myself as though he can see me naked. I try desperately to push back the memories, but they won't go away anymore. With Carlos right here, yards away and leering at me, the corners of his mouth twisted into an evil grin, the past becomes all too real. Folding his arms over his black leather jacket, he looks indignant and cold. A contrast to his gold watch and ringed fingers catch the sunlight and cause orbs of light to dance around the otherwise dull box I'm trapped in.

"Well, look at you now, precious, all dressed up and looking damn glamorous," he drawls, his voice catapulting me backward in time.

"I swear to God, if you come any closer, I'll call the cops." I fumble inside my tote for my phone, my eyes still locked on Carlos. He's not as tall as I remember, and he has aged badly, his face craggy and his eyes sunken. His curly black hair is still the way I remember, trimmed and short at the sides. But the growth now continues down the sides of his face, ending mid-cheek and joining his disgusting mustache, giving him a more pimpish look than ever. He glances around the container as though in fascination. But I've pulled out my phone, ready to call the cops. I fumble with the cover, trying to flip it over without taking my eyes off Carlos and end up dropping the photo I'm still holding.

"Relax, I ain't gunner touch ya." He watches me closely as I bend to pick up the photo. "What you got there?" he comes farther inside, making me hurry so I can move away from him, again looking for a non-existent escape route.

"None of your business, just go away and leave me alone." I slide the photo into my tote and out of sight. "Why are you even here?" I snap.

"Maybe because I own this show." He moves quickly toward me.

"You do not, these are my mother belongings, not yours."

"The yard, dumbass," he says in a tight condescending tone, marching straight at me, his legs weaving easily between strewn boxes.

Backed up as far as I can go, my hand shoots out, warning

him to stay back, then my eyes dart to the screen of my phone. I swipe, then try punching in the passcode as fast as I can. Why did I put the stupid thing on it in the first place? Damn it!

Reaching me, Carlos snatches the phone then grabs my tote all in one swift movement.

I scream at the top of my lungs for help.

"Calm the hell down." He moves away slightly, then looks inside my bag. Pulling out the photo he looks at it briefly then shoves it back in my tote along with my phone. He dumps the bag at my feet. Then he's retreating, looking around the space again, checking everything out.

"Where you been, kid?"

"Nowhere." I bend to pick up my tote, dazed that he doesn't seem to be an obvious threat anymore. "And there's nothing here that's yours, so don't bother looking."

"Is that right, and how the fuck would you know, not like you were around."

"What did you expect? You raped me. I was a child for God's sake. A child!"

"You were a woman. Old enough to bleed, old enough to butcher, bitch."

"You're disgusting," I seethe, almost hissing at him.

He huffs.

"Know who's in that photo?" he asks, gesturing to my bag.

"I don't care, just get away from me. Get out."

"You should care, you little bitch. He was your brother."

Certain he's telling the truth. I don't question him.

Kicking a box out of the way, Carlos bends to pick up a Tupperware container, then peels back the lid. Finding nothing worth examining, he tosses it on the dressing table noisily, knocking empty perfume bottles over and sending at least two smashing to the floor.

"Your old man made her give him up. Did you know that? Then when she went looking for him, she found out he died."

Lost, I have no idea what Carlos is talking about. I take a step toward him, my eyes scanning for a clear path, hoping to outmaneuver him.

"I don't care. Just get out of my way, I'm leaving, do what you like with this crap. I don't want any of it anyway." Then I remember Sheree's Bronco jersey. Reaching into the box, I quickly tuck it under my arm.

"That bastard killed that kid, and you don't fucking care?"

"What are you talking about, Carlos? Why would my father kill his own child?"

"Wasn't his kid. He might not have strangled him himself, but he put him in the hands of someone who did. Broke Mavis's heart."

"She had no heart."

"Never had a heart? What about your prick of a father? What kind of man snatches a kid from his mother and hands him over to murderers?"

"What kind of man ties a young girl to a bed and rapes her?" I yell back. "Why are you even telling me this anyway, it's not like I had anything to do with it."

"Thought you should know what sort of asshole your old man was. That you were better off without him and you should've had more respect for me."

"Respect? You're the asshole. You and my mother. I'm glad she's dead. She never cared, she always treated me like I was shit on her shoe. My brother, if what you're saying is true, was better off dead. Mavis didn't know how to be a mother. Look what she let you do to me."

"Your old man made her that way."

"You're not exactly innocent, Carlos, it's not like you loved her."

"Hey, I fucking looked out for Mavis." He comes at me so

swiftly, I haven't got time to think, let alone move. Gripping me by the shirt, he bunches the fabric up in his fist, pulling me in so close, I'm only inches from his face. His stale breath reeks of cigarettes and rotten teeth. I almost dry retch it's so pungent. "I brought work in for her. Without me, the pair of you would have starved."

"Yeah, well, that would have been a thousand times better than what I ended up having to endure. You're a disgusting pig, I hate you. Now let me go," I scream back in his face, and push on his chest.

"Everyone had to earn their keep, bitch. Ain't no free rides on this fuckin' planet." Shoving me backward, he lets go. "You were the devil's spawn to your mother."

It feels like Carlos has sliced straight through me with an ice sword. The confirmation that she truly hated me is crushing.

"You all right in there?" Mr. Pilkington calls out, startling me. "Rocket said… Oh, you're here, Mr. Mendez." He looks a little confused by Carlos's presence.

Distracted, Carlos hardly notices when I bend to pick up the hatbox then scoot past him.

"Hey!" Carlos calls out, trying to grab me as I slip by. "Who said you can take anything. She's got money owing. That all became mine the day she stopped paying."

"Take it up with her when you see her in hell, Carlos. I don't owe you a damn thing," I yell back over my shoulder, moving as quickly as my legs will carry me. I glance back several times to make sure I'm not being followed, almost stumbling into the safety of my car. Once inside, I start the engine and plant my foot, sending the car speeding off without so much as a backward glance. And only then do I let go of all the years of fear and anger I'd held inside. Using every inch of my lungs, I scream wildly until my throat is burning, and every tear and ounce of anxiety has left me.

Half an hour later, I'm pulling up under a large carport that's occupied with what I assume is Sheree's Subaru and Darby's Ford pickup. I gather quite quickly why Sheree is so happy with her new man and the lifestyle he is keen to share. Sitting amidst acreage is a beautifully renovated colonial-style house, complete with sweeping verandas that overlook whitewashed holding paddocks where thoroughbred horses are prancing about. It's Sheree's dream come true.

Checking myself in the review mirror, I take out my compact and do a quick makeup mend before getting out of the car. Glancing around, it's hard not to get drawn in by the spectacular view. The whole time I lived in Ponderosa Park, I never realized just how pretty this side of town was. Large pine and oak trees provide shade around the house and horse stables, with more dotted around the yards.

Not bothering with my belongings just yet, I make my way past the house entrance and down a rock path that leads to the holding paddocks. In the distance, I can see someone in a blue jacket tending to the horses with flakes of hay. Night rugs appear to be strewn over the white rail fences, and gathering by the amount, someone has a large task ahead if they are to get the horses rugged before night crawls in.

"Hi, you're here. I was getting worried."

Sheree comes down the stone path to join me. She's changed in to jeans, boots, and a heavy brown jacket. She looks true country, and I can't help but grin. "You suit this place, Sheree." I smile despite the sense of foreboding that crawls in and wraps around my spine.

"I know, right." She grins back, giving me a hug. Her long blonde hair is twisted into a loose bun, and the bitter afternoon air has made her cheeks pink and her eyes, so much like her father's, glassy. She looks radiant, and I wonder for a moment if her father, if he were to see her, would be proud.

"I'm sorry I took so long. I got lost amongst my mother's things. I'll tell you about it later, because, I mean, look at this place. It's amazing, Sheree." I keep walking until I'm at a fence "Is that Darby over there with the horses?"

Sheree joins me by the fence and leans her forearms on the rail, then looks to where I'm pointing.

"That's Ian. He's Darby's right-hand man. These guys are full-time work." She's referring to the fifteen or so horses pawing impatiently by their feed bins.

"You always wanted this growing up." I'm so pleased for her. Though I must admit, I am a little jealous.

Sheree nods, taking in the sweeping landscape with pride then turns her attention on me. She pushes my loose hair off my shoulders.

"So, what took so long? Did you have a lot to sort out?" She links our arms and guides me toward the house.

"No. It was because I ran into Carlos, he was there."

Sheree stops in her tracks. "You don't mean—Carlos, Carlos? What was he doing there?"

"As fate would have it, he apparently owns the yard."

"Christ, creepy. Are you all right?" Knowing how much I hate the man, she squeezes my arm reassuringly and pulls a tight smile. I didn't say it aloud but, no, I wasn't all right. Carlos surfaced horror I wanted to forget, actions I regret, and lies I no longer felt like hiding behind.

I have so much going on in my head, I'm having trouble processing everything. And being here with Sheree, in her own environment, I feel the years peel away and I want so desperately to feel the closeness we shared as kids. But there were still so many lies in the way, big lies, enormous lies.

"I will be, there's just a lot to process right now, and I've got so much to tell you."

"If you're referring to Alex, I know you've been having an affair." She says this triumphantly, like there's no escaping her psychic abilities. Something I wish she had. Then I wouldn't need to explain my deceit.

I involuntarily let out a groan. "Yes, there's that, and more."

Sheree resumes walking, guiding me along slowly as I take in the sweeping veranda, the wrought-iron wall art, and the hanging pot plants.

"Well, let's get you inside and settled first. Where's your luggage?"

"Still in the car. I'll get my things later. Right now, I'd love you to show me around."

A tour around the gardens and horse facility has me both thoroughly chilled to the bone and envious as hell. The place is astounding. We make our way back to the house, and once inside, Sheree sheds her jacket and boots and I make my way over to the huge stone fireplace that dominates the open-plan living area to warm myself by the flames.

"Do you want a cup of tea?" Sheree offers, heading straight to the cozy kitchen where a large table dominates the center.

"How about hot chocolate, do you have any?" I smile, wondering if she remembers the times we sat on the front porch at her parents' house in the dark, talking for hours, drinking hot chocolate from a thermos so we didn't need to keep going inside.

"Ahh, the old hot chocolate, you must have some serious things to get off your chest. Should I add the mellows too?"

She totally remembers.

"You better," I say, admiring a photo frames on the mantel.

"Ooh, now I really am curious." Her lighthearted attitude is nice, but it just makes me feel ten times worse.

"This is a beautiful photo of you and your mom, Sheree." Picking up the frame, I stare at it for the longest time until the uncomfortable feeling of envy I became so accustomed to surfaces. Placing it down, I go quiet while Sheree fusses around the kitchen, banging cupboards and putting away dishes until the milk is ready.

Heated through from the fire, I meander around the room looking at more of Sheree's and Darby's life together, making small talk until she comes back through with two steaming mugs.

"All righty, are we going to address the elephant in the room?" she asks, handing me a mug.

"Are you calling me an elephant?" I take the steaming cup from her.

"Not at all, at least not yet, check back in several months from now, when you've got cankles."

I only manage a half-hearted chuckle because the reality of my pregnancy is just too surreal at the moment.

"Sorry, Paige, it's just I hate seeing you so… Miserable. It's depressing. What's going on? Why aren't you happy about the pregnancy? I mean you've been with Gerard for ages, isn't it about time? You, are planning on keeping the baby, aren't you?" she asks in a stern voice.

We take a seat facing each other on the couch.

"Gerard won't be happy that I'm pregnant. He—doesn't want children with me."

"Oh, Paige." Sheree reaches for my hand and gives me a squeeze. "Maybe he'll change his mind."

I look down at my lap, ashamed, because that's not even the half of it. There's a tightening in my stomach that's making me nauseous. But I've already decided that this is the time for confessions, regardless of the outcome. Sheree needs to hear everything.

"There's so much to tell you, I don't know where to start."

"Do a Julia Andrews then."

"A what?"

"You know, start at the very beginning." Putting down her mug, she gets up to poke the fire and tosses another log on. "Darby won't be in for at least another half hour, so offload your troubles my friend, that's what I'm here for."

"The beginning. That's harder than it sounds."

Sheree takes her seat again, curling her feet beneath her and patting my leg. "Just blab away." Then she's grinning from ear to ear and squeals. "I can't believe you're actually here. Sorry." She composes herself then taps on me again. "Go. Tell me what's going on with Alex, so, you're having an affair, could the baby be his? Is that why you're not happy about it?"

"No, it can't be Alex's we've been using protection, well except for once, but I'm on the pill, so I don't even know how I got pregnant. Fuck," I cuss when the reality hits again. "Gerard will freak out, and I'm already on thin ice because he found out I've been seeing Alex behind his back. Gerard went ballistic."

"As a man would."

"Yes, but you know how he found out?"

"How?" Sheree reaches for her mug again.

"Cameras. He has cameras all over the beach house."

"What, why?"

"I don't know. Security maybe? Anyway, it's over now. I've ended it with Alex."

Sheree pulls a sad face and gives my leg a rub. "It's for the best. And you never know Gerard might surprise you." She sounds hopeful, but it's useless trying to convince me, she doesn't know Gerard like I do.

"Sheree, do you remember when I said Gerard wanted to talk with me and Alex, together, you know, after I confessed to him?"

She nods.

"I didn't tell you everything that happened that night, I couldn't, it was too weird, and I didn't think anything was going to come of it anyway." Leaning forward, I put my cup on the coffee table and expand my lungs. "Gerard wanted a three-way."

"Oh, okay!"

"Okay? What, you're not shocked?"

"Gosh no. Not really, just about everyone is doing it these days. I had a three-way with Amanda Leverman and Dan," she says with a giggle, then looks around to make sure Darby is nowhere in sight. "Do you remember Dan? God he was cute."

"You did? You never told me." I'm a little shocked by her confession.

"Yeah, well, you went all funny around that time. Then my folks broke up, so it hardly felt like a thing really, which reminds me; Mom is hoping to see you. She was looking forward to catching up after the funeral."

My heart accelerates, making me groan and close my eyes.

"Are you all right? You've gone pale. I'll get some water, you're most likely still dehydrated. Do you need something to eat, I've got dip and crackers?" she rushes back into the kitchen and returns with food on a tray.

"Here, eat and drink, woman. I'm worried about you. I can't believe how thin you've gotten, not like me. Thailand did nothing for my waistline. The food was so good. Anyway, go on. The three-way—do tell!"

"I can't, Sheree. I've already told you too much of what you don't need to know, and I'm scared you will hate me."

"Hate you, why would I hate you?" She grabs the tray and shoves it forcefully at me. "Eat!"

"Because I've been lying to you for so long." I take a

cracker, so she can put the tray down, but I stare at it between my fingers, wishing it were a knife so I could just slit my wrists instead. "You're my best friend and I wish I could have told you the truth, but it was so complicated and then it was just easier to leave. To start fresh, but my past followed me, Sheree, and then I got caught up in the illusion, the possibility that I could make it work."

"Make what work?" Sheree asks, resting a hand on my leg in reassurance. But her touch feels scalding, like liquid ice, making me leap to my feet and start pacing.

"My marriage to Gerard. I was so in love with him, Sheree, and now I think I've screwed it all up because I'm realizing it wasn't really love, because what I feel for Alex is so much more, so much more real. I'm not hurting anyone by loving Alex, well maybe Gerard, but then, he started it. He shouldn't have pushed me there, manipulated me so I felt like he'd be angry at me; that I was letting him down if I didn't do it."

I stop pacing and toss the cracker on the table then put my hands on my hips and stare at the ceiling, "Christ, why does he have such a hold on me?" Then, as if it was a legitimate question directed at her and not the heavens, I look at Sheree. "No, don't answer that, I know why, because I owed him, he saved me, if it wasn't for him…"

"If it wasn't for him what?"

"Argh. I've got to get my stuff out of the car. I have something to give back to you, then I'll explain." I say, calming myself before my mouth flies away on me. What I need to tell her requires tact. Sheree could very well be the ally I need right now. Not waiting for a response, I head out of the room before I can change my mind.

9

SPEAK UP SELAH

Outside, I take the path back to my car where the nippy breeze from the west cools my hot face. I shouldn't have blurted like that. She'll hate me if I don't explain it properly. I rummage around the interior for my suitcase, tote bag, and then, the hatbox. She'll understand, she will. I just need to explain it properly, like she suggested, from the beginning.

I'm struggling back up the path toward the house, ladened like a packhorse, when Darby comes from around the side of the house, startling me. In a flash, the hatbox falls to the ground and everything spills out.

"Whoa, sorry about that," says Darby.

Both of us bend to retrieve the contents of the box before the wind scatters the dozen or so photos, cards, and...

"My diary!" I exclaim, picking it up and standing. Leaving poor Darby to put everything back in the box on his own because I'm so transfixed on the diary. I run my hand over the still glittery cover.

It only takes Darby a moment to finish the task before he

too is standing, box in hand, staring at me as I flick quickly through the contents of my book.

"Ha! I thought I lost this years ago," I chuff, meeting his gaze, his dark brown eyes smiling at me with a mixture of amusement and warmth. "Sorry. I'm Paige. And you're Darby." I thrust out a hand which he takes.

"I am. It's a pleasure to meet you, Paige. Sheree never stops talking about you."

"I hope she's only telling you the good stuff?"

"Always."

Sheree wasn't kidding when she said Darby is gorgeous. I'd only seen him in the few photos she'd posted on social media, which hadn't done him justice. He's a mixture of what I think is Native American and Mexican. His long black hair is tied, and his wide mouth breaks into an even bigger smile when I crane my head around him to see for myself, how long the ponytail is that trails down his back.

"Whoa that's long," I state the obvious, making Darby chuckle.

"My pride and joy. After Sheree that is." He smiles. "Got anything else to bring in?"

"Nope, that's it," I say, moving forward to take the box from him, but he shakes his head.

"I've got it, you grab the rest of your things. Sorry to hear about your mother."

"Thanks. Sorry to barge in on you guys like this. I hope you don't mind me staying. You've got an amazing place. I can see why Sheree is so happy."

"You bet. It is my real pride and joy. After Sheree of course," he repeats his joke. "My Grandfather worked here years ago." We walk the length of the veranda. "I came to visit often. Loved it so much, I swore to one day own this special place."

"Wow, and here you are."

"Yes. There are still some things to improve. Sheree helps when she can. Right now, see over there?" He points to a steel frame some six hundred yards to the left of the stables that looks massive. "That will be our new arena. I plan on breeding soon." Darby smiles proudly.

"Oh, and does Sheree know she's soon to be a mare." I can't help but giggle.

"Ha, funny, I mean horses."

"Figured that. Well, I'm sure Sheree will be in heaven. Growing up, all she ever wanted was horses."

Darby holds the door open for me then leads me down the hall to what I presume is the guest room where I will be sleeping.

"My God, what a view." Dropping my belongings on the bed, I marvel at the scenery from the large bay window that overlooks the yards and valley of pine trees.

"Oh good. Thanks for helping Paige, D," Sheree says, coming into the room. "Think you'll be okay in here?"

"Are you kidding? It's gorgeous." I look around the room appreciatively.

"Just turn off the oil heater if you get too hot." Sheree checks the dial on the heater that is to one side of the queens-size bed, covered in what looks to be an heirloom patchwork quilt. I brush my hand over it while taking in the rest of the space. A large pine wardrobe sits to one side of the room, and two chairs face the bay window with the view. Heavy sage green drapes have been tied back with rope, giving the room a rustic look.

Kissing Sheree, Darby excuses himself to go and get cleaned up.

"He's nice, Sheree."

She smiles then catches sight of the pile of things on the bed.

"What's this?" She takes a seat on the bed and touches the hatbox. I join her on the bed then pull the box onto my lap.

"Some of my mom's stuff I wanted to go through, but I wanted to return this to you." Peeling back the lid, I pull out the Broncos jersey.

"Hey! It's my sweatshirt. My dad said he threw it out by mistake. Where'd you get it?" she says, excited and holding it out in front of herself. "Gosh look how small it is. Do you remember I used to wear this everywhere? How uncool," she giggles, burying her nose into the fabric.

"No, you were cool, believe me."

"How come you have it?"

For a moment, I think about lying, telling her my mom must have found it somewhere, but I'm so tired of the lies, and I'm not about to tell new ones.

"You remember earlier when you said I was acting weird around the time your dad left?"

"Sorry, I didn't mean weird, you just went all quiet. You remember, you got your nose out of joint because of Lisbeth and me hanging out. But she was Dan's buddy's girlfriend, you know? And we sort of clicked." Obviously curious, Sheree glances in at the contents of the box. "Oh wow! Is that your diary? I still have mine too." She reaches in to take it out, but I stop her, shoving the box quickly off my lap and out of her reach. "How crazy we both still have them," she intones, frowning at my reluctance to let her look at it.

"Sheree, it wasn't because of Lisbeth I went all weird, and the reason I have your jersey is because… Do you remember the day I wanted to stay behind at the bike park because Peter Moriarty was finally paying attention to me?" I twist myself to face her better, and when she nods, confirming she remembers the day, I go on to tell her about the incident.

"Please tell me they didn't do something horrid to you," she says, looking distraught when I'm done.

"No. But I'm pretty sure they would have if your dad hadn't turned up."

"My dad? What was he doing at the park?"

"I don't know. I thought maybe, *you* might have told him I was still there?" I widen my eyes at her.

"I don't remember, but maybe? He liked keeping an eye on you." There's a slight bitterness in her tone, making me painfully aware how difficult this conversation will be.

I nod in agreement. "Well, anyway, he stopped them. He gave Peter a warning. My shirt was all ripped, and he told me to put your jersey on, so I did. I was going to give it back, I promise."

Sheree screws up her face and shakes her head, "Gosh, who gives a crap about the stupid sweatshirt. Why haven't you ever told me this?"

"I didn't feel like I could. Argh, there's so much you don't know. I've made a mess out of everything, Sheree, my whole life is a lie."

"Your whole life? That's a tad melodramatic isn't it?"

"Maybe." I look around the cozy room, and suddenly I feel overwhelmingly tired. "Would you mind if I took a couple of Tylenols and laid down for a while?" I ask, needing to collect my thoughts.

"Not at all." Sheree pats my leg and rises. "I need to get meals ready for the men anyway, we'll talk later then."

When I look confused, she offers more. Telling me about the stable hands who live on-site, then leaves to get started on their meals.

When she closes the door, I shift my belongings off the bed and kick off my boots. I unzip my jeans to make myself more comfortable, thinking how strange it is that as soon as the doctor mentioned I was pregnant I felt my stomach bloat. I'm worried now that the other clothes I've brought, might be too tight.

Opening the hatbox, I grab the book with a unicorn embossed on the front, then prop myself up against the pillows, stretching my legs out in front of me.

Taking a deep breath, I open my diary.

Dear diary,

Today is my 11ᵗʰ birthday. Dad gave me this book. He got me a cake as well. He's gone to work again so he will be away for ten days. My Mom didn't get me anything, as usual. My best friend is Sheree, and she lives two blocks away on Sycamore Cres. I live on Redcliff street. I'm in middle school. I don't have any pets, but sometimes I play with the neighbor's cat when it comes looking for food. I'll write more tomorrow. Good night.

I re-read the first entry over and over, uncertain I want to go on because there's a nauseous feeling brewing. I lay the book down and rest my eyes, thinking about my mother and the photo I found. Why wasn't I told about the child she had before me? How is it that I know so little about my mother? I reach for my diary again, and over the next half hour I read random entries. With each passing month, then year, I feel a sorrow so profound it has me despairing for the little being growing inside me.

Dropping the diary beside me again I rub my abdomen. "Sorry about all the shit I've been doing lately, it's just, I didn't know you were in there," I confess, feeling extremely guilty. Then I'm shaking my head. God what am I doing? I can't get attached. Argh. My hand leaves my bump and goes to my forehead instead. I need Tylenol. I claim my tote then search through its contents, finding medication and my phone. I check the recent calls and see I've missed several calls from Gerard, and before I can talk myself out of it, I press call. He answers almost immediately.

"For crying out loud, Paige, where have you been? I've been worried sick."

I stay silent because I don't know what to say. I'm hoping he hasn't figured out that I've left the hotel.

"Are you all right, why haven't you been answering your phone?"

"I've been sleeping. I needed a doctor last night."

"Are you sick?"

"No. I was distraught. It wasn't a very pleasant experience waking up to find police at my door."

"Well, why were you at the Cold Springs? I checked you in at the Caledonian."

I let out an exhausted sigh. "I didn't care where I went. I just wanted to sleep." Rubbing my sore neck, I let the silence stretch out before us. I'm waiting for him to say whatever it is he needs to say.

"Paige." Remarkably, his tone is soft. "It's because I love you, I get so angry." He pauses and draws in a deep breath then rushes his words. "I know I have a problem keeping my temper in check, and it was deplorable of me to upset you like I did. Especially in your time of grief. But…" I roll my eyes and draw in a noisy breath that I'm sure he hears, because he clears his throat and continues. "No. You… You have every right to hate me. I'm a weak man for hitting you. For swearing and belittling you. I know I need help. I've… I have decided." He chokes out a sob.

Pulling myself up, I start pacing the room, waiting for him to finish blowing his nose so he can go on.

"I know I need to see someone. Someone who can help me get over the cheating," he says. "To help me understand why you betrayed me. Have you any idea how hard it's been for me?" he questions softly.

I screw up my face because he's breaking through my resolve.

"I need to work out how to get over someone they love cheating on them. You crushed my heart, Paige. When I saw you with Alex? Christ," he breathes out. "I just wanted to end it all. I just keep seeing it over and over in my mind. I should have cooled off before I called you. I'm an adult. I should have conducted myself better. I should have reminded myself that you are young and perhaps prone to bouts of recklessness. Can you forgive me, honey?"

I stop my pacing and then take a seat by the window. In my silence, it sounds like Gerard is still trying to compose himself with a tissue. He gives a little cough. "Are you still there, Paige?"

"I know what I did was wrong, Gerard. You have every reason to be angry and I promise it's over with Alex." I let my words settle in then, for Alex's protection I add, "You're right, you've been right all along, Alex wants his freedom. I don't really know what I was thinking, but it wasn't to directly hurt you. But I need to be honest... I just don't know if I can... Gerard, you've been scaring me with the things you say." I can almost feel him nodding. "And I mean... camera's? That's so wrong. I can't be with a man who..."

"Don't. Please don't say it. I need you, Paige. I can't live without you and thank you. Thank you for taking ownership, that means a great deal to me. I can forgive you when I know how sorry you are. Are you having a good time?" He quickly changes the subject on me. "Has the place changed much?"

"I haven't been out, really. But from what I can tell, it's much the same. Gerard, we need to talk properly about this. I don't want to lie about us anymore." I'm starting to sound desperate. I need him to understand the depth of our problems.

"Oh. Well, maybe tomorrow after the funeral you'll get a chance. What time do you fly back in on Sunday?" he says, ignoring my concern.

"I'll check." I go to my bag to find my ticket. "But Gerard you're missing the point. I think…"

"I miss you Paige, and I know there is so much more to discuss. But I love you. Do you know how much I cherish what we have? I really want to work through your infidelity more maturely. Would you… Do you think you'd be willing to go to counseling with me?" Gerard stammers, sounding maybe a little uncomfortable. More like the man I married. I press the ticket against my forehead and crush my eyelids closed. Why is my stomach twisting in knots?

"My flight gets in at two. And yes. Yes, I'm willing to go to counseling."

"We can sort this out. I know we can. I won't annoy you anymore tonight, and I'm sorry if I've disturbed you. What are you having for dinner? How does the menu look there?"

"I don't know yet. I haven't decided if I'll eat in my room or at the restaurant."

There's a long pause. "Gerard?"

"Oh sorry, I was just distracted for a moment, there's a car coming up the drive. I'll see you Sunday, honey and don't forget. I love you." He disconnects without waiting for me to say goodbye.

I look down for a moment at the one melting Tylenol in my hand, trying to sort through the conversation. I'm confused about what I just agreed to. Do I even want to stay with Gerard without Sheree knowing the full story? I want her in my life. I need her in my corner. If things turn bad again with Gerard, I feel she's the only one who can truly help. I reach for the packet of Tylenol and pop out another. It feels like this headache has been a constant one for months now.

In the kitchen, I find Darby and Sheree being intimate, arms around one another and leaning against the bench, they're smiling and teasing each other.

I halt in the doorway as they both turn to look my way before separating. "Sorry, I was after some water."

"It's fine. I need to get these meals to the guys, anyway. I'll leave you two to catch up," says Darby, picking up a thermal bag in one hand. "I think I'll have a couple of beers with the boys. I'll see you both later."

"Did you sleep?" Sheree asks, as Darby leaves through the back door off the kitchen, letting in a rush of cool air that causes me to shiver. Sheree begins cleaning away the mess she made.

"No. I ended up going through stuff, then my diary." I take a seat at the table.

"Anything interesting? I should get mine out, and we can swap. Unless you've got deep dark secrets you don't want me to read?" She arches one eyebrow, but from the look on my face she can tell it's anything but a joke. "Are you okay?" Sheree throws down the tea towel she been using and takes a seat opposite me.

I shake my head but stay silent, looking at the pain relief and trying to find the right words. In a heartbeat, Sheree is up, getting me a glass of water, then hands it to me.

"Is it safe, do you think, I mean for the baby?" I open my palm again, and she takes a seat.

"A bit won't hurt."

"I've most likely caused damage anyway. I had Molly the other night." I down two pills and chasing them with water, avoiding Sheree's concerned look. "Made the sex club interesting." I drop another bomb on her, still staring at the glass in my hand.

"Shit, Paige. What exactly has been going on? Has Alex or Gerard been making you do things you don't want to do?"

"Maybe. No. Oh, I don't know."

"Christ, Paige. Will you just get whatever it is off your chest? It looks like it's about to kill you."

I finally meet her gaze, but I still can't fess up. Getting to her feet, she pulls me to mine then leads me to the sofa in front of the crackling fire.

"Sit, and then out with it," she demands, curling up on the plush fabric amongst a pile of cushions then waits expectantly. I remain standing, looking down at her, feeling like I'd rather run than spill my guts like this.

"That day after the park. Your dad saved me, only for Carlos to nearly go and do the deed instead." I mumble.

"What do you mean, deed? You're not saying…?"

"Even in front of my mother, that disgusting man was going on about my virginity. Telling her how much a virgin hole can earn. Then the creepy bastard was trying to rape me. You wondered why I didn't want to see my mother? She was a fucking bitch, Sheree. They took me to the lake house, so Carlos could rape me."

And there it was, out. In an incoherent rant I offload onto my unsuspecting friend.

Sheree's color vaporizes, and her eyes dart between mine, searching for more—an explanation, a reason maybe, but she and I know, there isn't one. Rape is rape.

"Christ, Paige." Sheree is shaking her head, trying, I assume, to understand what I just said. "I'm so sorry, what a horrible, horrible day that must have been. How, why? Oh Gosh, no, don't answer that, that's stupid of me, it's just… I don't know what to say. I'm stunned, why didn't you tell me, and what do you mean the lake house, do you mean our rental?"

"It's long and complicated, Sheree. The first time it happened I was…"

"The first time? What the fuck! Paige, no." She lunges up at me, wrapping her arms firmly around. "No wonder you took off," she says, searching my eyes again, her own brimming with tears before holding me tight again. "You poor thing, and here I was all caught up in my own shit to even question what was going on with you."

"No, I kept it from you, Sheree. It happened more or less right after your dad left. Carlos trapped me at home late one night. I just couldn't tell you about it. I still don't know if I can explain it all." I slump into the sofa, leaving Sheree standing and reeling.

"Hey! Stuff the hot chocolate, we should have had shots."

"I wish I could. All I feel like doing is getting comatose and sleeping for an eternity, because that, Sheree—is just the beginning."

"All right, so I've been thinking about it while I was in the shower," Sheree says, making her way across the slate floor, combing her wet hair until she's standing in front of me at the large dining table.

We'd stayed silent about my confession over dinner, talking instead about mundane things. Sheree informed me that her aunt Casandra was back from Africa and how excited she is to finally meet the niece she hasn't met. And Darby expressed his dreams to own a racehorse one day. Sheree filled me in on her job and her plans to revamp Darby's house. I explained how I'd helped Alex renovate the beach house, which seems a lifetime ago. I even suggested that she and Darby could vacation there, even though I thought it an impossibility, given I knew what was about to go down.

"Carlos is a dog," Sheree continues, putting her comb down and taking a seat at the end of the table and close to me, "He needs to die, that's a given. I think you should report him, get his ass thrown in jail. Not only was it rape, you were only fifteen. A child."

"They wouldn't jail him. It's too long ago now."

"You could try," she says, sounding optimistic. "Why didn't you press charges back then, Paige? You should have told me. We could have told my parents; they would have helped." She's angry, sounds frustrated, and I love her for caring so much, which makes my betrayal all the worse.

I stare down at my hands. "Your dad knew about it. Well, at least Carlos's first attempt."

"What! Well, why wasn't anything done about it?" she whines, grabbing my hand off the mug I'm holding.

"Your dad said he'd get off, and I figured he knew what he was talking about. But it gets worse, oh God it gets worse, and I need to tell you about it. I can't live with it any longer. I trusted your dad, Sheree. He was always looking out for me, and I didn't mean for it to happen."

"For what to happen?"

"Sheree, he was always looking out for me. Do you know how many times I slept in your shed while he was working in there?"

"Slept there?" She recoils and screws up her face. "What, overnight?"

"I formed such a crush on him. You have no idea."

"What? But he was old." She's still frowning and waiting for me to explain myself. I look down, feeling rotten to my core because I've only just begun explaining, and already she's distraught.

"He wasn't really that old, Sheree. He is an attractive man," I say, calming myself a little, twisting the tissue in my hand.

"Yeah well I wouldn't know. I haven't seen him since he walked out on Mom and me."

"I know, and I'm sorry, Sheree."

"You're sorry? You've got nothing to be sorry about."

"Yes, I do. Believe me, I really do. Ever since Alex, all this shit from my past is surfacing, and now, I'm here dumping it all on you. I'm really struggling, and God…" My head drops into my hands. "I keep forgetting about the pregnancy," I mumble into my hands, then startle when Darby's voice booms in our direction.

"Who's up for a movie tonight?" he cheerily shouts out, entering the kitchen, not realizing he's interrupted an important discussion. Abruptly, our conversation ends, which suits me fine. Because I've decided I just can't bear telling Sheree what she has every right to know.

It's around midnight when the deception must finally sink in. I hear a door close quietly and the sound of feet padding past me and down the hall. Putting my diary that I've been reading over and over on the coffee table, I pull the blanket tighter around me.

When Sheree doesn't find me in the guest room, moments later, she is standing in front of me, staring down with a piece of paper in her hand. Her face holds absolutely no expression.

"I couldn't sleep and then I remembered his name. How could I forget his name?" Drawing in a lungful of air, she shakes her head in disgust. "My father was always secretive, that's for sure, but you—how did I not realize what you were doing? I must be dumb, deaf and blind." She waves the document that I know must be her birth certificate in my face and lets out a sarcastic chuckle. "Do you know why I didn't care after he left?"

Shaking my head, I look down at the floor.

"Because whenever we were together, all of us, my mom barely existed and neither did I. He would hang off your every word. Praise you more than me, and you lapped it up.

Even though at the time you made me think you hated his attention, you secretly loved it, didn't you?"

I look back up at her. "I had no one else, Sheree, and you and your mom were so mean to him. He just wanted you two to be proud of him. I could see that."

"Proud of him. Do you know why he annoyed me and my mom so much? He was controlling, and verbally abusive and, obviously, he's a fucking sexual deviant. How could you have fallen for that?"

"He spoke to me as though I was an adult, smart and interesting. He was kind, and I was scared, Sheree. You know what sort of home life I had. I interpreted his attention as love. I couldn't see that it was wrong. It never felt wrong to me, only keeping it a secret from you felt wrong."

"No." Sheree shakes her head wildly back and forth. "That's what he wanted you to believe. Don't you remember the times he made you sit on the bank, watching, telling you that next time we came skiing you could have a go, making out we ran out of time. I thought he was doing it because he was being selfish, like you didn't deserve it because you weren't his kid. I could never figure out why he kept getting me to bring you along and then not let you have a turn. He was making you worship him. He was fucking grooming you."

"What? No. He said he didn't want you to feel put out. That once you got bored with skiing, he would teach me."

Sheree looks at me like I'm pathetic.

"He was." She lets out a deep disgruntled huff. "No. Correction. He is a manipulative asshole. For years after he left, I used to tell myself it was because he was so young when him and Mom had me, but now I know the truth. He was born that way. He is a conniving asshole. Show me." Sheree thrust out her hand.

"Show you what?"

"The photo I know you have."

Reluctantly, I reach for my phone and produce a photo for her to see.

She looks at the screen for a long time, studying the two smiling faces from a time not so long ago, then tears slowly slide down her beautiful face, making me cry as well. Handing back my phone, her eyes cloud, look haunted. The light inside has died, and with her final words on the subject, she blows out the last remainder flicker of hope in mine.

"I'm sorry that Carlos did that to you, Paige, I really am, but in the morning, I want you gone."

Through blurry vision, I watch her walk away, then stare down at the image I showed Sheree. A handsome man wearing a pale blue polo shirt that smelled of butterscotch and powder. His hand is captured midway as he pushes back blond hair from off his face. His smile lights up the entire screen. Perfect straight white teeth behind luscious lips that whispered the sweetest words the girl beside him had ever heard. And those blue, blue eyes. So iridescent they sparkled like expensive gems that held her captive. The young girl looks dreamy-eyed. Forest-green eyes stay fix on the man as she twists her face, trying to capture the moment without losing sight of him. She's not gorgeous or stunning, nor is she plain, just pretty with the reddest hair framing her pale round face in waves. She's wearing a sloppy gray sweater that looks new. Her smile doesn't reveal her teeth, but her mouth is curved as far as her muscles will allow. Two smiling faces that once looked like the perfect couple to me.

Now all I see is a man firmly holding a young gullible girl around her shoulders. A stupid young girl who chose a man over her one and only true best friend—Sheree.

NOT GIVING IN

The following morning, I'm gone from Sheree and Darby's place before either has woken. Then I wait the time out at the Caledonian Hotel until half an hour before the appointed funeral service. I speak briefly with the pastor who assures me he will pass on my apologies and speak on my behalf. Sadly, I believe he'll be addressing empty chairs.

My mother's casket is a simple unstained pine box with rope handles and not a flower in sight. As soon as I see it, a horrid, choked sob leaves me, and I grab the back of the chair to stop myself from crumbling to my knees.

It's what I arranged, I know—the cheapest available box above cardboard. But seeing it now, knowing that inside lays my mother, all I can picture is the woman holding the little baby boy to her breast, staring down with all the love she possessed, and suddenly it seems so inadequate for anyone. She was once a little girl, then a teen, then a young woman, until life twisted her insides, tarnished her soul, and she became an empty vessel that she filled with poison to numb herself.

I can feel her pain.

I start sobbing and fall into the chair. I should hate her, totally despise the woman for how she treated me. For allowing Carlos to rape me. But I can't. If it's true, that my father forced her to give the child, my brother, her first-born son away, that would be like tearing part of her soul right out of her body. I reach for my stomach. How could my father do that? Then I hear Gerard telling me about men and claiming women as their own. Like a damn lion. Are we honestly not that far removed from animals? Was my little brother killed deliberately or was it an accident? Where did he go?

I pull out the photo of him and stare at it until I can feel the love my mother was giving him. Then I pretend she once looked at me that way.

Suddenly, I can feel her in the room. I look around in sorrow, then whisper goodbye to a woman I hated, yet now pity. After taking a copy on my phone, I slip the photo of my half-brother and her book of beautiful drawings inside her casket and leave. I have no other words for the woman I never really knew. She lived behind a veil of resentment, alcohol, and perversion instead of dealing with her demons. If there was one thing to learn from her mistakes, I was not going to make the same ones. I just needed up until now, to figure it all out.

The flight to LA the next day is a blur. That is, apart from the ten minutes waiting for my flight to board when I looked up the Planned Parenthood website and booked an appointment for two days' time. I forced myself to eat everything that was put in front of me, and I dozed.

Reminiscent of my last night with Alex, it's raining when

the plane lands, and as if God's tears are suggestive, I find myself pulled up outside the beach house, desperate to see Alex. There is only one reason I am here though. To tell him everything so he will push me away in disgust. I just don't have the strength to hide anymore. I made my bed. It's time I lay in it.

All the scaffolding has been removed, and from what I can tell, Alex has finished with the renovations, at least on the outside. Unsure of the locations of the cameras, I opt to park and wait out the rain. When it finally lets up, I walk down to the beach and pace the front of the house hoping Alex will spot me. After an hour of treading the sand, staring at the house and picking up shells to toss back in the ocean, I plop down defeated on the wet sand, ruining my white jeans, and then my sweater when I stretch it over my drawn-up knees. Mindlessly, I stare out at the choppy gray ocean.

The sea smells heavy of seaweed and salt, and in no time, the whitewash is lapping at my sodden, now discolored tan boots. I rest my head then close my eyes and listen to the calming sound of waves as they shush one after the other. I don't know how long the ocean lulls me, but then it starts to rain again. Heavy and hard and relentless. Soaking my hair straight and filling my sponge-like clothes to capacity until I feel the wet against my skin. The sand beneath me liquefies, and I'm sinking deeper and deeper until the sand washes back over the soles of my boots. But I don't care. I just wish the ocean would swell up, for a huge, unexpected wave to engulf me, and then drag me out to sea. Then all my problems…

"Jesus Christ, Paige, what are you doing out here?" Pulling me to my feet and wrapping an arm around me, Alex turns me toward the house. He's trying to hurry me, but my whole body feels like lead. We meet Tony halfway with a blanket and only then do I seem to come to my senses and start jogging with them toward the house to get out of the rain. We rest under the cover of the lower level, which is the upper-story decking, so the rain still sprinkles us.

"Come inside. Shit, are you nuts? It's freezing. How long have you been here?" Alex asks.

"Not long enough. I decided I'd wait for the tide. You should have left me there."

Alex pulls me in close, his arms wrapping around me so tightly he absorbs half the wet from my clothing. He goes to make a move again, twisting me toward the stairs to the upper story.

"I can't come inside Alex. Gerard has camera's everywhere."

"What?" Alex stiffens, and I pull out of his arms. Turning, I see the stunned look on Tony face before he wipes it and the rain away. I look from one to the other, then unwrap the blanket.

"I just came to tell you that. I need to go." I hand a still stunned Alex the blanket.

"Like bloody hell." Alex snatches hold of my hand. "Tony, is your place cool?"

Tony nods.

Without a pause, Alex is thrusting out a his other hand. "Where's your car parked?"

"I would have called straightaway, but Gerard deleted your number, and I couldn't remember it. I could have called Jenna and asked her again but…"

"Don't worry about it," Alex says, tugging me along the sand and up the pedestrian stairs from the beach to the parking lot. "I—I didn't—didn't realize you—you had—a private number." I continue through chattering teeth. "He—he saw us. All those—those times we—we were together he was—he was—was watching us."

It's like Alex isn't listening. He leans me against the car then goes to the driver's side, unlocks the door, and starts the engine. He turns on the heat and then opens the trunk. The rain has let up at last, apart from the odd spray that comes from nearby trees when shaken by the breeze. Alex looks at me briefly then opens the back door of my car and throws clothes on the back seat. Quickly turning, he pulls off my sweater and helps me out of my jeans.

As he's drying me off with one of my shirts, I squeeze at my drenched hair. I can't take my eyes off him. Alex doesn't speak or look at my face, he's just totally focused on the task of getting me out of my wet clothes and dry. He pulls a tee-shirt over me, and I'm forced to slip into shorts because they're the only thing left that's clean. After wiping my legs again, he peels off his gray sweater that's still reasonably dry and pulls it over me before encouraging me inside the car. He gathers my wet stuff and throws it in the trunk with a slam. Shaking the water left in his hair, he gets in the driver's seat then turns to me and holds out his hand.

"Give me your phone."

"What for?"

"My number. I'll punch it back in."

I stare at him for a moment then shake my head. It needs to end here. On this day. "No, Alex. I don't want it. We need to stop seeing each other. This is over. No more. I can't do this to you or him. He'll kill you."

"No. I'm going to kill him. I swear to God I will kill that motherfucker in the worst way possible." He ignites the engine and makes it roar. "Fuck!" Alex slams the heel of his palms against the steering wheel. "They were our moments,

Paige, not his. What's his fucking reasoning? Did he tell you? How did you find out—where are they—are they everywhere? I need to know, because if he saw any of my clients half-naked. Fuck! Fuck, fuck, fuck." Alex slams his palms on the wheel in time with his cussing. "He could frame me. He could say I set it up. Can you imagine? My clients could sue my ass off."

He barely looks at me, just shakes his head until he seems at a loss then slumps back in the seat. Alex huffs then smirks. "He's smart. He's so fucking clever, isn't he?"

"Yes. And I've been selfish and stupid. I did this, Alex. I came after you, and he knew I would. He warned me, and I didn't listen. You were like a drug I couldn't get enough of, and now… Even Sheree hates me."

Looking out the windshield, Alex shakes his head again, as if he can't bear to hear any more. But he needs to hear everything. That way, I know he'll hate me, and if he hates me, I'll be able to leave him alone.

"I'm taking you to Tony's, you're not going back there. We'll both be able to stay until I can find us something. I'll drop you off first, then I'll come back and pack everything up. I don't care about the money anymore. He can jam his dirty fucking money up his ass."

"No, Alex. I have to go back."

"What do you mean? No, I'm not letting you go back to that psychopathic asshole. No, Paige I won't fuckin' let you."

"Alex, I have to. He will do what you're afraid he'll do. He's already threatened that he'll do something to you, and I believe him. But…"

"What?"

"Well. When he mentioned seeing us, he said nothing about the massage. So maybe he didn't put any cameras downstairs. Maybe he only saw us when we were in the main house." I may be overly optimistic, but still, it reinforces the fact that I need to push Alex away. At least that way, he might avoid Gerard's retribution.

"He said he wanted to go to counseling so we can work this mess out. I owe him that, Alex. I owe you that. You were right in saying you're not the right man for me, because I don't deserve someone like you, Alex. I'm damaged in so many ways. I've done things I'm not proud of, and I hurt my best friend in the worst way. This is all my fault. It's as simple as that."

"Don't you dare say you're not good enough for me."

"But I'm not. I'm tarnished, Alex. I have secrets that will disgust you."

"Nothing about you would disgust me Paige."

"You say that now, but if you knew."

"Let me be the judge. What's this disgusting thing you did that would repulse me so much I can't stand to look at you? What, you murdered someone? You sold your body? You were drug-addicted. You raped someone? What? Tell me what you did that was so bad that you hate yourself so much and won't let someone who really loves you rescue you."

"I thought you said you weren't here to rescue me, Alex."

"Well, I changed my mind. Now, we're going to Tony's, and that's the end of it."

Alex puts the car in gear and twists his head around to back out.

"I made Sheree's father take my virginity when I was fifteen so my mother's boyfriend Carlos wouldn't try to rape me again or sell me off as pure." I rush the words out.

Midway through reversing, Alex slams on the brakes.

"I fell in love with him, and when I went to Sheree's the next time, I acted like a lovesick girlfriend in front of Sheree and her mom, and so he left. He deserted his family because of me. Then Carlos tied me down and raped me while my mother watched re-runs in the living room."

Alex cringes and slides the stick into park.

"Paige." He reaches for my hand, but I snatch it away. I don't want his sympathy. I don't want his love. I don't want anything from anyone anymore. I just want this disgusting black goo out of me. So, I keep going. Contaminating Alex's mind so he understands the vileness that is me.

"I ran away. There was a man in town who was an old friend of my father's. I don't know why I went there, but it seemed like it might be the only place I could find refuge, and I was hoping he might know where my father went. He didn't, but he took me in and promised to keep it from my mother." I glance at him quickly then look away and push myself harder against my door. "For about a year, I worked at the roadhouse at nights after school. I didn't even tell Sheree what was going on. She was so wrapped up with her boyfriend at the time because her father had left. And even though she didn't know the real reason he left, I felt to blame so I avoided her."

Alex puts the car in gear and returns to the car spot we'd vacated and turns off the engine. Within seconds, the windows are misting over with condensation. I look around, dazed for a moment having forgotten where we are.

"It's okay, Paige, keep going. You need to let it all out," Alex encourages and grabs my hands.

"I needed to get out of that town, so I convinced myself I'd do anything. One night." I pause to choke back a sob. "One night—One night…" I take in a deep breath then in a rush blurt, "One night, I offered the man who took me in sex in exchange for money." Tears start blurring my vision. I press my lids tight, hoping to get rid of them.

"Paige?" Alex says in a gentle tone.

"Alex, he was old. Like old, old." I pull my hands away to cover my face. Alex pulls them away. "It didn't happen though. He wouldn't." I sniffle back my useless tears. "But the fact is, I was going to do it. I was prepared to do it. My dad's friend sat me down and made me promise I would never, ever lower myself to do that. That I was better than my mother, and then one morning, he left an envelope for me full of cash and a bus ticket to LA."

"Why would I judge you for that, are you forgetting I took money off Gerard? Seems we're peas in a pod."

"But I was selling myself just like my mother. You took the money for a whole other reason."

"Paige, you were prepared to do whatever you had to do. Christ, and does Gerard know about all this? Is that why you think you need to stay with him, because you told him, and he still loved you? Who is this fucker Carlos anyway? What's his last name?"

"Carlos Mendez. God, I even saw him when I was there."

"What? You went and saw him?"

"Not deliberately. When I went to see what things my mom had in storage, he was there. I didn't know it at the time, but he now owns Samuel's Storage. As soon as I could, I was out of there."

Alex nods. "Okay. Well, we're still going to Tony's. Gerard can't hold that over you. You've got nothing to be ashamed of." Alex starts the engine again. When he turns to look at me, I'm shaking my head.

"Why the hell not?"

"He will come looking for me, Alex, and I haven't finished telling you everything."

"Well, you can tell me on our way to Tony's then." Alex says firmly. I don't argue with him. Maybe it's better he has the driving to focus on. Once we are cruising along the freeway, I tell him about my visit with Sheree. About her life and our friendship when we were kids.

"I was so envious of Sheree, Alex. I wish you could have met her. She's gorgeous. But I stole her father away."

"You didn't steal him. He used you."

"He loved me."

"He did not."

"Alex."

"He took advantage of a young girl's crush. He was a dirty old perv."

"He wasn't that old."

"He had a daughter the same age as you. That makes him a dirty old man as far as I'm concerned."

I take in a deep breath. "Well, that makes me sick as well then."

"No. You were young. The old geezer was most likely grooming you all along. What did you see in him anyway?"

"Everything. He was handsome and caring. Smart. He'd help me with my homework on the nights I slept in their garage."

Alex does a double take.

"You slept in a shed?"

"Just when things got tough at home."

Alex can't take it. He pulls the car over and turns off the engine again.

"Sheree's father let you sleep in his garage?" he asks warily.

"Well, Sheree and I had a clubhouse in there, and it was warm and quiet, and I didn't have to listen to my mom going at it all night with strangers."

Alex massages his head. "Go on."

"He brought out food and would talk to me. Taught me things."

"What sort of things?" Alex snaps his head around.

"No, not like that, just things about the world and stuff. He cared. Like a lot. He was looking for me the night some guys tried doing stuff to me at the park."

Alex is shaking his head, but with a hand, he gestures for

me to keep going. I fill him in on my past and the lake house and how Sheree's dad burst in the room and pulled Carlos away from me. How I was scared, and I didn't want to go home. That he let me stay the weekend at the lake house to make sure Carlos stayed away from me.

"It was nice. He was nice. It was me who kissed him first that night. I wanted to thank him for caring so much. That's when I suggested losing my virginity to him would stop Carlos. It's not like I hated it. In fact, it was everything I imagined. I fell in love with him, and because of that, he deserted his family. It was my fault his family fell apart."

"Paige, it was still wrong. You were just a girl—he was an adult."

"I know, but I loved him, Alex. I trusted him, and he was there when no one else was. Then I saw him again, Sheree's Dad. He came into the coffee shop I was working in. We acted like we didn't know each other at first. Like that time before never existed. I felt all the same feelings I felt back then, Alex, and so when he introduced himself using his real first name, I went along with it. Somehow that seemed to push away the ugly past and I was free to love him. He was no longer Sheree's dad. He was just, Gerard Richard Whitmyer, a reputable lawyer from LA." Saying it out loud reminds me that that's exactly how Sheree would have read it. Over and over on her birth certificate.

Alex is wide-eyed for the longest moment, his eyes darting around the interior of the car. Finally, he settles on somewhere outside and I think he starts to cry. Instantly his palms are pressing firmly into his sockets and his body heaves several times. Then something seems to well up inside him, and he leaps out of the car. Traffic screams past him with the blaring of their horns. Then Alex is at the front of my car, punching the hood with one fist over and over, leaving large dents in the metal. Screaming, swearing and using Gerard's name with such venom, my blood runs cold.

I get out of the car slowly and inch toward the front, my hand reaching out over the hood to calm him.

"Alex, no, stop. Please, it's all right. I just wanted to explain myself to you. You needed to know the truth, why I feel I owe Gerard, and why you shouldn't care about me anymore," I say calmly now.

When Alex looks at me, it's like a million shards of ice get hurdled my way.

"Shouldn't care. Shouldn't care?" he screams. "I can never stop caring about you. Jesus Christ. I had no fucking idea he had a family before you. He never said a thing. The man is a lying, cheating asshole. You can't go back to Gerard. Look how he has manipulated you and me. All these years, he was grooming you, Paige, and I became part of it. I feel fucking sick." He lowers his body and rests his hands on his knees.

"It wasn't like that," I shout. Alex was supposed to hate me, not himself.

"No? No! Then how was it? A fucking thirty-something-year old father sweet talks a child until she's old enough to have consensual sex. You don't think that's grooming? Um, that's statutory rape at best, Paige. That's why the pig ran. It scared him that you'd tell Sheree. He let you carry the shame, the blame. You." He jabs a finger at me, "Cannot go back to that man. He planned it, he planned it all. He used me, and he used you—is using you. I thought you first met in Los Angeles when you were nineteen, which I could barely condone. But at least you were an adult, but no, not this. This makes it all wrong. So—so, fucking wrong."

"Alex, please, you don't understand. I have nowhere else to go."

"You have me, Paige, me." He jabs a finger to his chest. "I've always been here waiting for you, but you had to make the break without me, or you'd just be jumping from one person to the other. I didn't want to be the rebound." He leans forward, clenching his fist on his thighs in what I think is frustration or maybe he really does feel ill. I know I do.

"Well, isn't that what you'd be now if I left him, the rebound?"

"I don't care anymore." He moves toward me. "Let me be the rebound, anything to get you away from him, just don't go back to him, please," he begs, grabbing the top of my arms, searching my eyes, his pained expression killing me. I look to the ground to gather strength.

"No, Alex. Because if you hadn't come along." I twist out of his grip and pull off his sweater. "I would still be respecting the man I fell in love with years ago. I would have been happy. Now I need to go home and fix things with Gerard. He needs to know you're not a threat anymore. That I plan on being faithful." I thrust the garment at him. "Otherwise he will punish me and put you back in prison. I know he will." I state firmly.

"So that's it? You dump all that on me and it's over."

"Let me do something right," I cry out when his eyes turn cold on me. "I love you, and you just don't understand. If he does anything to you, Alex, I will kill myself. I swear to God I'd rather die than let him hurt you. I messed up everyone's life." I punch into my thighs, still sobbing and screaming, causing cars to slow down as they go past. "I've been selfish and indulgent and crazy. I don't even deserve someone like you."

"All right. It's okay. I know, I get it. I get it." Alex rushes at me and pulls me in. Finally, he seems to understand the pressure I'm under. He strokes my head and tries shushing me when I bury my face into his chest. I breathe his scent in deep, my arms wrapping around him tightly.

"I love you, Alex. If I could change things, I would, so please, just don't make this harder than it already is."

"It's okay, it's okay, I won't. I promise." He kisses the top of my head once then looks into my eyes, searching one then the other. "I never knew you were so strong, Princess." He presses me against his chest again, cradling my head with his large hand. "Boy, did I have you pegged wrong."

BLACK SEA

If I hadn't glanced at my tote bag falling to the floor the moment I rounded the curb, I may have kept going when I noticed the eight or more cars parked in our circular drive. Creeping along, I take in the mixture of monotone BMWs, Volvos, and even one pearl white Bentley.

Parking in the garage, I take my time getting my luggage sorted. I'm hoping Gerard comes out to greet me and explain the collection of vehicles. When he doesn't, I'm forced to enter the house and speculate about the group of men sitting around our large dining table. No one notices me at first, but their roars of laughter are splintering the usually quiet house and sending shivers up my spine.

The kitchen counter is littered with chip packets, plates, and empty snack boxes. The place is a mess. If I didn't know better, I'd say Gerard has been entertaining while I've been in Ponderosa Park, not away on a work-related trip at all. Not even remorseful or concerned over his aggressive behavior toward me, that he was hoping to make amends for. The sight of all those loud men sets my heart galloping, and any residual near-hypothermia earlier evaporates in the sweltering room. When I put down my suitcase, my presence is noticed.

"Ahh. Here she is," Gerard sings out, throwing down his hand of cards and pushing out his chair and rising.

The room falls silent when all eyes turn on me, the smile I pull feels chapped and tight.

There is a chorus of hellos before everyone turns their attention back to the game, each picking up their hand of cards that are suddenly interesting. They reduce their voices to something more orderly.

I don't recognize anyone.

"How was your flight?" Gerard grabs up my case and sweeps an arm around my waist, easing me forward to guide me out of the room and into the hall. "Play on, everyone, and help yourself to more drinks," Gerard suggests over his shoulder.

Once we are out of sight, Gerard becomes affectionate. Stroking my messy hair first before planting a kiss on my forehead. "What took you so long? It's after four." His hot breath against my brow smells of alcohol, and by the glassy look he gives me when I pull away, it's obvious he's had too much to drink.

"My car got damaged while it was parked at the airport. I was putting in a complaint, and it took forever," I lie.

Gerard jerks back. "Damaged how?"

"On the hood. Was there a storm here when I was away? Because it looks like something heavy landed on it."

"Did they check surveillance? It was most likely some deadbeats that broke in, I'd say. Was anyone else's car damaged?" Gerard asks, mounting the stairs quickly. As I follow behind, we discuss theories then he watches me put my things away. Dumping the bag of wet clothing in the bathroom, I turn and tell him I'd like a shower to freshen up.

"That's a good idea. I'm sorry to say, but you do look a mess." He smiles at me from the doorway.

"I got caught in the rain. Who are all those men?" I ask, stripping off my tee.

"Just some people I know. I got bored home alone. Carter and I finished up by Friday night, so we came back early. How was your mother's funeral?" He leans himself against the door frame. I turn on the shower then strip off my shorts.

"I didn't stay for long."

"Oh?" He eyes me in my underwear then pushes himself off the wooden frame and moves toward me.

"I thought it would be better if I didn't see Sheree at all. I went in early, said good riddance to my mother and left before the service."

"Really? I'm surprised Sheree let you get away with that."

"I texted and said my flight got changed. She seemed to buy it. Besides, she's busy with Darby."

"Probably for the best, don't you think? I missed you," Gerard whispers, encircling his arm around me and murmuring into my hair, his chin sliding back and forward across my skull, getting harder with each pass. I press my eyes shut. "Hmm, I could fuck you right now, Paige. You feel so good." He steps back abruptly and lifts my chin. "But we'll wait until later." He arches his eyebrows then pecks my lips. "There's still more fun to be had first." His full smile sends more shivers running through me. Something is off. Letting me go, he walks toward the door then turns back. "See you downstairs. Oh, and if you're not too tired, do you think you could make us something to eat?"

Taking hold of the door, I give a slight nod then wait for him to leave before closing it and stripping fully.

Under the water, I try grounding myself. Keep my thoughts together. Focus on how my life used to be when it was just me and Gerard. Five years of calm routine. A time when I wasn't afraid. Wasn't haunted. Wasn't lost. Five years of love and protection and adoration. Gerard seems fine. But when my head comes out from washing the suds from my hair, I can hear the roars of laughter from the table full of men below me, and an uncomfortable knot settles in my stomach. What are they even doing here? Gerard has never had friends over. Not like this. I'm reluctant to get out of the shower, and for a long time after I'm clean and warm, I just stand there under the water, taking long deep breaths and looking at my slightly rounded abdomen.

Suddenly, the water is freezing. Not gradual, just snap, cold. I know it's because someone is using the tap downstairs. Probably someone who doesn't realize the effect it has on the shower. When I'm waiting over thirty seconds, I know with certainty, that someone is Gerard, no doubt hoping to hurry me along. It wouldn't be the first time he's used that trick.

Dry, and covered in a robe, I step out of the bathroom and into our bedroom then halt. There, sprawled out on our bed—is a deep purple dress I wore to a cocktail party on a yacht last year. A dress I've come to hate because of all the attention it drew. Not just from Gerard who couldn't keep his hands off me all night, but also from many of his work colleagues who felt the need to whisper inappropriate remarks when Gerard's back was turned. There's no way I'm going down into the kitchen to cook in that dress, if that's what he's suggesting.

With a racing heart, I hang the dress and find something else to wear. I blow-dry my hair, stopping the dryer several times to grip the vanity and remind myself to breathe. Why would he lay that dress out for me? Is it a scare tactic, or am I just being melodramatic? Does he really want me strutting around downstairs in the sexiest dress I own? Why would he want me parading around all those men on the night of my return? When are they leaving so Gerard and I can talk about the counseling we need? With thousands of questions going through my mind, I move about on autopilot, doing makeup and finding shoes.

When I'm done, I come out of the room and make my way downstairs. When I've reached halfway, Gerard suddenly appears from the living room with a drink in his hand. His friends are still swearing and laughing noisily. I stop. There is something in the way he's looking at me and instantly the chills return. Gerard doesn't have to say a thing. He just points. I shake my head because I know what he's implying. He wants me to go back up and put on that dress. I'm horrified to comprehend what's going on. These men aren't just here to play poker. When Gerard looks to the floor, I call his bluff and descend. But then his head flicks up, and he starts coming up the steps. Panicked, I turn and jog up the stairs as quick as my heels will allow, shutting the bedroom door and wishing to Christ it had a damn lock on it. I rush into the darkened walk-in closet and quietly close myself in. Pushing under my coats to hide, I instinctively cover my stomach and slide down the wall, drawing my knees up for further protection. I'm shaking so hard the wood panel I'm leaning against is clunking empty wooden hangers together.

Light bursts into the closet when Gerard pulls open the door. He searches for a moment then comes at me.

"Please, Gerard, I beg you with everything I am. Please don't make me go down there to do anything with those men. I promise I'll be good. I promise I will never betray you again. I— I— I can't— can't take anymore. I'll— I'll kill myself, I will. I won't be able to live with the disgust." I try catching snatches of air through my sobbing, but too soon I'm hyperventilating and feeling faint. Groaning I fall onto the carpet. What am I doing to my poor baby?

I start wailing, readying myself to tell him about the baby but then he's rubbing my back and soothing me.

"Good Lord, Paige. Stop, stop. Calm down. What's gotten into you?"

But I can't calm down. My head is swirling, throbbing, thinking crazy thoughts. He pulls me into a hug, and then I hear him whispering. "I'm not going to make you do anything. You just need to lie there while I watch them fuck you. Bite your nipples as they all have a turn at sticking their cocks inside your betraying little cunt." I pull back, wide-eye and mortified. "What? Don't look at me like that. They're all willing to pay." I don't know if he's saying that or if it's my imagination. His lips are moving but they don't match the words I'm hearing. I'm nauseated to the core. Are they real words coming from his mouth? Instinctively, I know that's exactly what he wants to say. My revulsion turns to rage.

"Nooo," I screech, leaping up at him, my fingers clawing at his face. I pull at his hair and slap at his cheeks. Punching at his chest, my mouth goes wide, as my teeth snap. I try to catch one of his arms as they flail through the air in defense until he stands. I lunge myself at him again, pulverizing his chest with my fists.

"Paige, what are you doing? Stop." Gerard grabs my wrists with a look of dismay, and beneath his concerned eyes, thin lines of blood trickle down his cheeks, scaring me. I'm trying to pull away, but he won't let go. I fall to my knees again, dragging him down with me.

"I can't do it. I can't do it. I can't do it. I can't do it. I can't do it. I can't do it."

"Do what?"

"Please don't let them hurt me." I sob weakly.

"I'm not going to let anyone touch you. Why would you think that? Christ, I'm not a fucking animal. They're here to play cards. We've been playing all weekend. What on earth would make you think I'd let them touch you?"

"You just said it. Just now. Horrible things." At least I think I heard him say it. It sounded like he said it, or maybe I was reading his mind? Either way, I sense the charade.

"What?" Gerard lets go of my hands and sits on his haunches. "I never said anything."

Still cowering, I look up at him. "You said you were going to watch them fuck me." Gerard's hair is all over the place, and three deep bloody scratches mar his face on one side. My gaze drops to the floor and I cry harder, the look of horror on his face embarrasses me. I think I'm losing my mind. My accusations suddenly sound stupid.

"I'm sorry. I'm so sorry. Look, I hurt you." I reach for his face, but he pulls away.

"I'll be all right, but I'm worried about you though. I didn't say anything. Do you want me to call someone, a doctor, or Annabel? Do you think this is about your mother's funeral?"

"But why? Why did you lay out that dress?"

"Because it's a nice dress."

"But it's too sexy. Why do you want me looking sexy in front of all those men?"

"Oh, Paige." Gerard gets to his feet, pressing fingers to one cheek and flinching. "You'd look sexy in a sack."

"Why did you tell me to go back and change then?"

"I didn't tell you to go change."

"You did, on the stairs."

Gerard frowns. "I was holding out my hand for you. Why are you like this? What's happened to you?"

I feel like I'm going mad. He pointed. I swear he was pointing. I run a palm over my forehead. "I'm sorry. I—I thought you were... The things you said the other day and then the police and... You... God, I'm so confused about what you want."

Gerard nods. "Yes, you have a lot to sort out in that head of yours." Turning away, he heads toward the bathroom.

Slowly, I get to my feet. "I—I think you're right. Counseling will be good for us. I need to see someone. Have you found someone?" I ask in desperation from the bathroom door, watching as he washes blood from his face. He stares at himself in the mirror.

"Not sure how I'll explain this." Gerard dabs with a towel, leaving bloodstains on the fluffy white fabric. "I hope they didn't hear you screaming. That would be embarrassing." He flicks me a look.

"I'm sorry."

"No need to be. Just putting on that lovely dress will make up for it." He tosses the towel down. "I better get downstairs or they'll think I'm keeping you all to myself." I feel what little blood is in my face drain away. Gerard chuckles then pauses to kiss my forehead as he moves past me, a glimmer of amusement following him. "Oh, and about therapy." He stops short and faces me. "I'm not sure about counseling anymore. I don't think it would serve me to know what sort of crazy you really are. Sort of creeps me out, really. Especially after that little episode."

Gerard is a big fat liar. A true tyrant. An insane psychopath. I want to find the rock I've been living under and smash it to smithereens for letting me hide beneath it. The men can't keep their eyes and hands off me. When I clean up the kitchen, two introduce themselves as Wayne and Garth then stifle a chuckle, asking me if I need any help. Then they accidentally brush against me and drop things at my feet. My heart can hardly keep up with my emotions, and the kitchen feels like the interior of a volcano. Part of me is praying I will spontaneously combust just to get away from what I feel is happening.

I keep looking over to Gerard who pretends he's not aware of what they're doing, instead he calls out that seeing as they're up, could one of them get him another scotch. As if he hasn't already had too much, but at least the task sends them away. I'm so uncomfortable, I take the garbage out and stay outside until Gerard calls me back indoors because the frozen casserole I put in the oven, smells like it's burning, which is an outright lie.

I scan the bench where I left my tote so I can grab my phone to send an SOS text to someone, anyone, cursing to myself that I should have taken Alex's number from him. But my tote has miraculously found its way to the back of Gerard's chair. When I look toward it, Gerard smiles and asks me how the food is coming along.

When the meal is cooked, I place plates around the table in front of the men, nearly all of them make an obvious show of checking out my ass, along with a libidinous murmur. How does Gerard find people like this? Where do they come from, and why are they having such little respect for me? I've done nothing to them. Has Gerard told them this is some game I like? That when I flinch and act scared, I'm just pretending? Well, I'm not pretending, and if they take their intimidating behavior any further, I'm won't hesitate in taking a knife to them all. I don't even care if I'm killed in the process.

Thankfully, they all seem to settle while eating the meal I set out for them, and I retreat to the living room and pretend to watch television, with my ass perched on the edge of the couch, chewing my non-existent nails the whole time. When it seems they're done, Gerard calls for my attention to clear the plates. All in his sweetest tone.

"Come over here, honey," Gerard calls when I'm done stacking the washer. When I don't move, Gerard repeats himself louder causing all eyes to fall on me. Reluctantly, I hang the dishcloth, then meander over until I'm by his side, watching the men carefully before Gerard is pulling me onto his lap. Stiff as a board, Gerard needs to shift me until he's comfortable.

"Not only is she beautiful, but she can also cook." Gerard kisses the top of my bare arm. "Thank you, honey, that was lovely."

There are murmurs of appreciation and glances from behind the fans of cards. I don't even take in anyone's features, they just become a sea of leering eyes that have me in a cold sweat.

"I'm winning." Gerard whispers squeezing my waist. "You must be my lucky charm."

"Your wife would be anyone's lucky charm," the man beside Gerard say, running a finger under my thigh and grinning. I yelp and leap off Gerard's lap and take hold of the chair.

Everyone bursts out laughing.

It only takes me a split second and I'm grabbing the leather strap of my bag and heading straight for the French doors.

"Hey, where are you going, honey?"

"Annabel's."

"No, come back, you're my lucky charm," Gerard says, stretching out his arm and laughing along with the rest of them.

Ignoring him, I slam the door in my haste and walk to my car as fast as I can without looking like I'm fleeing for my life.

~

Seeking refuge at Annabel's turns out to be a waste of time. I haven't seen her since the fundraiser and I'm disappointed when instead of my dear friend answering the door, Maude is there with a flush-faced, red-eyed Katie by her side. Neither of them seems happy.

"Mom's gone," Katie blurts then turns away.

Looking every bit Stuart's mother, Maude's dark eyes droop. My tears are instant, and my hand covers my mouth. "Oh God, what's happened?" I breathe through my fingers until Maude is pulling my hand away.

"No, Paige, darling, it's not that. Annabel and Stuart have separated."

"What? No!" I gasp, pushing past Maude and going inside.

Stuart is on the couch watching TV. When he spots me, his expression crumbles.

"Stu, what happened? What does Katie mean Annabel's gone? Gone where?"

"Packed her bags and took off." Stuart gets up off the couch and heads to the kitchen. I watch as Maude shoos Katie out of the room, instructing her to say goodnight. I turn in both directions, not knowing who to address first, and before I have time to hug Katie in reassurance, Maude has whisked her away.

Stuart goes straight out the back door with a beer in his hand. Obviously, I'm intruding and resurfacing things even watching television is having a hard time blocking out. He glances over his shoulder at me.

Taking the hint, I follow him outside. It's chilly, and when I rub my arms, I remember what I'm wearing.

"So, I gather you haven't spoken to her?"

"No. I only just got back. When? When did she leave? And why?" I rub Stuart's back before he steps away and takes a gulp of beer then folds his arms, still looking out at their small backyard.

"I guess she just had enough. She was always saying she felt like she was competing with Corrin's ghost," he says, referring to Katie's biological mother who passed away shortly after separating from Stuart.

"Corrin? I don't understand. Why would she feel like that? Annabel said it was you who left Corrin, why would she feel like she's competing?"

"No. I think it's more to the fact that Corrin had Katie."

"Oh, Stu, I'm sorry. Maybe she just needs some time apart. She'll come to her senses. When did she leave?"

"Thursday."

That was the same damn night I was visiting sex clubs and screwing my brains out. I want to crawl back under my rock, this time in shame. I've been so self-centered lately.

"Has she called? Did you talk? I'm sure…" I cover my heart to stop it from shattering. I can't believe Annabel would do this. "Oh, Annabel." I breathe out heavily. I knew she was struggling a little, but to abandon Katie. Annabel is all she's ever known. It's not right.

"She left a note that said it all. I really don't think she'll be back. Katie is heartbroken. Jesus, Paige, Annabel is mom to her. All Katie understands is that her mother walked out on her. Why couldn't Annie just be happy with Katie? I mean, I got lucky—why push it? Want a beer?" he asks, draining his bottle.

I decline but wait as he gets another. Stuart sinks onto a lounge chair and encourages me to do the same.

"Stu—what do you mean you got lucky with Katie. Like, I know you're lucky, she's beautiful and I can…"

"I shouldn't have children, Paige. It's a decision I made years ago, right after my baby brother died." He looks down at the beer he's holding, taps the top of the glass bottle with its cap. "I've got a screwed-up gene that runs in my family. Corrin knew, so I was shocked when I got the call after she died in a car accident. She listed me as the father on Katie's birth certificate. Corrin wasn't the type to lie, Paige. I'm happy of course. Especially since Katie's been cleared of having the disease. I mean, that's luck. But I wasn't prepared to risk having another child."

"Well sure, that's understandable. But why would that upset Annabel? She never wanted kids anyway."

"Are you serious? She's been nagging me ever since we got married."

"What?" I'm so surprised my head jerks back.

After talking and hopefully reassuring him, I ask for Annabel's phone number, so I have it again, and promise to let Stuart know if I manage to get a hold of her.

Inside my car, I repeatedly try to reach Annabel until it just looks ridiculous how many times I've tried. My frantic behavior reminds me of Einstein's quote about insanity and makes me question mine again.

Why is all this happening? Where is Annabel? Is she safe? I try her number again then growl when it goes to voicemail. How can she just go?

Exhausted, I fall back against the seat and close my eyes, my hand rubbing over my belly, feeling scared and mentally unstable. Tears are on my cheeks again. I swipe them away, annoyed I'm so pathetic, that I can't stand up for myself. That I'm not smart enough to know what to do.

My phone lets out a ping, startling me. Sitting up, I'm relieved that it's Annabel texting.

Annabel: Oh. Paige sweetie. I'm so sorry I've done this to you, to Stuart and Katie. I know it wasn't right, but I just can't lie to myself any longer. I'm not in love with Stu, not anymore. I just wanted to let you know I'm fine. I'm in good hands, and I'll call you soon. Right now, I just need the space, okay? Love you.

Me: Where are you though? I want to help. What can I do? Please, you can't desert your family like this. Annabel, I need you.

Annabel: Don't hate me, but I'm on a yacht in the middle of the ocean.

Me: What? Who with?

Annabel: Ronald.

Ronald Klaneski! The pinstripe suit guy from the fundraiser? Mister suave who was bidding on my donated photos. Is she for real? They obviously found that dark alley and she lifted her skirt. Part of me is in shock, the other part amused. Annabel, you little hussy. My fingers get busy again.

Me: I'm calling you. Pick up.

I tap on her number, but she doesn't pick up. What the fuck! How can she just shut all of us out like this?

I grip the phone with two hands then look out the windshield then back at the phone. Is she shitting me? Just like that, she tosses everything away to go sailing with a stranger. Leaving behind her perfect husband and gorgeous child when I can't manage leaving a tyrant. Where's my goddamn spine?

Then Gerard is calling, making me jump. I almost let it ring out before answering.

"I don't mean to interrupt, but I'm just letting you know the game has ended and they've all left. Not before I took all their money though." Gerard laughs. "Sorry if they made you feel uncomfortable, they can be a rowdy bunch. How are Annabel and Stuart? Did he mention the gift I gave them for Katie?"

"What gift? What do you mean?"

"The envelope I gave you to give to Annabel. It was to help out with Katie's school fees."

"Her school fees?"

"Yes. You're always telling me how stressed out Annabel is with money issues. I thought I could help. I arranged a scholarship through my firm. I thought it would make you happy."

Me happy? What the hell?

12

LOVELY

When I push open the glass doors to the main reception area of the Planned Parenthood Clinic, I recoil. Why would they bloody well put up pictures of babies? Cute newborns and the growing fetus depicted in graphics. How the hell am I supposed to stick to my decision with the perfection of life staring me in the face?

While I wait to go in for my appointment, I try burying my head in a home decor magazine, but the constant chit-chat between mothers and their small children keeps diverting my attention. I home in on a young mother with a book resting on her protruding stomach. She's reading to a four- or five-year old girl sitting beside her, who's presumably her daughter. Her fine blonde hair is pulled up into little pigtails, which makes her look positively adorable. Every now and then, she slides off the seat and tickles, albeit annoyingly, at her little brother in a stroller. He's sucking fiercely on a pacifier and his eyes are locked onto his mother's phone, watching a show that keeps repeating the names of colors. At least it's educational, I surmise.

"Mrs. Whitmyer." My name is finally called by a nurse

who presses a clipboard against her white jacket. Her hair is pulled into a bun at the nape of her neck and she reminds me of Annabel. She smiles when I rise from my seat, gripping her stethoscope in one hand like it's a scarf around her neck then turns to lead the way. After gathering my purse and lightweight jacket, I follow her down a long corridor.

In the consultation room, I'm relieved to see posters warning of STDs instead of babies, pregnancy, and babes on boobs. But soon, they too become confronting on a whole other level when I'm thinking over the sexcapade I witnessed at the sex club five nights ago. Not to mention kissing Rebecca and then having amazing sex with Alex. I try blocking everything else out when I take the seat I'm offered.

The nurse runs through the preliminary checkup. Blood pressure, weight, temperature, and asks me a bunch of questions regarding my general heath, then queries the date of my last known period. "I have no idea," I tell her, as I'm still experiencing regular cycles, or at least I was until the doctor told me at the hospital and I stopped taking my contraceptive pill.

She reassures me that it can sometimes happen, and an ultrasound will give them a better idea of how far along my pregnancy is. When I protest, because I'd rather not know or at least pretend the baby isn't real, she tells me the sonographer will keep the sound off and the screen facing away from me. That I'm free to wear headphones and listen to music if I'd prefer, but it's necessary to accurately gage the fetus because they cannot perform a procedure after the maximum twenty-four weeks gestation. She stresses, "The sooner a termination is carried out, the better." I have to agree.

I try appeasing my own conscience when I tell her I've also been using condoms. The nurse, whose name is Judy, informs me that no protection against pregnancy or disease is one-hundred-percent, although I am in the minority, she says.

"Just my luck."

Many tears and tissues later, when I explain my circumstances and my decision to terminate, I'm led to another room where an ultrasound is performed. The conclusion. The fetus is estimated ten weeks and three days old, but the earliest booking is two and a half weeks away.

I cry all the way home, thinking of little fingers and tiny toes. Then I climb into bed, still crying but consoling myself that it really is better this way. Exhausted, I finally fall into a dreamless sleep.

Even in my unconsciousness I sense him. Jolting awake like I've been caught in the middle of a crime, which is how Gerard makes me feel these days, he is standing in the doorway with his arms folded, watching me. I pull myself into a sitting position and reach quickly for my phone to see the time. I've slept for over five hours.

"Hi. I didn't hear you pull up. I only meant to have a quick nap." Pushing back the blankets, I swing my legs over the edge of the bed and rub my face. My cheeks feel gritty from my salty tears. I push back my hair, switch on the lamp, and look at Gerard. "You're home early. Is everything all right?"

"I'm not sure yet."

"What do you mean?"

As I rise and make my way to the bathroom, Gerard pushes himself off the doorjamb and follows me. I keep glancing over my shoulder as we cross the floor while he proceeds to remove his jacket. He flicks on the closet lighting and hangs it just inside the doorway.

"I know where you went today."

I stop midway from shutting the bathroom door. "Pardon?"

"The clinic. You went into the city today to a clinic. Why?"

"I needed to renew my script." I say, closing the door and sitting on the toilet. My heart starts racing. How the hell did he know I went there? "Are you following me or something?" I call out. My tone implying I'm joking with him.

Gerard opens the door to the bathroom, making me jump. I'm still sitting on the toilet with my panties at my knees. "Gerard!" I quickly wipe and flush and make myself decent.

He watches me intently as I wash my hands. I try to appear calm and study my reflection before splashing cold water on my face to wake myself up. I need my wits about me.

"Yes. I'm having you followed."

Snatching at the hand towel, I spin around. "What, why?"

He arches a brow.

"Gerard, I told you, you can trust me. I'm not seeing Alex. I promise."

"Why were you at the clinic? And please don't lie to me."

I rehang the hand towel before facing him squarely. After the night of my return, we'd been getting along. I've been playing the compliant wife, biding my time until I can work out a way to get out. It's the only way to keep Alex safe. I don't want to tell Gerard about the pregnancy. The termination is my choice. I won't allow him the last word on my decision.

"I needed a new script for the pill."

He huffs. "But—you've still got some."

Heat rises to my cheeks because he's right. But only a few. I never thought he might monitor that side of things, I must remember to pop them out daily.

"Well?" he snaps out.

"Well, what?" I push past him and head toward my jewelry case where I returned the near empty packet after traveling, making an obvious display to prove him wrong. But when I lift the lid to my case, I gasp loudly and step back. All my jewelry is missing. I swear it was there this morning when I changed earrings. But now, only the redundant pill packet remains. "Shit. My jewelry is gone. Gerard?" I spin around as he makes his way into the walk-in closet. I reach for my phone on the bedside table.

He comes out, loosening his tie. "If you're calling the police, don't bother. I have your jewelry in a safe," Gerard says, slipping off his shirt and kicking off his shoes.

"Why?"

"Really? You're asking me why? Because we were robbed last month, Paige. If you haven't realized, your jewelry is worth a fortune."

"I know, but what if I want to wear something? I mean, my engagement and wedding ring were in here. I want them."

"I'd like to think you do. I'll get them out for you in the morning, but I think it would be best if we put them away each night."

"I think that's a little over the top. They're mostly on me anyway. And what's not, I'm sure is secure inside the box when we're home. I'll put everything in the safe when we go out."

"No, that's fine. I'd like to be the only one who knows the combination. Your ex-lover is a thief, afterall. And now that he knows he can't have you, maybe he'll seek revenge by trying to steal other things that belong to me."

"Gerard, this is ridiculous," I whine, closing the lid of the box.

Gerard stares straight at me, his eyebrows arched. "Is it

though?" He turns and heads for the shower, leaving me reeling, because again it seems he's read my mind and is one step ahead of me. Damn it. Plan A of my escape, to sell my jewelry, just went down the drain.

$$\backsim$$

I barely leave the house all week, apart from my early morning run, which turns into a jog that slows to a walk because I feel so drained. It's not that I have the desire to go anywhere, anyway. When I sighted the silver car that followed me to the dry cleaners, I realized Gerard wasn't bluffing and is monitoring my movements. I hadn't heard from nor seen Alex since my return, and while thoughts of him make me teary and crush my chest, I refuse to bring him into my mess. In time, I'll forget. Just stick to the mundane, I instruct myself on a loop.

"Morning, Delilah," I call out when I see the avid gardener at her mailbox. I give her a little wave from the opposite side of the road. She is minus her sombrero today and looks dressed to go out.

"Oh, Paige, darling, wait." When I stop in my tracks, she hastily opens the gate. I don't feel like a chat this morning, but before I know it, she's crossing the road, waving her mail at me as if I might change my mind and run off.

"What a beautiful morning."

"It is."

She shares pleasantries, telling me about her daughter's visit and where she's off to today. Then she gets to the point of holding me up.

"There's only one left now."

"Sorry?"

"Kitten. He's a sweet little thing. Marianne named him

Napoléon. But I'm sure you could change that. Have you spoken with Gerard?"

"Oh." I look away, feeling ashamed. I hadn't given it a thought after we parted company the other week. There was no point really. Gerard doesn't want a child, let alone a kitten.

"Oh dear. I'm so sorry, I didn't mean to upset you." Delilah reaches for my arm when I use my jacket sleeve to wipe my eyes.

I chuckle at myself. "Don't mind me, I'm just a bit teary lately. The truth is. I'd love a kitten, Delilah, but Gerard wouldn't tolerate a pet."

"Really. Who doesn't like pets? Well, never mind. I'm sure we'll find him a home eventually." Delilah gives my arm a rub. "I better get a move on if I'm to make the bus. Those garden tours wait for no one. Have a nice run or jog or whatever it is you do," she says in her usual parting way, waving a hand over her shoulder and giggling.

I wait until Delilah is safely back across the road and through her gate. She waves once more as she closes her front door. I stare ahead, down the curving road leading home. I want to be old. Live in a house on my own with a cat. I want to go on gardening tours. I want to go to our beach house. I want to go back and see Sheree. I miss my friend. I want to tell her how sorry I am. I want to see Alex. I need Alex. Suddenly, I'm sobbing and running. Nearly stumbling over my own feet. When I turn into our drive, I finally stop, skidding to a halt as the silver car drives past me. Why is Gerard doing this to me? I promised I'd be faithful. Why won't he believe me? But it's a stupid question I have no right asking. Even to myself.

I jerk open the mailbox, nearly pulling the top off its hinges. Who am I kidding? This is insane. I don't love, Gerard. I need him, but I don't love him.

I pull out letters and wrapped magazines, a parcel and stupid flyers. "It says no fucking junk mail, goddamn it." I shout, slamming the lid and looking down the road as if I can expect to see the postman, though I know he's long gone.

I march inside and kick the door shut, dump the letters on the table, then take a shower. Minutes later, I'm standing in front of the open fridge, willing myself to eat something. I'm not hungry, but my conscience keeps screaming at me that the baby needs food. But I'm not having a baby. I slam the fridge shut and stare at the closed door.

Suddenly I'm at the lake house, staring at the closed fridge door after getting everyone a cool drink. Filling large glasses with ice and chilled homemade lemonade. I'm pretending I'm not listening to their conversation. I was always trying to make myself small and unnoticed.

"But it's a stupid idea. If I wanted to study medicine or law like you, sure, but I don't want to be a doctor or a disgusting lawyer."

"Sheree, that's enough," Teresa snapped.

I snuck a look at Gerard. His mouth was pulled tight, his knife and fork upright in his clenched fists. When he glances at me, his expression softens, and he places his utensils down, then turns his attention back to his wife and Sheree.

"Is horse training all you'll aspire to, Sheree. Are you aware of how little trainers make?"

"I don't care. It's what I want to do. It will make me happy," she argued.

"Life isn't about damn happiness, Sheree, it's about being of purpose."

"Richard," Teresa said softly. "You can't be serious? She's fourteen, let her have dreams."

"Dreams are for no-hopers. Get a career. Strive to become someone I can be proud of. I've been working my backside off and studying to get a good career so you can have a good education. Now you're saying you'll waste all that and become a horse handler." He shook his head in disgust, staring down at his plate of food.

"You would have done that with or without me, Dad. You're the one who wants a fancy life with fancy people. Me and Mom are happy here."

I tiptoed back into the dining area carrying a tray full of drinks. I placed it carefully in the center of the table and looked to Sheree, who was rolling her eyes before reaching for a drink.

"Thank you, Paige," Teresa said, before I took my seat again. Gerard's eyes were straight on me, and he reached for my hand.

"And what about you, Paige? Are you going to disappoint me also?"

I looked around at the expectant eyes and slowly pulled my hand out from beneath his to reach for a cold glass of lemonade. Thankfully, when I brought the glass to my lips, Sheree answered for me.

"Paige wants to be a veterinarian. Don't you Paige?" Sheree said, picking up her toasted sandwich and biting into it. Through a mouthful of food, she added, "That's a doctor? Will that be good enough for you, Dad?"

Gerard picked up his cutlery. "Please use your knife and fork, Sheree, just because you want to work with filthy animals doesn't mean you can't act like a lady at the dinner table."

"It's a sandwich—Dad."

I'm still staring at the closed fridge door. Tears have been sliding down my cheeks, remembering the hollow feeling inside me that day. Sheree wasn't good enough. I wasn't good enough, and the only reason Sheree's mom was good enough was because she was supporting him while he studied.

Later that same day, he'd joined me on the front porch

where I was reading. Sheree and her mom had taken a walk. They hadn't invited me along, so I stayed behind to read. I knew they must have been discussing Sheree's future by the conversation they'd had at lunch.

Gerard put his arm around me that afternoon, pulled me in close. I shut the book up and rested it on my lap.

"I wish Sheree was as smart as you, Paige," he began. "Vet science is an extremely challenging career path. I didn't want to say anything in front of Sheree because she's jealous of you. Have you chosen your subjects for next year to support that path?"

"No. I've been waiting to talk to the careers counselor. It will be hard though because I'm relying on a scholarship in track and field," I answered, flattered that he was interested.

"That's right, you're a distance runner, aren't you? That's another thing I'm disappointed about with Sheree, she's lazy. I mean, you're our guest, and yet you're always helpful." He kissed the top of my head and squeezed me tighter. When his arm came away from my shoulder and reached for the book I was reading, he rested his hand there, right at the apex of my legs. The feeling was electrifying and made my lungs freeze mid-breath.

"Anne Frank?" he said, studying the title, his hands moving just the slightest, so he was pressing into me a little before he was lifting the book up and away then flicking though it.

"The school makes us read it." My breath came out in jarred pulses between words, and I shifted on the seat so he wasn't touching his thigh with mine anymore.

"You enjoy reading?"

I nodded.

"Sheree doesn't. All she thinks about are boys. Do you have a boyfriend?"

I shook my head.

Standing, he placed the book back on my lap and looked down at me, smiling.

"I wish I was younger."

"You do? Why?"

"Because I would have given anything to date someone as smart and beautiful as you."

He waited a split second, seeing if I'd respond. When no words came out, just my face catching fire, he turned and walked away. His hands went into his pocket, and his shoulders rolled forward. He looked sad. I was never able to stop thinking about his words that day and the buzz that lingered between my thighs.

Conveniently shaking the memory away, I grab a slice of quiche from out the fridge and take a seat at the table to sort through the mail until all that's unopened is the parcel. Expecting to find it addressed to Gerard, I'm surprised to find it's for me. Ripping open the plastic satchel, I pull out a gray sweater. Following it, is the scent of Alex. I instantly bury my nose into the fabric and hold it close to my chest. His smell drops my stomach and an overwhelming ache pools there. I look inside the plastic bag and find a small box and a note.

To the Princess on Solsbury Hill,

Something to remind you of me. I bought it when I got out of prison. I liked what it said.

I hold the sweater at arm's length to study it harder then turn the garment over. And there it is, the words 'Solsbury Hill.' Alex told me to Google it, but I never did. When I read the writing scrawled over the back on what looks like a scroll, they seem to be lyrics.

I keep reading the letter.

I never meant to hurt you, Paige, and I never knew what kind of evil was inside Gerard. Years ago, he asked me to do a job. He told me the young girl he wanted to scare was someone who stole a watch from him. I didn't know it was you he was trying to scare, not until you mentioned it after seeing your friend in the store. I would have never agreed to anything had I known about him. It wasn't me who stole from you that night, but it was me who organized someone to do what Gerard paid me to do. I hope one day you'll find the strength to leave him. You need to find out who you truly are and what you want in life. You deserve to be happy. You did nothing wrong. It was those around you who wronged you, including me. The only thing you ever did was fall in love with people who don't deserve you.

Love Alexander X

And Solsbury Hill is a song. It's about being prepared to lose what you have for what you <u>might</u> get. I thought I could teach you that.

I grab the sweater again and breathe him in. I want to see him so badly there's physical pain everywhere, but then I open the small box and gasp. Conflicting emotions run through me like I've just been hit up with poison in my veins. Simultaneously, I feel like clutching the pendant inside the box to my chest and throwing it across the room. I can't believe what I'm looking at, and the turmoil inside is deadening. I place it on the table and bore my eyes into it. The cat necklace with the onyx eyes, that my father bought for me.

13

SIRENS

There are eighty-five roses on the plaster cornice that joins the ceiling and walls of our bedroom. Fifteen of those roses are on my side of the room alone. I know because I count them over and over every night and first thing in the morning. The roses are joined by a long continuous stem with leaves. I haven't begun counting the leaves. Yet.

Tonight, I only get up to thirty-two before Gerard comes from the bathroom and I roll onto my side, ending my compulsive behavior. My cold shoulder does nothing to deter him though, and within seconds, he has killed the light and is spooning me from behind, holding a naked me tightly against his chest. His arm goes around my waist, then a hand fondles my breasts. His breath, heavy and pungent from scotch is making me gag, or maybe it's the insistence of his jabbing cock that's trying to enter me.

"I want to make you come like you did with Oliver," he whispers against my ear. Gerard may as well have thrown a bucket of ice water over me. I'm surprised to be lubricated enough to accommodate his cock when he finally slides in.

His hand reaches lower and pulls my leg over his to give him access. Spreading me, his fingers find my sensitive spot. I'm dry there, and his touch is unpleasant.

"Don't worry about me," I say, stopping his fingers, pushing him away then pulling myself out of his tight hold so I can breathe, but it also helps him penetrate deeper, making him moan. I grit my teeth and bear it, hoping he will become more aroused by the position and get this over and done with.

He murmurs and sucks noisily on his fingers before his hand resumes trying to pleasure me. But I've lowered my leg again, and I'm hunched forward and out of good reach.

Instead, he slides his hand between my butt and without warning, slips a wet digit into my ass.

"Gerard," I yelp and jerk away.

In a heartbeat, he pulls away, and I'm rolling onto my back and staring up at his grinning face.

"I don't like that."

"But I want you to come for me."

"Well, that's not going to do it," I snap.

Ignoring my snide remark, Gerard keeps grinning, then moves to position himself between my legs, slipping his hands under my knees and pushing forward. His movements are primordial and cavalier. Aware of the growing life inside me, I'm hypersensitive, and his actions feel disgusting. I try crawling up the bed to give myself some distance, but he follows me. In the semi-lit room from the hall light left on, his features are clear. His desperation and hunger are disturbing. Every night, he wants to have sex. I'm wondering if he somehow found out about my pregnancy and secretly, he wants to fuck the baby out of me. My vulgar thoughts repulse me and put me on the verge of tears. Throwing my arm over my eyes, I bite on my lips and take hold of the sheet in one hand, gripping it into a fist, the threat of a scream inside clawing its way from my gut and up my throat.

Gerard doesn't care that I'm cringing. He dips down, tasting me, and buries his nose between my folds. I let out a groan and reach for his head with both hands, calming him when he muzzles my clit and dips his tongue inside me. The sounds that escape me, resonate like moans of pleasure, but are really groans of agony instead. I detest him touching me now. If it weren't for his insistence that I come to bed naked, I'd be dressed in clean running gear, ready the moment the sun peeks over the horizon so I can be out the doors and running.

Gerard's efforts to arouse me are futile.

"Please, Gerard. Just make love to me, I'm not going to come."

Inserting a finger, he's then sucking on me. The familiarity of his action reminds me of Alex. I know he's mimicking Alex. My insides go cold, realizing that I've been deliberately blocking out the reality of who this man has become. What lengths he has gone to claim me, to keep me, to control me. My legs slide slowly down the bed until they are straight.

"Stop," I say, pushing on his head. "I don't like that."

"Mm, but you taste so good." Gerard lifts his head and smiles salaciously. Palming his face dry, he crawls up toward me, his knees spreading me again so he can position himself at my opening. "I'll be gentle," he says, kissing my forehead and sliding inside. Why would he say that? But I don't even consider refusing him. After his drunken, abusive night, which feels like a lifetime ago, I now know what he's capable of—docile has become a super tight second skin I'm in.

I grab hold of his hips, making sure he doesn't penetrate too quickly or get rough, that he doesn't lose control. Ha!

How things have changed. Once upon a time, I craved him losing control. But now my mind is so scarred, by fear, uncertainty, and shame. Lies. It's all a lie. Everything. Him, me, our life together—this baby. Everything is a lie and has always been a lie. I threw myself blindly into his traps because he pretended to adore me, and I fell for it.

My mind slips away somewhere while Gerard does what he needs to do. He demands nothing from me. I'm just a vessel for him to use now, and he becomes sweaty from his effort and the lack of mine. He stoops to kiss me, but I turn my face away. It doesn't seem to discourage him though, and in minutes, he is grunting and thrusting to completion.

Rolling off, Gerard's arms go behind his head. "You could have at least shown some enthusiasm. That was like fucking a corpse." He twists his head to look at me. "What am I doing wrong now?"

"Nothing. It's me," I say, pushing back the blankets and going to the bathroom. I use the toilet then splash water on my face and get a drink, stare at myself, at my glassy dead eyes.

I can't do this. I can't live like this for the rest of my life. I reach down and cup my slight belly and pace the room, feeling nauseous. Looking up again, I stare into my eyes. I need to find a way out. I think of women's shelters that I could go to or how I could beg Sheree to take me in until I get on my feet, but every idea I come up with strikes fear inside. I need Alex. I want Alex. The impulse to go to him is so fierce, I shake from the idea of it forming in my mind.

I don't know how long I'm in the bathroom, sitting in the upholstered chair with a towel around me. I just know I don't want to go back to bed until I know Gerard is asleep. His touch, his smell, his voice, everything about him repulses me, and the second he is asleep, I plan on grabbing my clothes and leaving. I don't want to involve Alex, but knowing what I know now, I suddenly feel like he owes me.

When Gerard's phone rings and I hear him talking, I can conclude he's not going to sleep in a hurry. Standing, I move toward the shower. I want, no I need, to wash him off me.

Suddenly, the door flies open, and Gerard is standing naked, mobile phone in hand and looking pale.

"That was the police. The beach house caught fire." Gerard looks around the bathroom frantically. I suspect looking for clothes before going toward the walk-in closet. When there's no response from me, he does a double take, supports himself with one arm against the door frame. "Did you hear me? The beach house has burned to the fucking ground."

Suddenly, I'm overly naked. The evidence of Gerard is between my legs, and I feel dirty. I turn toward the shower. I don't want to hear what else he might say.

"Paige." Gerard steps forward, grabbing me before I have time to reach for the taps. "Paige, listen to me. The police said they think there was someone still…"

"No." I pivot on my heels, my hand covering Gerard's face and pushing him away. "Just no. You will not. You will not do this to me. Don't you dare say anything about Alex."

"It's not me. The police, they just called. They said the house went up in minutes."

"Shut up, shut up, shut up." I cover my ears, flop into the chair in the corner of the room again and start rocking, glancing up at Gerard repeatedly waiting for him to sneer and tell me he's joking. But he runs a hand through his blond hair, looking genuinely shocked. Putting down his phone, he splashes water over his face and looks at me through the mirror, still rocking. He grips the vanity and droops his head. "There was… his body was…"

"Shut up." I say, my hands still covering my ears and rocking.

"The police say the fire started in the…"

"Shut up. You're lying."

"… furnace room, and because of all the accelerants…"

"Shut—the—fuck up!" I scream and lunge at him, beating my hands on his chest before he catches my wrists. "You did this. You had him killed, didn't you? It wasn't enough that you have me back, you wanted to make sure he would never be there. Why? I said I wasn't going to see him anymore. It was me who betrayed you, Gerard, not him. You should have killed me, not him."

"Stop it, Paige." He shakes me by the wrists, holding tight so the anger searing through me can't inflict more pain on him. I want to rip his evil eyes out, claw at his face. I know he did it. All his threats. The belittling, the power games. "For the love of God. I didn't touch him. I've been right here." Gerard's face is a furrow of disbelief. "You've gone mad. Last week, you nearly clawed me to death, and now this." Releasing one wrist, Gerard reaches for his cheek.

"You had someone else do it. Just like you sent police to harass me and Kelsey."

"How dare you accuse me. Just who the fuck do you think you are, you ungrateful slut?"

"Get out." I rip my other arm away and turn toward the shower.

"You've gone insane."

"Get out!" I scream.

"This is not just happening to you. He was my brother. That's my fucking four million-dollar investment that just got burned to the ground."

"Get out, get out, get out!" I yell at him, stepping behind the glass.

"The police are coming over. They need to talk to us."

I ignore him, turn on the shower taps, and wait for the water.

"Paige, did you hear me?"

I step under the water and start humming him and his voice away. Gerard comes up to the glass, glowering at me.

"If you say anything stupid to the police, I will never forgive you. Do you understand? This has become an investigation, Paige. I hope you understand the severity of what's happened."

Disregarding him completely, I push my head under the water and let the warmth wash everything away. Everything until I'm floating above this hellish life and into some space that's nothingness.

Gerard needs to pull me up off the floor of the shower when the police arrive half an hour later. Turning off the taps, he then dries me hastily and pulls me through to the bedroom. I stand idle in the center of the room when Gerard races to the windows and looks behind the blinds. The headlights from the police car snap off, and the room is again lit only by Gerard's bedside lamp.

"It was a stupid idea to have a shower, Paige. The police are going to think you might have washed away evidence. Did you think of that?" He disappears into the closet then returns with underwear and my fluffy gown. He did it. Why else would he mention evidence?

I lift one leg at a time when Gerard helps me dress. Otherwise I'd still be naked in the center of the room. My lip quivers when I hear the banging on the front door, the reality hitting me that Alex might really be dead and they're coming to tell us in person. "Noooo," I wail, collapsing to the floor. My beautiful Alex. What have I done?

"Shit," Gerard cusses, lifting me so he can pull my gown around me and fasten the belt. "I need to answer the door. Go into the bathroom and dry off your hair, you're dripping everywhere."

When I don't respond, Gerard shakes me. "Paige, listen to me. Go dry your hair, the police are here." He bends to search my eyes. What he sees must concern him because he pulls me into an embrace. "I'm sorry, Paige. I truly am. I never hated Alex. He was my brother, I loved him."

The police fist the door again then ring the doorbell.

Gerard puts me at arm's length. "You need to pull yourself together, Paige. The police will want to talk to the both of us."

My head is nodding, but I don't know who makes that happen because I'm dead inside. I've gone somewhere away from here.

Gerard leaves the room, his mouth moving, but his words come out as a garbled mess that have no meaning. I walk into the closet. On tiptoes, I pull down a box and lift the lid.

In a daze, I pull out the gray sweater Alex gave me, press the folds of fabric into my face. My knees buckle until I'm sitting on the floor, rocking and crying and chanting four words over and over. I don't even register the sound, just the vibration in my throat.

Then I'm undressing and slipping the sweater on over my head and wrapping my body within the oversized garment. Alex's smell and essence envelope me immediately, and I draw in consecutive long breaths between moaning, "I'm so sorry, Alex."

I stop chanting and pull the sweater over my nose, clamping my eyes tightly, then breathe him in again. He's here. He will always be here, right here inside me. Slowly, I get to my feet. Methodically, I finger comb my hair and tie it back. I dry my face and blow my nose, then make my way downstairs, compulsively counting each step as I go.

The police interrogate me and Gerard for over an hour. By the end, I have my head resting on my arm, lying across the table, struggling to even keep my eyes open. The officers keep looking at me, concerned. One, a female, even gets up and makes me a cup of tea, which goes cold and untouched. I barely say anything, except yes, no, and I don't know.

The only things I hear apart from their direct questions are, 'accident,' 'accelerants,' and 'burned beyond recognition.' My beautiful Alex burned away. Into dust. A pile of twisted, charred body parts. I let out an achy wail. A howl that must stand hairs because the female officer rubs her arms before I rush out of the room. I don't care what they think. Don't care if I embarrass Gerard. I don't even care for my own life anymore.

I don't even get to drift off to sleep because Gerard starts calling me to come downstairs. I surmise the police have left by the anger in his tone. I lay still, hoping he thinks I'm asleep, but he calls out again and again. Then his screams get louder as he marches up the stairs.

"August twenty-fifth. Two days ago. You told him, didn't you?" Gerard, shouts at me, his eyes still locked onto his laptop, viewing his surveillance tapes from that date. Footage he neglected to disclose to the police that he had.

Exhausted, I try to exit the living area.

"Get the fuck back here."

I turn slowly and face him, my arms limp by my side. When I don't move fast enough, Gerard gets to his feet, grabs me by the back of the neck, and pushes me along until I'm in front of the computer. He taps a few keys until Alex's face takes up the whole screen, his hand giving the finger before the screen goes black.

I let out a sob causing Gerard to tighten his grip.

"That little bastard deliberately set fire to my house. You told him about the cameras, didn't you? And of course he wanted revenge. And here I was feeling bad thinking Max might have fucked up with the rewiring, but it's your fault. Again. Just as well the dumb prick set fire to himself, or I'd hunt him down and have him shot."

Still limp and crying, I twist out of his grip and stumble away. I climb the stairs and crawl back into bed, sleeping his accusations away while I snuggle into the gray sweater that I swear I'll never wash.

My heart is already racing when I hear a loud bang. I've sat upright, but even as my head flails in every direction, I can't see a damn thing. I can hear muffled voices and a door slam, but I'm blind and what's that familiar smell?

Suddenly, I'm yanked down, and someone grabs my hands. I try to scream, but something gets stuffed into my mouth, and then my legs are being jerked on. I tug my arms, but they are heavy and stiff, getting pulled out of their sockets the more I struggle. I rub my head against my arm that's pinned over my head, and there is a sliver of light now.

I feel something warm and wet dripping on my abdomen. Again, I try to scream but my throat is full and dry, and suddenly I'm chewing on a big tacky gob of gum. I want to spit it out. Pushing with my tongue, I press the large wad half out my mouth, but I'm having trouble breathing now. Panicked, my body flips from side to side, my chest heaving, but my legs are tied. I'm splayed wide open. Darkness tries to claim me. I'm slipping away, going to faint, and then I can breathe again. Alex is standing next to me. He has removed whatever it was in my mouth. I can't see him, but I can breathe now, and I know it's him, because I can smell him. His sweet, musky scent. My heart settles, and his hand caresses gently over my face, teasing me by pulling the blindfold up a little, then back over my face again.

He kisses me. But then… they're not his lips. The face is rough and smells of alcohol and cigarettes. The scent makes me gag, and for a moment, I have the same choking feeling. Then, Alex is there again, pushing the blindfold up a little and whispering, "Peekaboo." He laughs and pulls it down again.

"Alex, stop," I say, panic rising that all along he's been tricking me. Then, large scratchy hands, cold hands, are between my thighs. I don't like the sensation. My legs spring into action, kicking and thrashing to make them stop.

"Stop it." I lash out and twist away. But I'm still tethered and vulnerable. "This is not funny. Let me go." I kick my feet, roll and try to get the blindfold off my face so I can see what's going on.

Then Alex's scent is all around me again, and I stop struggling. "Alex," I whisper. "Please, can you untie me?"

There is a warmth on my face like sunshine, making me smile. "I'd do anything for you, Princess," Alex murmurs against my lips before kissing me. When I open my mouth to take him again, he's suddenly screaming right into my mouth with such force, he fills my lungs.

"Peekaboo. Don't be blind, he can fuckin' see you."

I gasp for air from the fright, and in the moment of silence that follows, the blindfold is suddenly ripped off, and I'm floating and staring down at myself from above.

I see a blindfolded me tied to a bed. I see Carlos pacing, staring down at my naked body before he crawls between my legs. I feel ill and try to look away, but then I catch sight of my mother in the bathroom. She's acting strange, like she's gone mad, thrusting out her hand to no one, and her mouth is moving.

The moisture dripping on my stomach brings me back to Carlos. It's his sweat. He's dripping sweat on me, and then he is sitting up on his knees undoing his fly.

"Carlos, wait," my mother yells from the bathroom. The body below me is thrashing from side to side, and I can hear my own muffled screams. Then Carlos is removing his pants. A loud thud resonates around the room as his belt buckle hits the wooden floor. Then he's between my kicking legs again. My knees bobbing up and down frantically. I want to turn away, but the pull toward the young me on the bed is so strong, I'm anchored to the room. The ropes are burning into my flesh, my head is thrashing. Carlos's arms are splayed close to my head, readying himself. But I'm jerking my legs so violently, he slaps my thigh. Once, then twice, then again until I'm sobbing and screaming into the cloth in my mouth. I can't breathe. My nose is congested, and I can't get enough air into my lungs. I stop struggling, try to calm myself so I can take in more oxygen to avoid passing out. Then Carlos is laying on me, a forearm pressing into my shoulder, digging into my collarbone and hurting me. Cupping my head with his hand, he's trying to kiss my wild sobbing face. I twist my head, thinking for a stupid moment I have teeth available to bite him.

Then suddenly, my eyes dart to the bathroom and I'm back in the body on the bed. The blindfold has lifted a little, and my mother is walking out smiling, nodding her head. "Well, that's impressive," she says in slow motion. Then I see him—there in the mirror—his reflection. He's seating himself in to a chair and staring at the mirror. He's watching. He is watching Carlos rape me. I go cold, so cold and heavy that my body sinks to the floor, then through it. Into the earth and deeper. Then I'm back in the bed again and the blindfold is over my eyes and I can't see any more. A numbing takes over my entire body, and I lay motionless and in shock. Terrified, my mind must be playing tricks. I let a haze cloud my mind, until Carlos thrusts his hard, rough, disgusting fingers inside me. Then everything goes black with a scream.

14

SECRETS AND LIES

"Good morning," says Gerard, straightening his tie as he strides down the hall, his polished shoes tapping loudly in his wake. He hangs his jacket on the coatrack, smooths his hair back and smiles at me. Gerard still cuts an exceptionally handsome figure for a seriously ill man.

"Is it?" I smirk, seeing I'm able to wipe the smile off his face with so few words.

"Christ, what now?" His pace quickens on his way to the coffee machine.

"You were there."

"What do you mean? I was home here with you."

"No. I mean, you were watching while he tried to rape me."

"Oh! So *now* you're saying Alex raped you? It looked to me like you were damn well enjoying it too much to say he raped you."

"I'm not talking about Alex. No, that was love. He loved me." I get to my feet but put the counter between Gerard and me as he makes a coffee.

"Oh, for God's sake, Paige, when are these theatrics going

to end? He's gone. We're moving on. Let's just forget any of that ever happened." He returns the milk to the fridge and picks up his coffee, looking around, frowning and feigning bewilderment. "Aren't you cooking anymore either?" He takes a mouthful of coffee, eyeing me over the cup.

"I mean you were there the night Carlos tied me up and tried to rape me."

"What are you talking about? That was years ago, Paige. Why are you still hanging on to that shit?"

"Because you were there."

"Well yes, I came there to save you from the disgusting pig. If I recall, I pulled him off before he did anything."

"Did anything? The slimy pig tied me up and violated me. You—were—there from the start."

Gerard marches around the counter, his hand in the air, ready to slap me, but I stand my ground ready to punch the fucker in the face. My eyes dart to the knife block, and Gerard follows my gaze.

"Oh, so our relationship has come to that has it?" he huffs and moves away.

"I could see you in the mirror when Carlos was hovering over me. You were there talking to my mother. You handed her money."

Gerard has seated himself at the table, pretending to read while sipping coffee. "Don't be ridiculous." He puts down his cup and opens the paper with both hands.

"I was petrified, Gerard! I thought my mind was playing tricks on me, but you were there, you paid to watch. God, how long had you all been planning it?"

"Paige, nothing ended up happening."

"It was a crime, Gerard, and you knew it, and yet you talked me out of going to the police." I hate that I'm crying but I can't help it. The reality that I've been living with a monster all along is gut-wrenching. "With all your knowledge about the law, you convinced me it would be pointless because of what those boys did to me earlier that day. You said the police wouldn't believe me anyway, that Peter and his friends would testify that I was a little slut and most likely wanted it. That's what you said. I looked up to you, I loved you. You convinced me… Oh God. Alex was right. You were grooming me all along, you took my virginity and left me."

Gerard has risen. He's walking toward me, his fists in balls. "Stop talking nonsense, Paige, this is all in your head. Why would I want to watch someone rape you?"

"Stop lying. You were there, I saw you, you walked in as it was still happening, pretending you were saving me. You were acting like you cared."

"I did care," he yells. "That's why I stopped him. He was being too rough."

"What!" I gasp. "You mean, if he had been gentler, you wouldn't have stopped him?"

"I paid a lot of fucking money that night. And all I got was a whimpering mess. Your whore of a mother stole my fucking money because that pig didn't understand the privilege I gave him," he snarls.

"The privilege you gave him!"

"I could have had you so many times over, it's laughable." An insidious smile crosses his face, and he folds his arms.

I try swallowing, but my mouth is too dry. My lips separate to speak, but no words come out. My entire life has been built on lies and sex. There are no words to explain the feeling of betrayal. Together, they stole everything from me, my innocence, my trust, my hope, my love, my friendships. How can someone be so desperate and depraved they don't care who they destroy in the process?

"The privilege of my innocence was mine to give, not for anyone else to take."

"Well, as I recall, you then gave yourself to me willingly. Paige."

"I thought you loved me. I thought letting you take my virginity would stop Carlos."

"Yes, and I lost my marriage and daughter because of your little idea. You, looking at me all fucking doe-eyed and lovesick. Teresa would have had my ass sent to prison if she found out what you did." He stabs a finger at me. "It was your fucking fault I had to abandon them."

I feel my strength leave me because he's right. It was my idea. After kicking Carlos out and consoling me, I threw myself at Gerard. Begged him to make love to me so I wouldn't be a virgin anymore. I'd been crushing on him so long I was blind to what was truly going on. And over the weeks that followed the incident, Gerard had avoided me to the point of leaving the house to play golf the second I turned up to see Sheree. And then he left for good. Abandoned Sheree and his wife because he didn't trust me with our secret. My secret. But that was before I knew the truth. The truth that he'd planned it all along. As if reading my mind, Gerard maneuvers around the bench and stretches a hand out to me. I step out of his reach.

"You owe me, Paige and you damn well know it. Don't you realize, I'm the only one who will love you this much? We've known each other for so long, you're like my own flesh and blood."

"Exactly, and that's why this has always been so very, very wrong."

I snatch my bag off the counter and head upstairs to change.

"Don't you dare walk away from me, you're my wife." Gerard races after me and grabs my arm.

"Not anymore." I pull violently away from him. "I'm leaving you." I look around for my phone and the car keys.

Gerard's face contorts before he comes at me, his hand going straight for my throat. "Like hell you're leaving. I didn't spend all this time and money to obtain you to let you just walk away. Not after the sacrifices I've made."

"Obtained me? Obtained me!" I screech, stepping back and slapping at his hand. "I'm not some damn possession you can acquire. No. No. You no longer have my permission to touch me, speak to me, or even know me."

It doesn't take much to subdue me. One solid punch to my face and the threat of him getting more violent and hurting our unborn child, snaps me back into submission. I stare at him in horror. My lip and jaw throbbing ferociously while he reminds me he has a person watching my every move.

Then, with a forceful hand to the back of my neck, Gerard marches me up the stairs and into our bathroom. To wash clean my bloodied face, with the tenderness of a loving parent.

15

SO FAR

I'm trying to figure out different ways to arrange the bookshelf. By taking all the items off first and placing them on the floor, then replacing them to resemble some sort of order. I've been busy on this task for the last two hours, and even though there is still a pile on the floor, I open the cupboards below to see what else needs straightening. Everything inside is a mess, or so it seems. I start pulling stuff out.

The aroma of baking is drifting through the house, and when I go to the laundry for a clean dusting cloth, I remember I need to iron. Then I'm contemplating what I'll cook tonight? What to wear? How long is it until Gerard gets home? Was it tonight he said we were going out with Oliver and Falon for dinner?

Halfway through unloading the washing machine, I'm searching for my phone to check the time. There's a surge of anxiety when I realize Gerard will be home in just a few hours. I need to get the chores done before he gets home. He likes tidiness and me being organized. I look down at my loose dress, willing the next two days to fly by, praying

Gerard doesn't notice how my breasts are changing before I end the pregnancy. A child does not need to be brought into what has become, a cold and sterile environment. I try calming myself with a chant to keep me from thinking. "This is who I am, this is where I belong. This is who I am, this is where I belong."

Somehow, I don't think affirmations are meant to make you cry, but still—I chant on while swiping at tears. I'll run out of them soon. Then I'll be fine. "This is who I am, this is where I belong. This is who I am, this is where I belong."

I'm skimming the pool when I hear her call my name. Then Jenna is rounding the corner of the house with something in her hands. "I was hoping you were home," she sings out, crossing the lawn that's still damp from mowing it.

"Hi," I say flatly, hanging the skimmer on the pool fence and coming out from the pool yard. Jenna looks to the ground as if that's where her smile went, but when I get closer, she looks up and recoils.

"What happened to your lip?" Her eyes have gone wide.

"Shower door hates me," I reply nonchalant, raising my eyebrows.

"Oh." She pauses for a moment, obviously doubting me. She thinks better than to press the issue. "I'm sorry to just drop by, but I wanted to give you this." She thrusts a large pot wrapped in a tea towel at me. "It's just a casserole. Just something to express our condolences."

When I don't take it, she pulls it back to her chest.

Picking up the bucket I was using to scrub the tiles, I head for indoors. I don't really want her or anyone's company. "Thanks, Jenna, but you didn't need to do that."

Jenna comes in behind me. "Yes, I did. Besides, I wanted

to see you. How are you? I—we... Nadal and I were expecting to see you at the funeral yesterday. Is—is everything okay?" She touches me gently on the back.

I stop at the back door, turn to stare at her, then exhale. "I wasn't allowed to go to the funeral, Jenna."

She frowns and jerks back slightly. "What do you mean you *weren't allowed?*"

"Gerard knew about me and Alex." I say flatly.

Jenna gasps, and suddenly her pot becomes awkward in her hands. She frees a palm and holds it up.

"Oh my God, Paige. Is that why the *'shower door'* hates you? I swear I never spoke a word to anyone."

"No. I know it wasn't you." I shrug but don't offer her any more. I'm sure if the casserole wasn't in the way, she'd now take that same hand to her heart, given the relief that now covers her face.

"Do you mind if I come in? I feel I need to apologize for how I delivered my response to your question the night of the fundraiser."

I step aside. "What question?" I place the bucket on the washing machine before accepting her food offering, putting the pot straight in the fridge when we get to the kitchen.

Jenna peels off her white leather jacket and hangs it over the back of the chair before pulling it out and taking a seat. "I didn't think you'd remember. You were very drunk and extremely angry. But I don't blame you."

"I don't remember much of anything at the moment," I say. And I didn't just mean from that night either. The brain has a splendid way of protecting a brittle mind.

"You asked how I knew about you and Alex in the shed."

Just the mention of Alex's name, my body tightens, and tears threaten. "Oh." I tuck a stray hair behind my ear then pull out a chair and sit. "No, I don't remember asking you that. But I guess it doesn't really matter anymore, does it? Would you like a hot drink?"

Jenna shakes her head and grabs for my hand. I'm just out of reach, and I don't make it any easier for her either, clasping my hands together instead.

She straightens.

"Maybe a confession will help clear my conscience then. That's if you'll forgive me. Because I didn't tell you everything that night, and I think Alex's death... Well, I need forgiveness, and I'm not going to get that unless I tell you what I did. Why we... Why he did it."

"Do you want water?" I push my chair out hastily and go over to the sink. I don't think I can listen. I don't want to be reminded about her and Alex. It was painful enough that I wasn't given the right to say goodbye when Jenna was. I was the closest to him. He was my lover first, not hers. Water fountains out of the glass when I lift the handle full tilt, sending a spray all over the bench, and even that reminds me of Alex. It takes all my strength to hold back the deluge of tears that want to follow. But I can't. If I start again, I will never stop.

I'm mopping up the spill when Jenna comes over and stands at the counter opposite me, insistent on telling me the details. "Like I said that night, I was going for a walk that afternoon..."

I should tell her to shut up, to leave, but I can't. She's bringing him back to life for me, and suddenly, I can feel. I'm not just numb anymore.

"... when I came past here, I glanced up the drive. You were heading toward the gardening shed, so I thought I'd pop in and say hello. I've always wanted to get closer to you, Paige. The truth is, I've always been envious of the friendship you have with Annabel, and well... I just thought I'd say hello, maybe have a coffee—try to put myself out there more." Jenna grabs the tea towel nearby to help me clean up, making me stop what I'm doing and look at her. She suddenly looks vulnerable and lonely.

"I'm sorry, I probably should have been more sociable. I just thought… Well, you're always so busy."

Jenna screws up her nose and wobbles her head, dismissing my lame excuse, as if she's not really that bothered. Finished with the towel, she folds it neatly, then looks me straight in the eye.

"I heard the conversation you were having with Alex that day, and then he was—he was talking about having sex, and that's when I ducked behind the shed. You were saying no at first. I'd taken my phone out of my pocket, getting ready to call the police, thinking he was about to do something against your will."

When I become shocked, Jenna looks down, refolds the towel again before smoothing her hair and looking back at me. "I peeked in the window and saw the two of you. I could still hear your conversation, and I need to be honest." She looks away for a moment, and when she re-establishes eye contact, she's flushed. "The way the two of you were looking at each other, the way I could see he was making you feel. It was the most beautiful, romantic, yet erotic thing I've ever witnessed." Her eyes glass over, and then it's me who needs to look away. "The two of you were so enthralled and hot for each other, I was afraid you would set alight the shed with all the combustibles in there." She chuckles, making me look at her again, and I can't help the small smile inside from reaching my face and a vague memory of her telling me some of this at the fundraiser comes to mind.

"When you went jogging one morning, I came here and saw Alex. I wanted to know, Paige. I needed to know what it felt like to be so desired by a man. I tried flirting with Alex, but it was clear he didn't have the same feelings toward me."

I look down at the sodden cloth still in my hands and squeeze it out. I try, I really try to hold back the tears, but they just come. Right there in front of her, and I let out a loud sob. Jenna reaches over the counter and grabs hold of my hand, and this time, I hold tight and look at her again. Her eyes are filling with tears, but she goes on.

"I'll be truthful, Paige, it hurt to be rejected by Alex." She pulls an awkward smile. "I know it's no excuse, and I don't know what came over me, but I bribed him. I told him I knew about the two of you and that I hoped my tongue wouldn't get away from me." Jenna lets go of my hand and fusses with tucking the front of her shirt back into her pencil skirt. "He got the message."

I remain speechless, and after a moment, she reaches for both my hands again. "You're one of the nicest people I know, and I tried to steal something so beautiful from you. Alex loved you. I know he did." She's nodding, her eyes glassy and full of remorse. "At the dinner party, after you left, all he could do was ask questions about you, and all I did was downright embarrass myself with him. I think if he had been anything other than the good guy he was, he would have put a restraining order on me I was so annoying. I hope you can forgive me?" Jenna presses carefully at her lids to stop more tears from escaping, then pats dry her cheeks and laughs softly at herself. We both sniffle and smile. I come from behind the counter to hug her.

"Thank you for being honest with me, Jenna. It really helps to know what you just told me. I loved him. I know I'm married, but I loved him with all my heart and soul and being and everything that is me. He was so beautiful and caring and kind and honest." I'm sobbing now, blubbering on and on while Jenna holds tightly and comforts me. The relief from the release is so soothing I laugh, then I'm crying again, slightly happier tears. "You're the only person I've been able to tell how I felt about him." She pulls me back and smiles. She is again as radiant as ever, and for the first time, I really see her, like really see who she is. I'm astounded to discover she is so much like me. An insecure and fragile bird living in a golden cage.

Later, once Jenna leaves, I go upstairs and change. And then —I run. I run fast. I run hard. Pounding the asphalt and allowing images of Alex to flood my mind, his voice to fill my ears.

"What are you reading?"

"A book."

"I can see that. But what's it about?"

His words reach right down inside, igniting my numb core, feeding my starved soul. I giggle at the memory, falter for a moment while the unfamiliar feeling of a smile lingers.

"I can't have you getting all hot and dirty—or can I?"

Oh, Alex. Yes, yes you could, and you did, and I loved it. I loved you so much. Every minute of every day with you I felt alive and desired, loved and respected.

Running harder with each memory, my slapping feet burn, and perspiration trickles down my temples

"Christ, Paige. Sneak up on a guy, why don't you?" I did, but I shouldn't have, but I wanted so badly to feel what I felt.

"Oh, I know how to tend gardens all right. Coral roses symbolize... desire." And he did. He desired me, like I desired him, with every fiber in me. I yearned for him, for his touch. And that wasn't wrong. It was beautiful.

"You frustrate the shit out of me. I can see you're unhappy. You're trapped. You should chase your dreams. Stop pretending you don't want something else." Yes. You were right. I am unhappy. I feel caged and obligated.

I stumble over a small rock but right myself and keep running. Past the playground and through the botanical gardens. Dash past mothers pushing strollers. Dodge cyclists. Jog through a band of pigeons, sending them soaring into a fluttering chorus.

"I've always been here waiting for you. I don't want to be the rebound."

Tears intermingling with sweat sting my eyes, making my vision blurry, but I keep running. My head is pounding, but Alex's haunting truthful words don't stop.

"I don't care anymore. Let me be the rebound, anything to get you away from him, just don't go back to him, please."

He begged. I see again the anguish in his eyes. See him thumping the car with his fist. The look of anger in his lined face.

I stop running—rest my hands on my knees, gulping air, trying to calm my belting heart, let the breeze under the trees cool my heated face. Lifting my tee, I wipe my face dry, then crouch, still trying to catch my breath while I study the gravel, totally lost in my own thoughts as people walking the track maneuver around me. Why would Alex burn down the house? Why not just leave? Standing, I look around, shocked to find I'm miles away from home in a neighborhood I rarely visit. And then it hits me. My own words to him that day. I search to find a bench and sit, thrusting myself into darkness when my face falls into my hands. I remember the words that were so hurtful. Words I didn't mean, echoing in my head over and over.

"No, Alex. Because if you hadn't come along, I would still be living my dream life and loving the man I fell in love with years ago. I would have been happy. Now I need to go home and fix things with Gerard. He needs to know you're not a threat anymore."

I let out a loud groan and look up. People are staring at

me. For a moment, I feel confused. Had I spoken aloud or something? One woman lets go of her stroller and comes to sit beside me, her arm going around my shoulder. Her touch is so unexpected I flinch and try to pull away, but she holds firm, her brow pinching, causing her eyes to droop. What's going on? Why is everyone staring? Do they think I'm nuts?

Suddenly, there seems to be movement all around. Another woman with a child comes forward, removing the lid from a flask and handing it to me. Still confused, I refuse to take it which has her taking a seat on the other side of me, insisting I drink. Then some guy starts pacing and talking on the phone, and I hear him say,

"Ambulance."

What?

I look around at the faces and along the path as though I've dropped a limb or something, check my hands and thighs, and that's when I notice it. On a beautiful sunny day in August. Amongst evergreens and orchids, flowering ash and oaks trees, chirps and children squealing, and the smell of the ocean in the air. All eyes are cast downward because my blood…

Is everywhere.

16

LOSE YOU TO LOVE ME

Something has changed in me this morning. I'm not sure what it is. Maybe it's because of the realization I have a bigger reason to fight rather than to give in to my circumstances. Like my situation wasn't just about me anymore, it was about all women and even men like me. People who have become pliable, moldable, and submissive toward their spouse, who are cruel and manipulative but essentially weak. Men and women who prey on their partner's vulnerability. Nourishing them with empty calories because their love is based on the condition that they yield whenever asked. And when they don't, they hold a mirror up and remind you of your own self-loathing instead of helping you to grow. To help you weed out your insecurities and remind you of your worth. That you are good enough and even sometimes great. That you're here to live your life according to your deepest desires, not theirs or anyone else's.

I thought when Alex first arrived, he would use my weaknesses against me. But he didn't. He drew out my strength. When I fell in love with Alex, it was the most painful experience of my life. It was more painful than my dad leaving, my mom hating me, what Carlos did, or how controlling Gerard has become. Because loving Alex meant learning to love myself despite all those things happening to me. He loved me unconditionally, so why couldn't I?

There's always a way out. You just need to believe you're worth saving.

Rolling onto my side, I stare at a devilishly handsome man. Most women find Gerard to be just—perfect. He's smart, wealthy and damn good looking. He's even mastered manipulation and degradation, all while being gracious, as if it were an art form in and of itself.

When he opens his eyes, I'm beaming at him. Right now, I think I'm feeling gratitude toward him. His destiny was to show me how weak I was. Alex's destiny? To show me how strong I am. How ironic.

"Good morning." I even kiss him.

Gerard rolls onto his back and places an arm over his eyes. "Why are you so happy?"

"I don't know. I guess I finally realize how grateful I am."

Gerard peeks out from beneath his arm. "Humph. You could have fooled me." He turns away again.

"What would you like for breakfast this morning?" I ask, rolling back the duvet and stepping into the bathroom. When I'm done, Gerard is out of bed and getting his suit ready. He tells me he'd like cereal and fruit, all in a gruff tone. He's not happy with me, but still, I practically skip down the stairs. I feel so light.

Over breakfast, we have a pleasant conversation, and he reminds me again about the new dinner plans with Oliver and Falon. I just smile at him and call his bluff. I know already he will announce, just like he did the other day, after I'd gone to all the trouble of getting ready, that Oliver called to cancel. After all, men don't go back for seconds, do they, Gerard? It's just him trying to intimidate and shame me.

After breakfast, and once he's in his jacket, I hug him, draw in his scent so I never forget it. I want to be able to smell it a mile away. I end up squeezing him so tightly, Gerard needs to loosen my grip.

"Okay, okay. I need to go." He frowns but smiles at me before lifting my chin to kiss me. "Why are you so affectionate this morning?"

"I'm just grateful, that's all." I still can't wipe the smile off my face, it feels like I'm high. Everything around me looks beautiful again, even the sun is spilling through the French doors and warming my feet.

I walk Gerard to his car. An unusual thing for me to do, so he keeps looking over his shoulder at me and frowning. "Did you want something?"

Pulling my gown around me, I tell him no, that I'm just seeing him off, that I hope he has a good day, and I'll cook something nice for dinner.

He looks skeptical. "Sounds nice. Does this mean I have my old wife back?"

No. It's more like, a *new* me. But I don't voice my thoughts aloud. Instead, I smile and nod. I've become an A student over the last few weeks, having perfected what he has taught me. I tell him whatever he wants to hear. When his car has pulled out and on its way down the drive, I wave, hopeful he can see me in his rearview mirror. "Goodbye, asshole. I hope you have a nice life," I mutter before turning to march back inside. All with a smile still plastered over my face, because secretly, I've been making plans.

~

"Paige?"

"Good morning, Jenna." I lean in from her doorstep and surprise her by giving her a hug. "I wanted to thank you again for stopping by the other week, you have no idea how much you helped me."

"You're very welcome. It was long overdue, and I'm glad I could help. Come in." Jenna pulls back the door, and I step inside then take the door from her to close it. When I don't follow her down the hall toward the kitchen, she pauses.

"Jenna I'm just going to come right out and say it and hope you don't get offended."

"All right." She crosses her arms over her chest, cinching in the floral mustard shirt she's wearing.

"I need both your financial help and a sworn oath and anything else you might be willing to do. Do you think you can help me?"

I've never seen Jenna so raw, so elated, so… real.

She nods and smiles. "Absolutely."

Over the next two hours I tell Jenna everything, and I mean everything. She goes through a spectrum of emotion from concern, shock, empathy, disgust, anger, then finally arrives at courage once she dries her tears. I can't believe the depth of her character, and by the time I'm gripping her front door handle, I'm leaving with a generous cash check and the promise that she has no idea where, when, or how I just… disappeared.

"I promise I will pay you back as soon as I get work."

"No. I don't want you to pay me back, Paige. I want you to go find happiness and love and have babies and remember me, that's all. Look." She gestures around the room. "We've got all and more than what we could ever need. I'll just be basking in the knowledge that I could help you get away from such a deceitful, cruel man, and I promise you, he will not be on any of my invite lists anymore. You've still got my word, my lips are sealed, but I won't condone what he's done to you by being friendly."

I nod and hug her goodbye. I'm suddenly sorry to be

going, knowing I'm leaving such an amazing friend behind and wishing we could have been closer sooner.

"Maybe one day I'll get to meet the precious little darling you have growing in there. Regardless of the man he is, I'm glad you didn't miscarry and that you changed your mind about terminating." Jenna steps back, her eyes still moist as she holds a palm to my abdomen. It had been hard convincing the doctors to not disclose my situation when I called and told Gerard I was in the hospital. But patient confidentiality ensured I had the final word, and instead he was told I had severe abdominal cramping. Which wasn't entirely a lie, just the bit they feared it may have been appendicitis.

"Take care, Paige, and don't ever let anyone make you feel less than worthy ever again."

I thought I might feel panicked when I got home, thinking about everything I needed to do before I leave. But surprisingly, I'm calm, and it's quick and easy to pack. I just leave everything behind that isn't me. The fancy clothes, shoes, and bags. I take what I love and what I believe is rightfully mine. I have one small suitcase. Basic clothing, essential toiletries, a pair of practical shoes. It's almost fun, and I'm surprised how excited I feel.

I go into the office to collect my camera but get confronted with the large photo of Gerard and me. It repulses me now that Sheree has seen it, and the truth behind Gerard's pursuit of me. Everything about it screams predator. I was blind because for so long, I wanted Sheree's life. I can see that now, and I gave away my soul to get it. I let her father claim me so I could feel special. Well, not anymore. I glance at the clock and see I have plenty of time. Lifting the canvas off the wall, I carry it out to the shed.

Inside, it still smells of grass clippings, fuel, and paint and the deep ache in my heart returns. Pushing the urge to stare at the space where Alex and I were first together, I search for the lighter fluid I know Alex kept whenever he needed to burn excess garden waste.

I move things around and lift up heavy canvas drop sheets that cover the bench to keep most things clean. Then I'm searching cupboards where I find some fuel. I'm just about to leave the shed when I hear something. An intermediate scratching. When it starts again, I creep around, trying to locate it until I realize it's coming from a plastic bucket under the bench. Bending, I peer inside and find a mouse. I tip the bucket on its edge to set him free and watch him dart straight out the door of the shed. I should have let him go inside the house where it's warm and he can find the best crumbs. Gerard would be irate just knowing I'd let the rodent live. I chuckle and shove the bucket back. That's when my watch catches the sunlight that bounces and reflects something back at me.

A little shove and push later, and I'm standing erect and shaking my head in confusion because of what Alex wrote in his note. And then it hits me.

"Oh my God, Gerard, you ultra-controlling son of a bitch!" I breathe out in disgust and reeling in disbelief. Because there amongst the gas fumes and clippings, the pool cleaner, and old paint cans, I just found my Apple computer and the golden glass egg.

Burning the canvas first, I then make a small ceremony of my departure. I set the table for one. Put a casserole in the oven and put on the timer. Then I place the egg in the center of the table. I put my credit card and all the change I have in my purse into a small glass bowl, then slip off my engagement and wedding bands and put them on the dinner plate. Alongside is a threat I've written, warning Gerard that if he comes looking for me, I will press charges. That, at the age of fifteen, when he was thirty-three, he had sex with me after witnessing my attempted rape. A rape he orchestrated. That he had surveillance cameras in his tenant's building without their knowledge or consent. That he wasted taxpayers' money, and law enforcements' time by staging a theft, not once but twice. Because I now know Gerard organized the break-in of our home and my apartment after Kelsey had left. That he also wasted time and money on scare tactics when police were sent around to my motel room under the pretense I was in danger. Yeah, in danger of him.

While I act brave on the outside, deep down, I'm petrified. Will he simply tear up the letter and send people to find me? I don't know. Most likely he will. But it's a risk I'm prepared to take now. I make two phone calls, delete all history, then pull out my sim card and throw it down the garbage disposal. I then put the phone on the table and lock up the house and throw away the key.

Knowing the owners aren't home, I tell the cab company to pick me up from the address of the property that joins the back of ours. After pulling back the tin paneling, I slip through into their backyard where I stay until the cab toots its horn.

Loading myself, the Mac and my backpack on the back seat, I greet the driver with a smile.

"Where to?"

"One West Bank on Sepulveda Boulevard please."

"Hope that thing don't shit in here." The cab driver says, gesturing with his eyes to the box I had him pick up first.

"He won't. Will you Napoléon?" I say, lifting out the most gorgeous kitten I've ever seen. "Are you ready for an adventure, little guy?" I whisper, tucking his soft head under my chin and drinking in the cuteness like liquid love that makes me sigh. "Because we're off to Cannon Beach."

17

I GET TO LOVE YOU

When I first met Quin, I welcomed him as Quintin. I thought it appropriate to use the formal version of his name, given he arrived three weeks early and still weighed in at a whopping eight pounds, three ounces.

He arrived on a Sunday.

Sheree and I were outside, digging in the garden bed, determined to get the weeding done before he arrived.

I didn't notice the contraction at first. Sheree had gone inside to get a cold drink while I collected my breath. I sensed my water breaking before I felt it, quickly turning as Sheree approached from behind.

"Oh my God," Sheree yelled, almost dropping the tray.

Quin would look different than how I had imagined him when the doctor had said, "He'll drop into position any day now." I pictured Quin with old-man features, a thin nose, lots of wrinkles, or a blemish crawling up the back of his wobbly neck. A bald head, perhaps. Well, I got the bald head right. But with the photos in pregnancy books as my only guide, I'd been at the mercy of my wild imagination, and I was sure Quin would be a force to be reckoned with, even with the assurance from the birthing coach that we're never given more than what we can bear.

"I'm fine," I replied, scanning Sheree's face, confused as to what to do next. Later, I would tell nurses I sat in the car while Sheree flapped around getting the last of my things together, reassuring me that everything would be all right. I don't doubt that now. I can guarantee Quin is an angel sent from heaven, loving us from the moment he arrived, assessing our life, calculating where and how he would steal our hearts.

Once I righted myself and offered the breast, Quin frowned. Through fair, thin lashes, his intense blue eyes reacted like he recognized me from somewhere or that I reminded him of someone. I wasn't sure if my heart missed a beat because I felt nervous, or because I was becoming intoxicated by his newborn smell. Soft, musky, and just reeking of love.

"Hello, my angel, you must be Quintin," I baptized, planting a small kiss on his small, wrinkled hand. "I'm your mommy. It's nice to finally meet you." Then tears sprung to my eyes.

I was uncurling his hand, still stunned at his early arrival when his father burst through the doors. "Paige…" he threw out my name, clasping palms around my face and smothering me in kisses, gesturing his surprise at Quin's unexpected arrival.

"He's here in the flesh now. I'm sorry you missed the birth, it just happened so fast," I told him, when I received a playful scowl.

"Christ, where's his hair?" he asked, caressing what little Quin had with his hand before dipping and placing a gentle kiss on Quin's crown, inhaling deeply to take in his wondrous smell before murmuring, "Hello, little man. It's nice to finally meet you."

HURRICANE

Life outside a secure marriage would be like free falling out of a plane after agreeing to a mystery vacation. Landing on unbuffered ground in unknown territory, not knowing what to do. Get shuffled along in an adrenalin-infused anxious daze, constantly looking over your shoulder, checking the news and people's faces as if there might be a cryptic message to determine what's next.

And life without an adoring, wealthy husband would prove to be a struggle. There was housing and work to find. A new circle of friends to make. Not to mention the lack of fine dining, fancy clothes, extravagant jewelry, or the nice car. Oh, and let's not forget the sex.

Life without love, devotion, and a purpose would be akin to taking a knife and slicing off both arms, leaving you scarred, broke and vulnerable.

At least, I hope that's what the bitch is experiencing by now.

"Hit me again, bartender." I say, tapping the bar as though I'm playing Black Jack, something I'd rather be doing than chasing a young, dumb, auburn-tinged brunette halfway across the country.

"Have you been working here long?" I ask the pretty-faced wannabe kingpin. From the way he keeps tossing the liquor bottle in his hand instead of pouring my drink, I'm sure he has a man-crush on Tom Cruise. He's irritating, to say the least.

"Yep," he states, finally pouring more liquor over my ice. He snatches the fifty I have on the bar, then spins on his heels and slides toward the register. When he slaps down my change, I swivel my stool to take in the desperate cluster of regulars scattered around the bar.

Three men hovering around a pair of broads in super short skirts and heels who are playing pool pique my interest. The way the men lean into each other as they try to catch a glimpse is amusing. So glib and unrefined, and yet, my cock still twinges when my thoughts wander, imagining one of those men pushing the blonde over the pool table and sliding her skirt up while the others watch on. I take a sip of bitter liquid, watching them over the lip of my glass.

"You from around here?" the bartender sings out. He's polishing a glass now, and his expression has changed. Creases now furrow his face.

"I'm looking for family," I inform him, placing my glass and forearms back on the bar, reluctantly aborting my musing in the hope of gaining some ground with him. "Sister. Unfortunately, she's remarried, and I don't know her new name," I lie, picking up the coaster that tells patrons they're in Warren House Bar as though we never thought to read the neon sign out front. "Maybe you've seen her?"

Taking my phone from my pocket, I thumb through the apps until the fair-faced beauty appears. "She most likely looks older, changed her hair perhaps," I hint.

Curiosity gets the better of him, and he leans across the

bar before I'm even turning the phone in his direction. I'm tempted to pull it close again just to embarrass him. But I don't. I need all the help I can get.

"Pretty," he comments, nodding.

"I guess." I shrug, hoping to appear indifferent. "Our parents died. She doesn't know yet, so I was hoping to tell her in person. I'm afraid we lost touch some time ago."

"You sure she lives around here? I see just about everyone, and sorry to say, I ain't seen that stunner."

It takes all my effort to calm the sudden inferno that sets fire to my skin. Taking hold of the glass, I stare at its contents and swirl it whilst I visualize hitting him squarely in the face with it.

"I guess you're no good to me then." I look up and pull a tight smile, turn my back on him and resume scanning the room. There must be someone here in this godforsaken town who has seen her. She can't…

Grabbing my attention, loud high-pitched hoots come from outside moments before the front door of the building thrusts open and a horde of what look to be university students tumble in. The rowdy bunch head straight toward me and within moments, are swarming around.

"Hey, Bro, what's doing?" a greasy jock asks, leaning close and grinning before his eyes dart to the bartender. "Yo, Mikey, my man," he screeches, fist pumping the bartender before receiving a scowl, his eyes darting to me.

"Hey, dude, give the guy some room, will ya."

My head swivels when a young woman whines that she needs to pee, before she's stumbling away with two other girls in tow. Then the man beside me is slinging an arm over my shoulder as though I'm now his new best friend.

"He's cool, ain't ya, dude? Have a drink with us," he suggests, ignoring the bartender's advice.

"Thank you, but I'm fine." I tilt my glass at him then slide a hand over my money, scrunching it in a palm and rising. "I'll give you and your friends some room, shall I?"

"Whoa." He laughs heartily, then turns to his two smirking companions, then sets eyes on me again. "Where the fuck you from, dude? Sounds like you're a long way from home. 'Shall I move?'" he mimics. "Shit yeah, you should move. This is our bar, Yo."

"Settle the hell down. Sorry, pal," Mike the bartender says, nodding to the far side of the establishment. "The booths over there might be more comfortable," he suggests, wincing.

I take my leave, leaving a chorus of slang and laughter in my wake. Never mind. He'll keep, the smart little cockhead.

Finding a quiet spot near the window, I take in the bar's reflection as the three girls emerge from the bathroom, all giggles and gropes. Two are rather plain looking, though I can appreciate the long legs on one. One girl then glances in my direction, her pouty, now bright-red lips curling up to one side, when I turn to stare. And I'm sure I notice she adds a little more swing to her hips as she sidles up next to her friends. The group huddle around, entertaining the bartender while he pours their drinks, singing out orders like they damn well own the place. I can't help but smile when the young blonde who eyed me as she came out of the bathroom turns and looks at me again. She's quite pretty in a poster girl kind of way. When her boyfriend the heckler notices, he throws me a look before resting a protective arm over her shoulder. I chuckle and look down at my drink and note that I need a refill, a smile playing on my lips. Dumb little fucker. By the end of tonight, son, I'll have that prized little pussy sitting on my face. My cock twitches in my jeans as a sign that seals the deal.

Losing interest, I turn to survey the other patrons. There are at least another fifteen people milling around, ones who might have information for me. But without an excuse, I'm struggling to see a way to extract what I need to know. All I need is a sighting, just one. I know she's here somewhere. It's the only place left to look. Although, I doubt she'd realize how astute I am, the silly girl she is.

Looking out the window at the near-deserted street, I can't help but let my mind wander. It's only been days, but already, I'm growing tired of this game. She knows where she belongs. Why make it difficult? I'd already found out she was using a fake name, no doubt getting fake ID off the internet. Not a surprise, really, in this day and age. Tammy fucking Anderson. I chuckle to myself. How stupid and unoriginal. Bob-cut brunette five-foot seven inches. Sounds about right. One thing I must accredit her for, however, no money trail. Smart girl. All cash. But she didn't factor in surveillance cameras in each service center though, and she's got to come out of hiding, eventually.

"Looking to buy someone a drink?"

Pulling me out of my reverie, a woman who was playing pool earlier slides into my booth opposite me. I feign ignorance and look about the establishment. "Who did you have in mind?"

She laughs. A deep, hardy sound that does nothing to arouse me. "Oh, you're a funny one. And cute."

"If you say so." I pick up my drink and take a mouthful.

"No, seriously, I'd love a drink. You buying?"

"No. But I'll gladly accept if you are. If fact, why is it that men always need to buy the drinks. Seems to me you're the one who wants a fuck."

She flings herself back and roars with laughter, and I must admit—she puts a smile on my face.

"So damn true. Right you are, drinks on me then. Same?" she asks, rising and pointing to my now empty glass. I tell her I'll have a beer, to which she salutes. It won't hurt as much when I reject her later, I surmise.

Carrying two beers, my new acquaintance does her best at sashaying back to our table, and I notice she draws the attention of the cute blonde still sitting at the bar with her friends. Pleasingly, she has lost her smile. She scratches her shoulder and turns away when I flick my brows at her. Seems it won't take much, to get that one eating out of my palm.

"Cartel."

"Excuse me."

"My name. Cartel."

"Oh, I see. Do tell, Cartel."

The busty woman appreciates my joke with another throaty chuckle, hands over a beer, and slides back into her position. "I will then. Thirty-six. Single. Three kids. Now you." She takes a sip of beer, her eyes still locked on me.

"Mmm. Where to start." I tap the table, pausing long enough to give her the shits and realize I find her intrusive.

"You're not from around here, obviously."

"Smart and sexy," I say, buttering her up nicely because she blushes.

She looks around, I assume to find the friend she was with, then addresses the young troop by the bar. "That kid give you grief earlier?"

"Not really. Just marking his territory, I suppose. Where do you work, Cartel?"

"I, good-lookin', work at the bakery on Emmett's Street. Been there ten years." She holds her palms up as though I need to count fingers to get the point before she reclaims her drink, leaving a film of froth on her upper lip. With a slight of tongue, she swipes it away and smiles seductively. I feel my cock retract from her salacious gesture. This woman is not my type in the least. I glance at Miss Peachy at the bar again to bring back the mojo I need to stay in this wretched conversation. I need the intel from a local, and

Cartel might prove worthy of my time. Everyone's got to eat.

"You have beautiful eyes, Cartel. I bet you see a lot around here?"

"If you're asking do I get around, I'm fucking clean all right."

"That's not at all what I meant. I'm in town looking for someone."

Cartel flops back against the cushioning of the seat, her hands falling to either side of her glass, looking deadpan.

"My sister."

Cartel perks up and takes hold of her glass again. "What's her name? Maybe I know her."

"Tammy."

"There's a Tammy where I work, actually."

My heart delivers me a jolt, livening me up and straightening my posture. Then Cartel smirks.

"But she's black. So, unless you're black under those clothes." She winks, "I don't think that's her."

Deflated, I frown at her. "That's extremely presumptuous don't you think?"

"Well, what the fuck is her last name then?"

"Anderson."

"Nope. That definitely ain't her." Cartel drains her glass and slides it into my resting palm. "However, maybe I might know another Tammy."

Point taken, I also drain my glass and head to the bar where the three girls are now sitting unchaperoned, their presumed respective partners having now claimed the pool table. I nudge up to the bar, keeping some distance between the blonde to my right.

The bartender, busy with others, takes some time before nodding at me to let me know he's coming. I steal a glance at the pool tables, see that the men are engrossed in their game and haven't noticed me. Blondie follows my gaze before we lock eyes. She smiles, then flicks a look at the bartender. "Bit busy tonight," she states the obvious but breaks the ice.

"That it is."

Her smile widens. "Sorry about my boyfriend, he can be a bit of a jerk." She glances at her lap and blushes. "He's harmless though."

"Well, it's not up to you to apologize, and really, no harm no foul."

My comment makes her giggle and squirm on her seat. She glances again at her girlfriends, then leans ever so slightly toward me. "I feel I should also apologize that you're stuck with Cartel over there." She gives me a twisted smile, and together we glance in the direction of the booth.

"That, I can assure you, *is* harmless." I give blondie a wink, quickly looking up as Mike the bartender approaches.

"Liquor or beer?"

Back in Cartel's company, I'm forced to endure a commentary of all the Tammys she knows. Some, not even in town. Though none, she explains, are Andersons.

"Maybe she changed her name," she rationalizes, though I believe she's just making up people, anyway. I hadn't wanted to show Cartel the photo I possessed for fear of her point-blank shutting me down. After all, 'Tammy Anderson,' is indeed stunning and doesn't look at all like my sister, even if we do now share similar hair color. However, time is money, and I'm already burning through it with this ridiculous search. I show her my phone. Instantly she is scrutinizing me, and now that she's seen it, I pray she doesn't know her. Women are cunning and have a tendency to stick together, as Jenna Martin had proven.

WATCH ME BURN

Cartel was a dead end. A waste of time and hard to get rid of once she became redundant. But I love a good hustle. So long as it goes my way. One round of pool with Cartel where I allowed her to beat me, and two hundred dollars on the table was all it took. Oh, and a few ever-so-gracious rounds of drinks to the heckler and his group. By midnight, his sweet little blonde was giggling and tumbling into me one minute, then making excuses to fight with her dumbass boyfriend the next. It was almost too easy. I even felt sorry for him when they all left the bar without sweet little Sonya. Sing-song Sonya, I find out.

"Because I like to sing in the shower," she explains, leaning against the elevator wall, swaying her hips.

"How old are you, Miss. Sonya?" I asked, unlocking the door to my motel.

"Old enough, wise enough, and good enough," she boasts, making me crave her even more. I slip my hand up her dress and pinch her on the ass, making her squeal and flounder through the open doorway.

Sing-song Sonya is impressed with the room, startled by the king-sized bed, but amazed by the ocean view.

She sheds her jacket and flings it toward one of the leather recliners but misses so it lands on the floor. Bending, I pick it up and hang it over the dinning chair where I hang my own.

"Wow!" she gasps, whipping open the sliders and stepping out onto the fourth-storey balcony. The strong sea breeze flutters her dress, and she thrusts her face into the cool night air. She's very sensual and playful. Liberated, and for a moment, I forget my search. Coming up behind her, I adjust my crotch to accommodate the erection that's filling my pants, and my arms come around her to clasp the railing and cage her in. Startling her, she jerks her head which collides with my lip. When I growl, she spins in my arms and apologizes, her glee evaporating.

"Getting rough already, are we?" I snap my teeth at her playfully. She relaxes her frozen look and giggles, looks down at our feet that are almost touching. She's tall, which I must admit I like. And curvy, just enough meat to take a good hold, and if I'm not mistaken, her breathing has quickened, meaning I turn her on. I'm even betting her panties are getting wet by now. My cologne seems to do it to them every time.

"I hope you don't think I'm a slut coming here with you because I don't usually do this sort of thing."

"Not at all. I hope you don't think less of me. I don't do this sort of thing either, but I just can't help myself with you." I brush the back of my fingers under her chin making her look up to meet my eyes. She has gorgeous eyes. Green and intense, they remind me so much of...

"Let's have another drink. We'll talk. I'd like to know more about you," I suggest, hoping to extract whatever information I can out of her, that is, if she has any. "That is—before I ravish you. You will let me ravish you, won't you?"

"Maybe," she teases, swiveling slightly from side to side, searching my eyes before slipping her arms around my neck, standing on tiptoes to reach my lips with hers, brushing them nicely with her tongue before locking on and kissing me deeply. She tastes of wine, mango, and her perfume is sweet. Cheap, I surmise but still, my cock throbs within its confines. I just want to bend her over and fuck her. Fill her up and pound into her, rid myself of this dreadful ache inside.

Stepping back and gripping the railing, she looks lost for a moment, her chest heaving, chewing on her full and pumped lips that are now missing their red gloss.

"I don't know if I can be bothered talking," she purrs out her sweet mouth, sounding every bit alluring.

I reach for the top button of her dress, twisting it deftly with a finger and thumb to reveal the lace of her bra.

"You don't want to know more about me? But we hardly know one another," I coo, undoing another button and squeezing a breast before diving in and kissing her neck, finding my way to her pleasure zone, just behind her ear. She moans and grips me tighter, reaches to take hold of my cock.

"Christ," I breathe. It's been too long. She's young and fresh. New and unblemished. I can sense it, and my need for contact is beyond words.

"You're not a virgin, are you?" I voice my suspicion, taking her cupped hand and pressing it harder against me.

"Sort of."

I pull back slightly and cock an eye. "How does 'sort of' work?"

She lifts onto her toes again, brings her face against mine, and whispers her sweet breath across my ear. "I want to stay a virgin until I'm married, so I only do it in the butt."

She expects I'll pull away because I feel her tighten to beat me at it, but I hold fast.

"I can respect that," I whisper back, both hands cupping her ass and lifting her slightly, nudging her face so she brings her lips back. I kiss her hard then soft, my tongue slipping in to caress hers, continuing to play until I have her moaning into my mouth. I feel her shudder, her legs weaken, and I take the opportunity to almost shatter her, quickly bringing a hand around and slipping it between her thighs, pressing firmly against her warm, damp spot. She falls away instantly, voicing her arousal and taking hold of the railing to lean back, offering herself to me.

In an instant, I'm on my knees, my hands sliding up both legs, reveling in the tenderness of her smooth flesh before ripping down her panties roughly. She gasps and takes hold of my head through the fabric of her dress when I dive underneath. She's pungent and ready and spreads her legs to welcome my experienced tongue, lifting one leg so it rests on my shoulder. The ocean breeze cools my groping hands on her ass before they take hold of her dress and rip the front wide open.

She screams out, momently freezing as buttons fly recklessly onto the concrete floor, but when my finger slides inside her tight ring, she sings out loudly and surrenders completely, crumbling to the floor and taking me with her.

Her soft wails mingle with the pounding waves as her climaxes come one after the other, her sweet nectar making me crave a holding for my throbbing cock.

Pulling her up and onto my legs, I rise and carry her into the room, lay her gently on the bed, and as I strip, she slips out of what remains of her dress.

"Leave that on," I instruct, when she reaches for her bra. I love that she instantly obeys me, rolling onto her stomach in waiting. She's so damn hot, but not yet submissive enough for my liking. But with a little more encouragement, I'm sure she'll do anything I ask. "Now touch yourself."

She throws me a look over her shoulder, then raises her ass in the air to give herself room, pushing her face well into the mattress, like an expert, making me question if she lied about her virginity. I stand back at the foot of the bed, take hold of myself and stroke while she pleasures herself, and I'm betting she's so tight in that cunt of hers, she'd damn near peel my skin off. The thought makes me harder, the idea digging a trench in my mind.

"Spread yourself with your fingers, lovely, I want to see all of you. Show me your delightful insides."

She stops. Sits up onto her haunches and looks around the room. "Is that your phone?"

Snapping into the present, I curse and move toward my jacket. "Don't move," I demand, pointing a finger at her, then finding my phone and exiting to the balcony. I slide my thumb to respond to the ring tone, noting who's on the other end.

"Sorry, I should have called. I'm here," I say.

"And?"

"And nothing as yet."

There is a heavy sigh on the other end of the phone. "She must be somewhere. How long is this going to take?"

"That's like asking, how long do you figure a piece of sting is?"

"Cute."

"I'm sorry. But I'm doing my best given the lack of information."

"I suppose. Right. Well, good luck then."

"It's not about luck, it's about due diligence."

"Christ, now you even sound like Gerard."

The phone goes dead. Thanks, Casandra, you're a true gem for reminding me why I'm here. I look out at the whitewash making its way higher up the shore. Then down at my waning cock. Then to where I left that hot piece of ass.

Marching in, I toss my phone on the bed and go straight into the bathroom, closing the door to both relieve and collect myself. When I come out, I'm just in time to catch Sing-Song standing and holding my phone. When she hears me, she looks up, not at all deterred, she looks down again.

"You're, like, not Tammy's dad or anything are you?"

Ignoring her momentarily, I reach back into the bathroom and secure a towel, then approach. She stares at me with those lovely gems in her face, emerald green and ever so alluring that evolve into concern when she realizes what my outstretched hand means.

"Shit. Like, sorry. I wasn't trying to pry or anything." She drops her head but lifts her eyes when I move closer, gently taking the phone out of her hand.

"What were you looking for?"

Placing hands on my naked chest and blushing she confesses she was searching for my number.

"Why?" I ask, seeming only half-interested, my gaze falling to the phone and the image she was staring at.

"I thought… Well… It's just… Shit." She expels heavily, lets her hands slide and steps away. "What if I want to see you again and you don't call?"

With one finger, I try to lift her chin. "Aww, and here I was thinking the same thing."

Her head snaps up to take in my warm, broad smile.

"You were?"

My-oh-my. So young and gullible, and just my luck she seems to know 'Tammy.' She makes me laugh and my heart sing. Even my cock seems pleased. I place the phone on the chair then whip off my towel.

"Sonya, Sonya, Sonya. You underestimate how beautiful and alluring you are. Come here you, naughty little girl," I woo, securing her tiny waist in my hands and backing her slowly toward the bed. With one shove, she's sprawled and giggling, bringing my cock back to life in an instant, and like the glorious little tease she is, she moves herself up the bed and leans back, spreading her legs wide.

She watches as I move around the bed, extract a condom from the bedside table, unwrap it, then place it strategically between her breasts. She glances at it—then me, a small frown furrowing her flawless brow.

"Don't let that fall off, or I'll spank you," I tell her playfully through gritted teeth. The thrill seems to ignite her eyes, and her legs fall shamelessly wider. She is such a goddamn tease, showing me that pretty pink cunt. That virgin hole that has a no-trespassing veil. When I take hold of my cock, her eyes dart there, widening as if it's the first time she's really taken me in. She sits up a little taller, her smile now looking strained.

"I promise I'll be gentle," I reassure, kneeling on the bed, then crawling toward her. When she retracts back, the condom slides off her chest. Our eyes dart in unison.

"Tsk, tsk, tsk," I scold, tapping her on her still bent knee before returning the sheath to its place and grinning. "You've got to stay nice and still, naughty girl."

Sonya seems to relax a little, slumping lower on her elbows, watching as my face inches closer between her thighs.

In minutes, I have her moaning and climaxing again, her tart syrup awash between her crack, lubricating her anus in readiness of my finger, which I plunge in. She arches and squeals, her hands snatching hold of the tangled bedding. I hold still, watching as the condom slides toward her neck, then disappears. This time I slap her harder. She yelps and tightens around my surrounded finger, making my cock throb and dig into the mattress. Ahh yes. I shudder. That's the way we do it.

Sonya wiggles around while I wait for her to find the condom and put in back in place, letting out a forced giggle before apologizing. She learns fast, this little Sonya. I may just have to get her number after all, I toy with the idea.

I latch onto her folds, my tongue finding her clit, flicking the pearl over and over, driving her insane because she knows she can't move too much or risk another slap.

"So, you know my little sister, do you?" I ask, thumbing her sensitive spot. She straightens her legs slightly, trying to absorb the sensation without discouraging me.

"What?"

I rub faster, make her whimper and squirm, her splayed palms pressing harder into the mattress to keep herself still.

"Tammy, you…" I hesitate so I can lick Sonya slowly right along her slit, making her shudder and still my head with both hands. My eyes dart to hers. "You recognized her?"

"Yes," she murmurs. I reward her by dipping the tip of my rigid tongue into her tight cunt. She gasps then looks at the condom, shimmying to her left before slapping it still and sliding it back in place. I pretend to not notice, instead I focus on her clit again, flicking it repeatedly before sucking. She responds by arching her back then slapping her hands over the moving rubber between her breasts.

"How do you know her?" I ask between licks, nibbles, and probing.

"My dog… I—She… Oh God, stop."

I continue teasing her, driving her into a frenzy with my lips and tongue and teeth, nipping on her inner thighs one second then lavishing her in oral pleasure the next. "Tell me where?"

"The vet, the vet clinic, I met her there," she pants, spreading herself wider. The greedy little thing.

I slap her.

Just because I can.

She shouts out and looks down at the condom still in place, then to me for an explanation.

"My bad," I say, wiggling my eyebrows and smirking, thrilled now that I've found out what I need to know while getting my rocks off. It doesn't get better than that. My cock pulses and throbs, becomes more engorged, and I just pray this little fox can handle me.

It becomes a game. I become more insistent, trying in desperation to make her jerk, so I can slap her. I like the sight of humming, flushed flesh. It's already there between her nice breasts, perky from arousal, but I want to see her hot everywhere. I slip another digit into her ass, push deeply, then extract quickly. She wails and rolls to one side, gasping and claiming my head with both hands again before I have time to invade her again.

"Stop it's too much, I can't stop moving," she says all hot and breathy. I find the condom. Wave it at her, then slap her leg again.

"Ouch," she squawks, rubbing the assault away. "Just fuck me. Please just fuck me."

"Are you sure?"

"Yes, yes. I'm sure. Just do it, but only in the butt." She snatches the condom off me. Pushes on my shoulder to make me sit up. Her movements are urgent, clumsy, but I let her go at it and I keep her fire roaring, my fingers teasing her lower region and the smell of sex filling the room.

She's on all fours in a heartbeat, twisting her head to look at me before lowering herself and spreading her ass cheeks apart. Her buttonhole looks glorious, still lubricated and waiting. I sidle up behind her, rolling over her so I can take her breasts in both hands, then pull down her bra to let her mounds pop out. The neat, hot handfuls of firm flesh fit sublimely in my palms and act like hand holds for a mountain climber. I'm desperate now to nail her, force her to take all of me. To feel the condom inflate when my seed erupts, sending a shock wave through her. Christ, I'm leaking at the thought.

Pulling her back slightly, my thrumming appendage slides between her folds, greasing my shaft up but frustrating the hell out of her.

I love it.

She leans back farther, almost sitting on my lap now as she jiggles and bobs. Her groans of vexation growing louder and amusing me. I'm almost tempted to excuse myself to get a drink, but I'm certain the little minx would chase me down and climb me, anyway. She's on fire, and I can't wait any longer to ride the little bitch.

Shoving her forward with a palm to her back, she readies herself, reaching around and spreading her juices over her ass. I can't believe how wet she is. If I don't get this girl's number by the end of tonight, I'd be a damn old fool.

One more slickening over my rod, and I'm lining myself up. My oh my, how I will enjoy this.

"Go slow." There's the tone of panic in her voice and she glares at me, her face still pressed into the bed.

"Nice and slow," I soothe, sliding a thumb in her ass, making her moan and backup toward me. I tease her for a moment, spitting on her ass and pulsing in and out with my thumb then a finger to help spread her. Bringing her closer, I position her just so…

Then enter her.

"Noooo," she wails, thrusting upright, her hands slapping on my thigh to push away, but I snatch her around the waist, hold her still so my cock can pop that sweet little cherry. The throb of my knob as her innocent skin protests around me is joie de vivre and almost has me ejaculating. The ecstasy not even wavering when I withdraw a little before pressing in again until she's taken a little over half of me. She's unbelievably tight. The sensation is exquisite and rare, compounded tenfold by the gentle sobbing of the not-so-sweet-anymore, Sonya.

"Aww." I stroke her hair with one hand while my other arm pushes her down harder by the waist, impaling her inch by glorious inch. "I'm sorry. Was that the wrong hole, *poppet?*" I soothe.

PUT IT ON ME

Twisting my wrist for the time, then checking the board, I see the flight has arrived but there's no sign of Jamison. His little trip to Cannon Beach has been an inconvenience and I don't appreciate him making me late for work. "Darn it," I lament, looking around the terminal.

"What's the matter, Mommy?"

I glance down and stroke Sophia's head then look around again, searching for a place close by where we can wait.

"Daddy's dawdling."

Taking her by the hand, I find a small café close to gate 16 to wait, and thankfully, it isn't long before I spot my husband. Not surprisingly, he's holding company with a tall brunette in a tight dress.

Not having seen us, he pulls up and chats freely, his hand sliding around her waist and laughing. I crouch down to Sophia's level. "Do you see him over there?" I ask, pointing in Jamison's direction. When she nods, I add, "Run over there and get him. I'll wait here."

"Okay," she agrees, excited to be sent on a task. I watch our six-year-old make the dash toward him. When he spots her, his hand falls away from the brunette, and he glances around. I assume for me. I turn slightly as though I'm interested in something else and haven't been watching, then glance back in time to see the brunette walk off in one direction, and my husband and daughter hand in hand heading my way.

Adjusting the shoulder strap of my handbag, I approach them, smiling.

"Casandra my love, I didn't see you there," he greets, kissing me on the cheek.

"I figured that. How was the flight?"

"Uneventful."

With the brunette having been aboard his flight, I highly doubt that.

"I'll need you to drop me off at work," I inform him as we make our way toward the exit. "Yvette has left something in the fridge for dinner."

"Daddy, did you bring me anything?" Sophia asks.

"Hey," I scold, jerking on her hand. She looks up and drops her lip. "It's polite to wait for surprises," I say softer. "And careful, or you might trip on that." I tap her lip before looking to Jamison. "So, no luck then?"

"No. Apparently, they don't give client information out," he says in mock surprise. "They wouldn't even give me a number."

"No surprise there. I suppose Gerard wanted you to wait it out?"

Jamison's lip curls and he draws air in through the gap in his front teeth, his eyebrows rising. "That he did. But I couldn't. I've a shipment coming in." He holds the door while I pull Sophia closer and brace us against the night air. "He thinks it might be an idea to visit Sheree."

"I gather you mean me?" I say, pointing in the direction of our car.

"Well, he can hardly go himself. She might have an address. You could casually ask if she still knows her. Whether they still chat. You know—that sort of thing."

While Jamison loads his luggage, I buckle Sophia in and hand her the iPad.

Once we're driving, and Sophia is distracted, I continue our conversation.

"I'm not sure I want to."

"Excuse me?"

"It's ridiculous how obsessed he is. He's a criminal attorney for crying out loud. I'm sure there are plenty of women who would be thrilled to nab him. If he weren't my brother, I think I'd ignore him completely."

"I'm sure you would. But we both know you owe him, so let's not upset him." Jamison places a hand on my upper thigh and squeezes while glancing in the rearview mirror. "She needs her mother."

A heatwave ripples through me, traveling swiftly to my face. I steal a look outside, giving myself a reprieve. It's getting darker, and an upward glance sees storm clouds brewing. "You realize he was the one who asked me to do it, and I feel guilty every damn day. I could have lost my job."

"I know, I know. Don't go getting yourself upset. It was for the best, and everything has worked out fine. I'm sure he won't ask any more favors once Paige is back."

I throw my husband a look, then pull down the visor, illuminating my features. "It wasn't right, he should have just taken on the responsibility, and it didn't turn out all right." Reaching into my bag, I give my lips a light gloss, then slap the visor away. "If anything, he owes me, and I have no idea why you're chasing Paige around. You could have said no."

Jamison tears his eyes from the road and onto me, then glances in the rearview mirror again.

"What can I say? He's become a good friend, and I don't

mind hunting. Reminds me of Africa. I miss it," he says, shifting in his seat and grinning.

I roll my eyes at him, cringing when I think of all the taxidermy he has in storage. But hunting animals of the four-legged kind, I suspect, is not what he really misses from our time living there. I twist in my seat to check on Sophia. She looks up from her iPad and smiles, her big green eyes so much like mine twinkling. Jamison is right, she needs me, but more than that, I need her.

"I'll think about it," I say, leaning in and whispering. "But I might just have to start calling his bluff. I'm getting tired of owing him. If he decides to rat on me and see his little sister in jail, that will be on him." Sitting straighter, I point to the next exit. "Don't forget you need to drop me off."

It's well after one in the morning when I finish my shift, the CHLA ward is now quiet, with the exception of the occasional wail from a newborn as I pass by their room toward the lobby. Freeing myself of my badge and swipe card, I stuff them in the pocket of my dark blue scrubs before readying my phone to call a taxi. There are a few stragglers seated around the lobby, most likely family or friends from the emergency department, so I don't notice him at first.

"Casandra."

Looking to my left, the sight of him causes a tremor to migrate straight to my stomach, and my feet to pick up speed.

"Casandra, do not walk away from me."

Slowing, I turn in his direction. "What do you want, Gerard? It's late. I want to go home." I bring the phone to my ear having pressed the dial icon for a taxi.

"Jamison said you'd appreciate a ride home. We'll talk on the way."

Slowing down, I throw him a look before putting my phone away. "Give up."

"Give up? She's my wife. I love her."

"Well, I'm sorry, but she obviously doesn't feel the same way. You tried. Your plan to make her jealous didn't work, so let her go. Alex is dead now anyway, so it's not like he's the reason she left."

"Don't fucking denigrate me."

I recoil from his venom before slipping through the automatic doors. Habitually, I look around for my car, shivering, then pulling my jacket tighter and folding my arms over my chest. I give him a shrug, hinting for him to lead the way.

"You may find this hard to believe, but Paige is my life. She is all I've ever wanted. I realize now how possessive I may have seemed. I pushed her too far, but jealousy can do that to a man."

Stopping in my tracks, I stare at my brother and heave a sigh. His sincerity is undeniable, and I truly believe he loves her. I just wish I knew why Paige went into hiding. My conscience wouldn't be able to handle knowing it's because he was abusive.

"She was infatuated with Alex, Casandra," he says, reminding me of his anguish. "I didn't handle it well. This way, I'm parked around the corner." He points and strides out to keeps us moving.

"Does Sheree even know about you and Paige yet? What am I meant to tell her, anyway?" I ask, buckling in and pulling the tie from my hair and shaking it out with my fingers. "You know, it's been hard lying all these years. You could have just come out. It's not a crime to love and marry someone younger."

"I deserted them, then took up with her best friend. How do you think that pill would have gone down?" Gerard fires up the engine then navigates around the parking lot and out onto the main road. "It's been almost ten years. It's too late to turn back now. Would you like coffee—something to eat?"

"No, thank you."

We remain silent for some time, lost in our own thoughts as the streetlights illuminate the interior of the car in flickers that radiate across Gerard's features as he drives. Looking at him, I can't imagine why she would leave him, unless there was more to the story than he's telling me. I care about my brother, but I worry he hasn't told me the whole truth. I shift in my seat and look at him squarely.

"Are you keeping anything from me, Gerard? Did you hit her?"

He does a double take, his expression hardening. "No."

"Did you cheat on her?"

"What happened between the two of us is our business. She's my fucking wife, and I want her back, and don't forget you..."

"What? Did your bidding. Swapped a few baby name tags here and there. It makes me sick—haunts me."

"Look, all you need to do is visit Sheree. Casually ask if you can use her phone because yours is in the car. Look under her contacts and get me a number. I can get her location from that. Then I'll go to Cannon Beach and bring her home."

"What did you do, Gerard?"

"I did nothing."

"You did something, I can tell. You're too desperate."

I notice his knuckles turning white on the wheel. Pressing my lips, I stare out the window again.

"She's the one who did something. She confessed to sleeping with Alex, all right. Are you happy now? That's right. The love of my life cheats then runs away in shame, and I'm the bad guy because I want her back." He pauses to calm himself, then glances at me with a pained look on his face. "She thinks she doesn't deserve me. I told her I forgave her, but she still ran."

"Oh."

"Yes, 'oh.' How do you think that makes me feel? I gave her everything. Then that bastard comes along, and, in a heartbeat, she fucks him."

"Okay, okay." I reach out and touch his arm. "All you needed to do was tell me that. I'll go. See what I can find out. Obviously, I expect you to pay though."

"Absolutely. And I'm sorry about what I said earlier. I know you feel bad about Jolene and the baby."

After checking in on Sophia, I shower and slip into my robe. Jamison is sound asleep when I slide in beside him. I inch myself closer to absorb his warmth, making him stir and clasp onto the hand I've thrown over him.

"Hmm, you're cold, my love. What time is it?"

"Almost two." I let my hand slide down until I'm holding him, hoping he's firm.

Jamison rolls over and pulls me closer. "Did Gerard drop you off?"

With a groan, I nod against his chest, twirl my fingers through his chest hair and then kiss where my fingers have been.

"Are you going to help him?" he asks, his hand traveling down my back, tickling me.

"I'm not sure how successful I'll be, but it will be nice to visit Sheree just the same. I've never seen him so upset. Did you know Paige cheated on him?"

Jamison slings back. "She did?"

Now I have the opportunity, I take hold of him again, but he pushes my hand away so he can pull me closer against him. He kisses my forehead and squeezes me tighter.

"I must admit, he is persistent. I can assure you, if she were mine, I dare say I'd slap her on the ass and send her on her way. No woman is worth the trouble."

I pull back a little, trying to get a glimpse of his gray eyes in the shadowy room to see if he's serious. "Not even me?"

"Not even you, my love." He rolls onto his back which gives me the opportunity to grab a handful of his chest hair and twist, making him growl and slap my hand. A smile creeps across his face and twinkles his eyes, the glimmer of light highlighting his teeth.

"When will you go?"

"I have a day in lieu. I'll go late next week. I insisted he pay."

"Of course."

"Make love to me," I beg, trailing a finger over his nipple.

"I'm rather exhausted to be honest."

"That's what you always say. You were away all week, I missed you." I roll away and onto my back. Jamison gives me every reason to believe he's unfaithful, but it's a question I'm too afraid to ask.

"Now you're pouting. It doesn't suit you. You realize I'm not as young as I used to be." In the darkness, I roll my eyes, knowing he can't see. Then turn back toward him with a sigh.

"Thought of Viagra?"

"You're cute."

"I'll be quick, I promise."

Jamison puts his hands behind his head and sighs with a grin. "All right, climb aboard if you must."

~

My niece is a striking-looking girl, having inherited her father's good looks, and when I'm introduced to Darby, who then wanders off, I admit he made me hot. Tall, tanned, and hair I could easily imagine tickling in all the right places.

"Mom says hello," Sheree says, handing over a coffee now we are indoors. She takes a seat opposite me at the oversized table. Too big for the space really, but it makes the kitchen homely.

"How is Teresa? It's been so long since I've seen her."

"She's good. She would have come today, but she had to work."

"Is she still nursing?" I ask, taking a sip from my mug and scalding my upper lip.

Sheree nods.

I glance around with interest. Pleased my niece has found her home and a beau to spend her life with. I almost feel jealous. Over the island bench is a collection of pots swinging in a breeze coming from the sliders being left open, bringing the fresh country smells inside.

"It's nice here. Do you have many friends?"

"Mostly Darby's. I don't really see many from school anymore. When did you get back from Africa?"

"About two years ago."

"I wish you'd brought Sophia. I'd love to meet her." Sheree rises from the table and fusses around in the pantry, then pops a tin of cookies in the center between us. "Is she enjoying school?"

I nod and smile, shift on the bench, feeling more deceitful by the second. Sheree takes her seat again and picks out a cookie to nibble on.

"I'll bring her next time, I promise. And Jamison. I think

he'd be impressed with your ranch. Did I mention on the phone that he bought a wildlife reserve in Texas?"

"No. What does he do with that?"

"It's open to the public. And although he denies it, I suspect he secretly breeds prey to send back to Africa. Those men and hunting. It's disgusting really."

She winces, making me wish I hadn't brought it up.

As I bring my mug to my lips, a clock suddenly chimes out and startling me, making me scald my lip again. Placing the mug down, I reach for Sheree's hand.

"Sheree, honey, I will cut to the chase. I've seen your father."

To my surprise, Sheree just nods. There's no expression at all. She's deadpan, her blue eyes piercingly bright and locked on me.

"Did he send you to see me?"

I can't lie to her. She's too gracious, too sweet. She's my niece, and I love her. I pull my hand away and wrap both around my mug, deciding not to answer her. My silence can speak for itself.

"I know he married, Paige."

My head pops up to meet her hardened gaze.

"Five years, if you can believe it. My best friend was lying the whole time. Well—no, she didn't lie, she just didn't tell me at all. He's going by his first name now. Imagine that! Paige would say his name over and over and I never realized. Not until she came for her mother's funeral."

"I'm sorry. We were in Africa—we didn't know he married her until we returned. And I know you were close. You must hate her."

Sheree shrugs, drains her mug, then reaches behind herself to place it on the sink. "She sent me a text not long ago, saying she left him."

"Is she well, is she happy? Do you know where she is? "

I'm hopeful Sheree will relinquish the information without me having to resort too snooping.

"Does Dad?" She raises both eyebrows, "Or should I say, Richard? Because I'm pretty sure I was disowned. No wait, it's Gerard now, isn't it?"

I feel my face scorch. "He just wants to find her, Sheree. She was unfaithful with Alex, his stepbrother."

"Alex. His stepbrother. Wow, that's new information." She nods. "Dad never mentioned him. Ever," she adds pointedly.

"He said he forgave her."

Sheree's face breaks wide open with a smile. "Is that right? Oh, okay. Well, here's the thing. Yes, I know where Paige is, but if he wants her address. He will hear it from me. Tell me where he lives, and I'll give it to him personally."

My look, I'm sure, is of surprise. "You'll do that?"

"Yes," she says, placing both palms on the table. "I want to see him." She nods, looking determined. "It's about time we get reacquainted."

I'm pleased to say, I feel my whole body relax. It's now out of my hands. And for the remainder of the afternoon, we speak about more pleasant things.

21

MAN OR MONSTER

I want to hate what I see, but it's impossible. There's a white picket fence, a long, curved gravel driveway, and the canopy of mauve is breathtaking. The house is weatherboard with gables and a high-pitched tile roof. My eyes dart to the gazebo and I can imagine Paige sitting out there reading while the ocean breeze blows in. Her long wavy hair would have been tied back and she'd have been wearing a white cotton sundress. She would have been happy here. It's big, it's clean, and it's a million miles away from her past. It's everything she dreamed.

When Darby squeezes my leg, and I turn, his face scrunches. "Oh babe, are you sure you want to do this?" He reaches across and gently wipes the tears off my cheeks.

"Look how beautiful it is. No wonder she kept it a secret," I say, turning away to take in more. I glimpse a pool, and in the distance a garden bed behind it where a multitude of shrubs and flowers flourish. To our left stands a garden shed, and a half-constructed pergola.

Drawing in a deep breath, I encourage Darby onward. The tires crunch the gravel beneath as we inch along the driveway, our eyes darting everywhere, trying to take it all in.

"Guess I can wait in there," he comments nodding toward the decorative, white-latticed gazebo.

"Shouldn't be too painful. Maybe the maid will bring out a beer. No, wait, that would have been Paige. Sorry bud, she flew the coop."

Darby chuckles and shoves me with his shoulder. I look at him again and smile. "I love you."

"And I love you. I can come in if you like," he offers, bringing the car to a halt. I shake my head and reach around to the back seat and grab my bag. "Nah. There's stuff to talk about that you shouldn't have to hear. But thanks." Leaning in, I kiss his cheek. "Just knock if you get sick of waiting. And if you hear any smashing sounds, it's mostly just me throwing a tantrum. I've got a lot to get off my chest."

"Can I at least come to the door and meet him? I mean I plan on marrying you and if he will be in your life, I think he should at least know what I look like."

Happy when I nod, Darby and I get out of the car and make our way to the front door, an imposing piece made of solid wood with a brass knocker, which I use—violently.

Darby laughs at me, then straightens out his flannel shirt before tugging on his belt buckle with pride. He's a pleasure to watch, no matter where the location or situation. I loop my arm through his and stand taller. My father will be pissed to the core to see me with a colored man. But I don't give a shit.

The butterflies in my stomach are wreaking havoc. I drop my gaze to my feet to calm myself but just then, the door is peeled open wide. My head snaps up in the same instant the butterflies turn to lead.

And there he is, my father in all his arrogant glory. His

eyes dart between me and Darby several times before he pulls a tight smile.

"Hello, Sheree."

"I draw in a deep breath. "Hello, Dad. This is Darby—my *fiancé*. Darby meet…"

"Gerard," my father says, thrusting out his hand. The men shake hands, then Gerard steps aside.

"Nah, I'll just wait over there." Darby gestures toward the gazebo.

"Certainly. Make yourself at home. Sheree can bring you out some refreshments if you like."

I raise my eyebrows, but chuckle to myself that he instantly insinuates I'm to be the hostess. The chauvinist hasn't changed one bit. Leaving Darby to his own devices with a smile, I close the door and follow my father down the marbled hall that leads to a staircase with an amazing wrought-iron balustrade. My eyes dart around taking in artwork and furnishings, a coatrack, and a lamp. Everything is beautiful—and expensive-looking. I plod along, trying to absorb everything while simultaneously looking at it through Paige's eyes. She lived here with him. Living this opulent life and she threw it all away to shag Alex, the gardener with nothing. She is either insane or my father is. My bets are on the latter.

"Impressed?"

"Sorry, what?"

"Do you like what you see? Did you notice the picture on the left?" He points to a black and white, a photo of a bridge obscured by fog. There are two joggers running away from the camera in the distance and trees overhang in the foreground. It's magical.

"Paige took that. Isn't it amazing?" He comes to stand beside me, so I take him in from head to toe, amazed he's not as big as I remember him. Probably because I was only a young girl when he left, who hadn't yet sprung to full height. Now I'm only about three inches shorter than him. "She's very talented. I had hoped to have a gallery for her. Unfortunately, the beach house was burned."

"And Alex," I add bluntly.

He snaps his head around, then steps away. "So, you know about that?"

"It was mentioned."

I follow him down the hall and we enter the family room. The kitchen sits off to the left while a dining table dominates the rest of the room, taking advantage of the large windows and French doors that lead out to a landing and the outdoors.

"Big table for two," I comment, walking past it and over to the granite counter bench. I glide my hand over the smooth surface, imaging Paige cooking meals, *his meals*. Ignoring my remark, he makes his way past me then switches on the coffee machine.

"So, you're engaged?"

"That's right."

"And what do you do?" he adds without congratulating me. So predictable.

"Darby owns a horse spelling ranch. Racehorses, mostly. Occasionally we get professional stock and endurance horses."

My father keeps his head down, pretending to be engrossed in the task of making coffee, which allows me the liberty of smirking.

"I didn't ask about Darby," he says, spinning around. "I asked what you did."

"Um—I help him." It's not my only job because I also do online admin for a law firm, but I'm not going to tell him that. Disappointedly, my sarcastic tone doesn't even make him flinch.

"Oh! Well, I suppose it's what you've always wanted to do. Do you have sweetener in your coffee?"

"Just one."

"Ah, same as me," he gushes then smiles.

Christ, he's smooth and cunning as a fox. This will be fun.

"Did you have a nice day with Casandra?"

"I did," I reply, pulling out a chair and sitting. I hang my handbag over the chair then take out my phone to check for calls I may have missed while flying. "I was hoping she'd bring Sophia."

"Oh, and she didn't?"

I shake my head then take the coffee offered. "I should have come sooner. Here, I mean. I would have caught you two. Paige and her 'mystery' husband." I let out a huff. "I never contemplated coming because... Do you remember when I got lost in the city as a child? Well, let's say it left me kind of scarred." I peer at him over my cup, hoping to guilt him because he was the chaperoning parent on the excursion who lost me. His own daughter.

He looks down at the table and flicks some imaginary crumbs away.

"Besides, whenever I spoke with Paige on the phone, she made such a deal about always being too busy, and her husband didn't enjoy getting visitors. 'He likes to keep a low profile. He hates getting his photo taken,' etcetera, etcetera." Dad doesn't respond, which is an inkling that I'm succeeding in shaming him. If he's going to get any information out of me, he'll damn well have to earn it.

"Paige and I bumped into each other in the city. She was working in a café my colleagues and I frequented and when..."

"I don't care how you met up again. For all I know, you both planned it. I mean, it wasn't long after you left that she hightailed it out of Ponderosa Park. The thing is—I shouldn't have been left in the dark. Did it ever occur to either of you I might have been happy for you?"

Gerard cocks his head a little to the side and palms his jaw, his brow rising before smirking, "Don't lie to me, Sheree. You would never have been happy with anything I did."

"You're probably right." Putting my cup down, I trace the handle. "Why haven't you asked about Mom?"

"Because I no longer care about Teresa."

"You should. If it weren't for her..." I look around his fancy house. "You wouldn't be here, would you?" I lock eyes with him over the big gold egg that's in the center of the table. My glare has the desired effect because he shoves back his chair and stands. I flinch for a microsecond, then reassure myself that Darby is just outside.

"Don't you dare come into my house making false accusations?"

"I didn't accuse you of anything. I just stated a fact." I take a sip from my cup, then place it down gently.

"I damn well earned my way here, Sheree."

I shrug. "Look, honestly. I didn't come here to argue. But she's fine, by the way."

He shakes his head and moves over to the windows, his hands thrusting into the pockets of his suit pants as he stares out into the yard. I glance around again. There's so much to take in and as I felt earlier, it's compounded because I'm still thinking of Paige as I investigate. Looking for anything that looks like it might belong to her. But the place is just filled with things. Designer things. Curiosity and the pause in the conversation gives me the opportunity to excuse myself.

"Mind if I use the bathroom?" I ask, standing.

"It's down the hall and on the left," he replies, his back still to me, turning only slightly as I leave the room. I think I might be getting to the man. I wish I could say I felt sorry for him, but I don't. He's a lying, cheating, sick man.

The second I'm in the hall I pick up speed, darting down the hall intent on peeking in rooms. There aren't many doors considering the size of the house, which I imagine makes every room large and spacious. The living room is opulent with the oversized suede leather couches and a huge bookshelf. I spot the ship in the bottle and chuckle. Next to it is a photo of him and Paige on their wedding day. I move over and pick it up. Paige looks stunning. Her flaming hair is loosely pinned with long curls trailing down to frame her face. Her dress is gorgeous. Champaign with lace and beads. I feel angry. Feel duped that I was denied the honor of seeing my best friend walk down the aisle. Feel hurt because we spent days and nights talking about that one special day, and I missed it. This photo is all I get to see. I trace a finger around her face, my eyes glazing over.

Putting it back, I spot the well-worn chair with script fabric. There's a small lamp table beside it and a book. I go over to read the title, curious whether it's my father's place, or hers.

The Liar's Club. Despite the irony of the title, I feel sad. I'm familiar with the book and I understand why Paige would read it. It most definitely doesn't belong to my father.

"If you wanted to snoop around, you could have just asked."

I spin around and place the book back. "Sorry. I got sidetracked and what can I say, it's a beautiful home. I'm sure Paige would have loved living here."

"She did. And she can always come back. Will you tell me what you know? I want to reassure her personally that she's forgiven."

"Sure. But let me use the bathroom first. I really needed to go." I dart out the room and go down the hall to where I was directed. Once I'm out, I find my father sitting in the living room, his elbow resting on his knees and staring at the carpet. I bypass him to go into the family room and retrieve my phone and bag.

Sitting opposite him, I dig into my bag to pull out a book and put it on the coffee table.

"Look familiar?" I ask, when his eyes dart to the sparkly unicorn, then back to me.

"I imagine it's something from your childhood. I may have noticed you carrying it around once in a while."

"No. This one is Paige's actually."

Gerard sits upright before pushing himself into the couch and crossing his legs, his arms splaying over the top. It's such an unusual pose. So open and receptive for a man who should cower in shame.

"Should you really be reading my wife's diary? That's a touch audacious, don't you think?"

"Not really. I think she wanted me to read it," I say, tucking my hair behind an ear. "Why else would she leave it behind on my coffee table when she came for her mother's funeral."

He stiffens, and his eyes turn dark. Leaning forward again, he clasps his hands together.

Now it's my turn to lean back and look smug.

"It's filled with a young girl's delusional fantasies, that's all," he says.

"And you would know that because you've read it, haven't you?"

"None of it is true. Ask her yourself."

I snatch the book off the table and open it to where I marked it and read.

"'Sheree's dad is nice. Not as nice as my dad, but he is more handsome. He said that because my dad was gone, I could ask him for help if I ever needed it. When I told

Sheree, she said she didn't mind, which I thought was nice of her because I don't know if I'd share my dad with her. She's my best friend, and her mom is nice as well. I've only got a nice dad, but he's not here, so now her dad—is kind of my dad.'"

When I scrutinize him, he just shrugs. So, I keep reading.

"'Sheree's dad picked us up from school today because her mom had to go to the hospital, and it was raining so we couldn't walk home. Sheree said her mom has something called a steroid but I think it might have started with an f. I don't know what it is, but Sheree said her mom will be away for a while.'"

I tap the page with my finger. "I only learned the truth behind this one the other day." I pause and stare at him hard for maximum effect. "When I read it out to Mom," I drawl sarcastically, watching him turn a shade lighter. "You told me she had a fibroid. Yeah right."

"You told your mother all this nonsense? Why would you torment her like that, Sheree?"

"Torment her! This gave her back her sanity. Here, listen to this one."

"'I'm so sad. I made Sheree angry today because her dad yelled at her because of me. Then he took me to the shops to get ice-cream, but Sheree wasn't allowed to come. I don't want Sheree to hate me, and I don't know whether to tell her he asked me if he could kiss my cheek. He said I was his special little girl.'"

"That's enough Sheree." He reaches forward to snatch the book from me, but I pull it away and turn to another page, the one I really want to read out. He rises from the couch, so I mimic his movements, walk around the coffee table as he comes around to my side, still intent on snatching the diary away. But I've found the page, the page that incriminates him completely because he wrote it. It's in his handwriting.

"'She's young and she's beautiful, so pure and divine. One day I hope to marry her because this girl is mine. P.S. It's just our little secret how much I love you.'"

"She was twelve-years-old then, you, pedophile. When did you start feeling her up?" I don't even bother waiting for an answer because apart from not being able to stomach the truth, I want to throw as many stones as I can before he tosses me out the door.

"You let her sleep in a box. You read about her fears. Carlos and her mother, and you did nothing. You should have told the authorities. And what's this shit about saving her from Carlos? That was a crime, and you could have put him in jail. Did you know he raped her after that? No, you wouldn't because you ran away and fucking hid!" I'm practically screaming the house down and I'm surprised Darby hasn't burst through the doors. "You're disgusting. And if you think I'm going to tell you where Paige is or how to get in contact with her, you're insane. I'm not handing over my best friend in the world to fucking Satan himself."

He flinches as if I physically threw shit on him, which is what I would have done had we been at the ranch. I would have gotten Darby to tie him up and feed him the stuff because my father is full of it. The man disgusts me to the core. "You're a heathen and you better brace yourself for the fall. It's never too late to press charges. And even if you don't do time, you'll be a registered sex offender. Take a good look around, Daddy and say bye-bye because if you go anywhere near Paige ever again, I will make sure this gets into the right hands." I slam the diary shut and stuff it in my handbag.

Stomping away, I'm a little unnerved that he doesn't follow or have a rebuttal. Even so, the rage in me is so fierce that when I spot the golden glass egg on the dining table on my way out, looking all shiny and pristine, I rush in and hurl it to the floor, sending millions of glittering shards across it.

Then I snatch the lovely black-and-white image off the wall so I can return it to its rightful owner.

Darby is at the door when I wrench it open, looking concerned and throwing his gaze over my head. When I turn, the asshole who I'm ashamed to acknowledge as my father, is standing calmly with his hands in his pockets, his face all waxy and expressionless except for the small curl to the left corner of his mouth. I'm so freaked out by his creepy, deadly stare that I don't even close the door. I just latch onto Darby and hurry away.

As soon as we're on our way, I voice my fears. "Change of plans. I think we should fly instead of drive. I'll see what's available. If we drive, there's a chance he'll follow us." I reach in my bag to get out my phone. "Christ, I can't believe what he's like. Paige must have been… He's a psychopath." I'm nodding my head and I'm sure I look dazed because I'm still in shock. "Did you see the way he was looking at us?"

Darby rubs my leg trying to console me. But I'm inconsolable. The rage I felt earlier has turned into a mixture of grief, fear and despair.

"I can't believe I shut her out. She went back to him because of me."

"She was giving you the runaround Sheree. You can't blame yourself."

"But that's what she does. She's afraid of hurting people. She came for help and I sent her away. Thank God she sent me that text. If she hadn't, I would have been freaking out that he'd done something to her. Now he's after her, and I don't think it's for the right reasons. Men like him just don't let go, Darby."

"Don't panic. We'll get to her before he does. He doesn't know where's she's at or else he wouldn't have wanted to see you. Just keep it together. What time does your mom's plane get in?"

22

SCARS TO YOUR BEAUTIFUL

When Sheree arrives, to my horror, she's with her mother. Teresa's elfin features had barely changed from when I last saw her, except her hair was much darker. It takes all my restraint not to go rushing up to them as if the last seven years hadn't existed. Instead, I stay where I am, shaking like a leaf, waiting for them to approach.

Walking side by side along the grassy lawn driveway, they glance at the unkempt garden beds that I haven't had the time to weed, then pass my car while sizing it up. There's nothing to be impressed by as they make their way to my back porch where I've been watering hanging pots. I put down the watering can and come down the steps.

My rental, though small and weathered, looks out over the ocean. It's a sight that halt them momentarily before they take in the exterior of my home that stands watching over the beautiful view. With shingled walls, in dire need of repair, the house doesn't really deserve the honor—even the roof leaks. But it's affordable, and it's my home, or should I say, sanctuary.

When I finally get the nerve to greet them, it's Teresa who

wraps me up in her arms and cries, making both me and Sheree tear up when I glance at her.

"I am so sorry, Paige baby. So, so sorry," Teresa says.

It's nice to feel her comfort, but after so many years of guilt, I feel dirty and ashamed she is apologizing to me.

When I pull back, stunned by her apology, her gentle hand continues to stroke my hair and her amber eyes take me in, but I look away. She has nothing to be sorry about. Looking up, I shake my head. "No, I shouldn't have married him. It was wrong and I've hurt you both." Teresa grabs me forcefully by the shoulders, trying to look in my wandering eyes, refusing to accept my apology.

"No," she says firmly. "I suspected something was going on, and I feel ashamed for not trusting my instincts."

Sheree comes closer, pulls me in to give the hug I really need. A hug that only a true best friend can give. One that settles the marching ants and knots of disgust and shame I feel for having betrayed the people I love the most. People who took me in and sheltered me. Fed me when I was hungry and tried to spray away the putrid stench of my lowly life without making me feel embarrassed.

"I love you sweet pea. *We* love you." She glances at her mother. "You're not alone in this okay," Sheree whispers. "And I'm sorry about the way I reacted. It just shocked me you would keep such a huge secret from me for all those years. God, I just fucking hate him," she cusses and pulls away, her features scrunching and marring her pretty visage. It's one of the few times I've heard Sheree swear. Growing up, Gerard drummed it into her, not to cuss. It makes me smile knowing she's deliberately doing it to spite him before it sinks in that both Sheree and Teresa are sympathizing not because I'm now separated, but because they'd *both* read the entries in my diary.

With my face catching fire, I pull away but invite them to have a drink.

After giving them both a quick tour of the house and sharing pleasantries, Teresa becomes concerned about me and the pregnancy, especially when I confessed to not seeing a doctor regularly. I'm still underweight and not showing signs even though the baby is now eighteen weeks gestation. I think in some way, I'm still in denial. I mean, I'm carrying my best friend's father's child. How much weirder can it get?

After bringing in bags, we sit out on the decking and watch the sunset together. It's the first time in weeks I feel happy. Pulling my cardigan around me, I listen as Sheree natters on about Darby who had flown home after picking up Teresa. I'm still a little shocked she is here. For me.

Teresa and Sheree sip on wine, while I indulge in a cup of tea. I feel like wine. I need a wine. Especially when Teresa opens up about her marriage to Gerard, though she continues to call him Richard.

It feels awkward hearing about the man I spent the last five and a half years with, as though he is someone else. Sheree excuses herself then slips indoors to prepare something to nibble on.

"He resented me for having a career. But nursing is easy to get into," Teresa says, now we are alone. "There's always a hospital looking for staff, you know. And I could study on the job. It was much harder for Richard. He's always been very smart, but he was young, and becoming a father when he was just starting out was not something he expected." She takes another sip of wine before continuing. "Even though we were only just eighteen—his father made us marry. To tell you the truth, I was madly in love with Richard, so I wasn't about to kick up a stink." She looks up at Sheree as she comes out the door with a plate of food and smiles, her pretty features lighting up with pride. "My parents were against it," she continues, resting back into the cheap aluminum chair. "And I think that's what made Richard agree. He hated not feeling good enough. His father belittled him every chance he got. So, as young people do, we jumped in boots 'n' all before we'd really gotten to know each other, which was a big mistake. We fought all the time."

"Really?" I ask, though I'm not surprised. Sheree was always whining about her parents' yelling matches.

"Tell Paige what you told me. You know, about Aunt Casandra and Dad," Sheree says, biting into a cracker with cheese. "So wrong." Sheree winces then chases down her food with a sip of wine.

"I don't think Paige needs to hear about that, Sheree. It was a long time ago." Teresa rises from her chair, takes her wine and leans over the railing.

"But it's why you guys broke up."

I snap my head around, feeling confused.

"Mom only told me the other day." Sheree turns to tell me, her big blue eyes going wide.

"It's a lovely spot you've found, Paige. If you don't mind me asking, how are you able to afford staying here?" Teresa asks, ignoring Sheree's rebuttal. Sheree pulls a face at me and mouths that she'd tell me later, making me deadly curious. I pull my cardigan tighter then answer Teresa.

"I work as a receptionist at the Sea Side Vet clinic."

"You do?" Sheree chimes in. "Good for you. Finally, you're doing something you love."

"I can't work with the animals while I'm pregnant, but I'm hoping they'll keep me on after the baby is born."

"Does Richard know about the baby?" Teresa asks.

I shift in my seat and place down my empty cup. I'm sure both Sheree and her mother think I've left because I don't love Gerard anymore. They're unaware of the gravity behind the separation. Even I'm having a hard time digesting it myself.

"No," I reply.

"And you don't plan on telling him? Do you think that's fair?"

I shrug, pausing for a moment to collect my thoughts, hoping to offer a tactful reply.

"Gerard... I mean—Richard, always made it clear he only ever wanted the one child." I throw Sheree a smile which only results in her rolling her eyes. It saddens me that still, after all these years, she still can't find a redeeming quality about him that she respects or even likes. Even without the knowledge of his behavior toward me recently, she still despises him. I think of my father, how I would give anything to see him again. To know him. To ask the thousand and one questions that swim around like piranha in my head.

Later in the night, over dinner, I learn more about Gerard as a child. I discover that before his mother died, the family moved numerous times because of his father's gambling debts. That his father took heavily to drinking and was prone to fits of rage. Casandra, his younger sister was sent away to live with her Aunt in Australia because neighbors had concerns that she was being molested and reported it to the authorities. Gerard was subjected to regular beating, but no one ever removed him. It's hard not to feel sorry for him given that his childhood had been laced with such trauma. He must have been forced to mature quickly or suffer his father's wrath. Teresa didn't spell out the specifics, but it's obvious Gerard was fragmented from the day they married. That he based his relationships on his role model.

Teresa leaves not long after dinner, returning to the hotel, where I had earlier assumed Darby was. But Sheree had sent him home, saying she wanted to spend some time with me. That is, if I didn't mind. Teresa was leaving in the morning, and when I protested that I didn't want to keep her from her family, she told me *I was her family too.* Truthfully, I'm grateful for her company, that she stayed, and as we clear up, we talk over what led up to me leaving. I leave out things Sheree really doesn't need to know about her father, things I am also ashamed of. She's scarred enough. Aside from all this, hopefully there's something in their relationship that might be salvageable, after all, it takes two to tango and I'm not innocent. I understand my shortcomings now that the veil has lifted. I betrayed Gerard over and over. He may have been controlling and perverted, but it was my fault for staying as long as I did. I had options. No one held a gun to my head and made me chase Alex. That was all me, and I knew I was hurting both men with my deception. It seems love is blind and the devil hides in plain sight.

"I've made hot chocolate," Sheree calls out from the kitchen when I come out from the bathroom toweling my hair.

"Do we need mellows?" I ask, giving her a smile and raising my brow. It's nice having her stay over. We need to share my bed and I can't guarantee I won't snore or get up at least a half dozen times to pee. It feels like old times too, that I have my best friend back. I'm not sure if I deserve her though. She curls up on the couch nursing her hot drink and we smile at each other.

"Sheree, why did you like me? I mean, back when we were kids. What made you come over and sit with me?"

"Your hair," she replies point-blank, making me chuckle. "And you looked like you needed a friend."

"Was it really that obvious?" Grabbing my mug, I curl up next to her on the couch and pull my fluffy new dressing gown around me. "Without knowing anything about me you just liked me?"

"When we met in grade three, you were hilarious. You kept coming out with all these silly jokes that you learned from your dad. Do you remember the one about Billy Big Balls? You know, about the bull and the farmer?"

I start laughing so hard I almost spill my drink. "Yeah, Billy Big Balls until he jumped the barbed fence and became just Billy," I say in a deep voice.

"See, there you are. That's the Paige I remember. I want to show you something."

Sheree pulls out two matching diaries from where they're wedged beside her. She must have gotten them out while I was in the shower. After handing me back mine, she opens hers and reads passages, reminding me of all the fun things we spoke about and did. "We had good times. You were fun and friendly and loyal. You always stuck up for the underdog. Remember that kid, Brian, the one with buck teeth? When you punched that Barnett kid for teasing him? Anyway, after reading your diary, I was gutted to realize what turmoil you were in beneath that funny exterior, I mean your mom, Carlos, those men always around. And then, Christ, my dad was…" she shakes her head and studies her half-empty mug before reconnecting with my gaze. "He lured you away from being a child. A child that laughed and was lighthearted. Despite your home life, you separated it from who you really were, you never gave in to your despair. But from what I read…" Sheree reaches for my hand and takes hold. "He was working on you from such a young age. It makes me sick to think of it. I know you thought it was love…"

I shake my head. Watching the sorrow and pain radiating from her eyes, now agreeing with her. It wasn't love, it was validation.

"Paige, my dad is a really messed up guy, don't you ever

think about going back to him. And despite my mom having reservations that you're keeping the pregnancy from him, don't tell him. He doesn't deserve the privilege of another child."

"You don't think she'll get in contact with him and tell him, do you?"

"I doubt it. I know she'd like to give him a piece of her mind, though. Like I did."

"You did. You saw him?" I feel nauseous.

"I didn't want to tell you over the phone. But I gave him a decent mouthful. Told him to stay the hell away from you."

I can't help but get teary. "What did he say?"

"Not a lot. I showed him your diary. Pointed out that passage he wrote."

When I frown, she recites it.

"I don't remember reading that," I say bewildered.

Resting her journal on her lap, she reaches for my book on the table and opens it to a marked page, then points to the passage, cleverly hidden between two of my own entries. I've never even noticed it before. Not even when I read it at Sheree's, having only glossed over it for fear of stirring up too many memories.

"It's proof, Paige."

"Proof of what?"

"That he was grooming you, that he's a pedophile. And I'll gladly swear it's his handwriting. So will Mom."

I don't know what to say, so I stare at her blankly for a moment before studying the floor. "But… Sheree, it was me. I let him take my virginity so Carlos wouldn't try to… Oh God I feel sick." I push myself back into the couch, not able to go on.

"Look, I know this is hard. But Paige, you need to understand you weren't to blame."

"Sheree, I practically threw myself at him, and then he felt so guilty he left you and your mom. I've had to live with that every single day."

"That may have happened, but he wanted it to happen. Did he... Had he touched... You know, like before the kiss, did he do more than that when you were little?"

Suddenly I'm on my feet and pacing. "I don't know." I look at her squarely. "There are times... Like I get these flashes now and then, you know. But then I think it's just me imagining stuff."

Sheree looks down at her lap, shaking her head. "Sounds to me like you repressed it." She looks up again and reaches out for my hand to pull me back on the couch. "You need to go talk to someone about it. I've been reading a lot of information about it lately. They say that sometimes you stuff it down so deep, it just festers there as shame. You end up going through your life making decisions based on that underlining shame, decisions you wouldn't normally make because somehow you think you don't deserve anything better."

Something about what she says makes sense but dealing with it now feels too hard. I wipe my cheeks and smile. "I get it and I will, I'll see someone. I promise," I reassure her. Now, what was that thing with your Aunt? The thing your mom didn't want to say earlier?" I ask, changing the subject.

"Oh yeah. Well, when my Aunt got back from living in Australia, she came to stay with us. Do you remember seeing her? Blonde hair and real pretty?"

I shake my head.

"Maybe you missed her because she was working with my mom at the hospital most of the time. My mom got her a job there as an aid, but some patients complained about her stealing things out of their room. When mom confronted Casandra about it, Dad hit her. Not just a slap, I mean a punch, which broke her nose. Mom left for a while. I was told she went to the hospital because she had fibroids or some crap."

I knew I'd gone pale because Sheree's face falls, and she reaches for my hand again.

"I'm guessing that's why you cut and colored your hair." She lifts her brow. "You didn't just leave, did you? You ran." She nods, concern creasing her brow. Sheree throws her diary at the table to hug me. Missing the table, the book, the one with the unicorn cover, the one identical to mine—falls to the floor and opens onto a page making us both look down.

"Oh my God," Sheree exclaims, reaching down for the book. "That's so freaky. That's her. That's Casandra and me."

There, glued to the inside of the page, is a photo of a young girl holding a baby. Her hair fanned around her perfect symmetrical face and piercing green eyes. She's smiling and showing off her perfect, white teeth and there's not a single crease in her high forehead. She's stunningly beautiful and youthful, but there's absolutely no denying it, I was staring at the fake Jolene.

23

WHO ARE YOU

"Paige, promise you'll keep in touch. Every day, I want you to call me," I plea, grabbing my bag out from the trunk of Paige's car. She nods with a smile, but I can sense her apprehension. "You can always live with me and Darby. We have room."

Again, Paige smiles then hugs me. "I'll be fine. Thank you for staying so long and helping me. The place looks so much better now."

"You'll get on your feet," I reassure her with a smile. Paige nods and tucks her hair behind her ear. "I wish you hadn't done that to your hair," I say, pouting. "I miss looking at it."

"Stop it." She swipes a hand at me. "You'll make me cry. Go already." Paige tugs my bag away from me and walks toward my newly rented car.

Moments later I'm watching her in the rearview mirror as I drive away, sorry to be leaving but happy to be heading home. Darby has been anxious about me being away for so long and I wish now I hadn't sent him home. Paige could have used his help around the dilapidated house. He could have at least fixed the annoying leak in the laundry. But I suppose someone had to be at the ranch to cook meals and tend to the horses.

I'd spent three solid weeks with Paige, helping her get sorted. There'd been things to buy, appointments to book, and I'm happy knowing she's seeing a doctor regularly now. I left promising her that I would come back again when it was closer to the baby's due date so I could be there for the birth. I wasn't going to let her go through it alone. A little flutter of butterflies makes me smile as I head along the highway to Portland to catch my flight.

So what if it's my dad's baby? I muse. A little boy we found out. Paige had already chosen a name. Quin. And after telling me the story about the older brother she never knew, I could understand why.

Reaching for my phone I try connecting to the Bluetooth so I can listen to my music during the drive, but the damn thing won't connect because I'm driving and haven't paired it.

Suddenly it sings out and startles me.

I put it to my ear. "Hello."

There is a long pause making me slow. I glance in the mirror to make sure there isn't a police car behind me. "Hello," I repeat, glancing at the screen to read the number, which is unknown.

"Sheree, it's your father," comes the quiet voice. I almost hang up immediately, but defiance swells the anger in me.

"What do you want?" I snap, before quickly pulling over to the shoulder in case I lose my shit and I can't concentrate on the road. My hands are already shaking.

"I called to ask for your forgiveness. I understand you're angry right now, and it may be hard to forgive me for walking out on you and your mother, but…

"I'm not angry about that. I'm angry that you messed with my best friend when she was a child."

"I did no such thing. I kissed her on the cheek. I never touched her until I married her."

"You're lying. I know you're lying. Paige remembers stuff. And what about you taking her virginity?" As soon as the words are out of my mouth, I regret it, and there is a long stretch of silence between us.

"All right. Seeing she told you that, I won't lie. She begged me, so Carlos would leave her alone. I was racked with remorse the moment it was over. But I cared about her. I always have, in fact—that's why I'm calling. Are you with her now? Because if you are, I need you to tell her that I'm here if she wants to reconcile. But if she wants to move on, she has my assurance that I will leave her alone. Tell her I love her enough to let her go."

Now it's my turn to remain quiet. I want to believe him, but instinct tells me he's lying. He's trying to set us up with a false sense of security, maybe so I will divulge more information.

"I don't expect you to believe me, but I promise I just want my wife to be happy."

"She's not your wife anymore. She wants to be left alone, Dad. So, if I hear that you're messing in her life, I'm sending the Feds on to you. She might not want to do anything about it, but I sure as hell do. I'm only staying quiet because it's what Paige wants. She just wants to move on."

"Fine. I understand. It's done. Does she need money? Can I talk to her at least? She left with barely anything. I want to tell her that I'm happy to pay alimony, will you put her on?"

"No! You're not going to speak with her, and she doesn't want anything from you."

"Oh." There's a long pause from him as though he's waiting for me to crack and change my mind. "Well alright then. Thank you for hearing me out. I wish you and Darby the best and say hello to your mother for me."

I can't help but screw up my face and when he disconnects, I throw the phone on the seat beside me like it's now tainted. "We don't need your warm wishes, creep," I mumble out loud.

NEVER SURRENDER

Talia Emily Perna is alone. Not nestled between two others like so many other sites I notice on my way to see what had captivated my wife, Paige. The other placements read of extended families who would miss them, and those who had preceded them, with many lying close beside. Most of the graves are marked with ornate and dominating chunks of granite or marble, decorated with fresh flowers or small photographs. But a small brass plate is all that marks Talia's grave, which is what I found my wife was looking at for so long. It's buried flush with the earth with a simple inscription that reads, *'Loved and cherished by all,'* and beneath her name are major dates. I must admit, I feel the teeniest, tiniest bit of remorse that I purposely had her son Alex buried in Los Angeles. But hey, he deserved it. He fucked my wife without me. I wish it was an offense punishable by law. But then that's neither here nor there now.

I glance up in time to see Paige getting into her car, a blue Mazda that looks well past its use-by-date. I miss her despite the fact she looks ridiculous in nothing more than plain clothes. Her hair is now sitting on her shoulders, and she has turned herself into a reddish-brunette. I wonder if she chose that color on purpose to spite me. My first wife Teresa, Sheree's mother, was a brunette, and I despised that dominating bitch.

It was a pathetic sight to see really, watching Paige only minutes ago, crouching down beside the grave of a woman she didn't know. I'm surmising she has a lot to get off her chest, and who better to tell your secrets and lies to but a dead woman.

Drawing in a deep breath, I pull up the collar of my windbreaker and thrust my hands into the pockets of my jeans, turning and pushing myself into the bitter coastal winds. I'd made sure to park where Paige wouldn't see, but it took a good ten-minute walk through the large pine trees that flank the perimeter to reach this spot. I know that by the time I get back to my car she will be well on her way. I'm curious where to, but I'm not worried about losing her. Not anymore. I know exactly where she lives—thanks to my daughter, who should know better than to leave her phone unlocked. Graciously leaving her cell on the table when she went off to snoop around my home, Sheree unknowingly allowed me to connect our phones. It was all too easy really.

Three weeks I'd waited, letting the dust and nerves settle before arranging time off work. Carter was understanding. It's not every day a man's wife runs out on him, leaving him distraught. I made sure I looked the part.

When I reach my rental car, a basic black Subaru with tinted windows, I fire up the engine and turn on the heat, waiting until a burst of warmth arrives so I can unfreeze my hands. I'm a little frustrated today. I was counting on Paige running through her routine. An early morning walk, not a run as I expected. Just a stroll with some mutt she seems to have acquired. Tea, toast and fruit on the back veranda while she gazes out over the ocean. A shower. Then off to work for eight hours. In the very same veterinary clinic Jamison had visited, thinking she was a client. Never again will I send a dipshit to do a man's job. If he had have done his job properly, I could have saved myself the inconvenience of seeing Sheree with that damn acidic tongue of hers. In the confines of the car, I chuckle to myself. She really is a chip off the old block.

With my plans to break into Paige's home, aptly named 'Apple Tree Cottage,' now redundant, I decide to play some golf while I'm here in Seaside. There are some interesting fellows at the club I've become familiar with who don't mind discussing their lives. Middle-class, they can be uncouth, but they and the staff are all very entertaining over drinks. It helps kill the time, which is what I need until I can figure out Paige's weaknesses, apart from the ice cream she seems to love now. Why anyone would eat ice cream in this weather is beyond me.

When I'm back in the house I'd secured through Airbnb, I change into something more appropriate, yet still in disguise. I haven't quite worked out who Paige knows apart from her work colleagues, and I can't be certain she hasn't described me to everyone, asking to be on the lookout. Most days, I get around looking almost like a hobo in jeans and a pullover, a jacket pulled up high over my ears and a baseball cap, hoping I'm unrecognizable.

With my clubs in the trunk and gloves on my hands, I head out to the nine-hole green.

❧

He's so pretentious it's a joke. Thinking he's unrecognizable in jeans and a jacket, even a new baseball cap can't hide that pretty face, and I'd know that walk anywhere. It's like he's got a pole shoved up his ass. I'd spotted him at the service center from across the road in the diner weeks ago. A man dressed in shoddy jeans and sneakers peeling himself out of a nearly new black WRX. It looked strange. He seemed nervous, too. Kept pulling down his cap visor and looking around.

I'd been waiting for him. Day in and day out, from my vantage point in town. The diner is always crowded, from early morning to close, so I knew I'd have good cover, and when I finally spotted him, I put everything into motion.

First, I needed a decoy, and fortunately for me, there was a young lady in the apartments where I was staying who struck a remarkable resemblance. She was the right height, slim, and had the dark haircut too, and when she slipped on glasses, I had to smile. She was perfect. A few dollars later, and she was up for the challenge. Prepared to float around town looking busy. Even going for walks with a dog she nabbed. I never asked how she managed that one, she just went in one door of the vet clinic and slipped out the other with a dog on a leash. I'd been watching Gerard though, and he was still watching the front door. All afternoon he sat there, the fucking psycho that he is.

Believe it or not, the decoy's name is Angel, which seems fitting. She's smart and on my side when I told her my story and how careful we had to be. Gerard watches Apple Tree Cottage like a hawk most days, so sending her out on an errand had to be timed perfectly because there couldn't be two Tammy Andersons getting around dressed differently. Angel was all over it, like it was some acting part in a movie. I just need to keep her safe. I doubt Gerard has ill-intent, but he makes me wonder why he hasn't just announced his arrival and gotten on with what he wants.

It's late afternoon when Gerard finally emerges from Seaside Golf Club's parking lot in his black car. Through my binoculars I see he's smiling, and I figure he's been drinking. Not a good thing. It seems he is getting drunk more often. Two nights ago, I'd seen him come out of some pub looking drunk and indecisive. I worried he would make a move, turn up at the cottage, and things would get messy. It made me realize I needed to get on with the plan.

Putting the car into gear, I pull out from my place of hiding and fall in behind. There's no guessing where he's going because I already know, but I follow him just the same. It's important I track and note his every move. It surprises me he seems so predictable. Well, no, maybe it doesn't. The man is wired in such a way that predictable is what he needs. He's out of his comfort zone right now, and he's prime for the picking. A few more confusing moves, and he'll be fucking all out of whack, at least I'm hoping so.

After a quick stop at his rental, Gerard is back in his car. He pulls into a drive-through for coffee, then heads toward Apple Tree Cottage where 'Tammy Anderson' lives, a few short miles out of town. He parks in his spot, and I park in mine. And now we wait, watching to see who makes the first move.

The lights are on in the cottage, and there's movement inside. The blinds are purposely left down, day and night. The thought makes me both nervous and pissed off, questioning everything that's gone on and why it has to be this way. Couldn't he just fuck off and find someone else?

My phone vibrates beside me. A quick glance tells me it's Tebor. I push my fingers through my hair and swipe my palm over my mouth. I'd been expecting the call, but now that it's here, a lump rises from my stomach and embeds in my throat, making me cough before I answer.

"Hello."

"Still need it done?"

I keep the phone pressed against my ear, stare down at

my lap while my hand rubs my forehead. I'm surprised I have doubts. Is this really the way I want it to go?

"Hey?"

"I'm still here. Did you get the brand?"

"Fuck yeah," Tebor replies a little too excitedly. "Cunt deserves it."

"Don't know how you can do it."

"Easy. Hold 'em fucking down and burn that fucker in the forehead. Mark the mother fucker for life."

As strong as I'm feeling, the thought still sickens me.

"When?' I ask.

"Midnight—tonight. They call that the witching hour," Tebor chuckles. "Is that soon enough for you?"

I glance toward the cottage that has an innocent occupant inside, then look toward the spot where I know Gerard is watching, the hood of his car barely visible.

"Right. So, all you need me to do is lure him out to the parking lot?" I start the engine, then readjust the rearview mirror.

"That's it. Unless of course you want to watch. But I'll warn you now, he'll scream like his dick's been cut off, which is what we should do. Then he'll pass out and piss his pants. Not necessarily in that order, but they always piss their pants."

Bringing the hip flask to my lips, I take another sip of scotch then light up my phone for the time. Eight o'clock. Paige should leave in about another fifteen minutes. Every Wednesday, she climbs into that bomb she calls a car and drives out of town to a building located between Cannon Beach and Seaside. It's some type of hall. I watch as she scampers inside, flicking her fingers down both sides of her head so her hair covers her face, acting suspiciously like she doesn't want anyone to know she goes there. I haven't been able to work out what she, and the other ten or so woman who turn up do in there. For all I know, she's turned gay and it's a secret club, though seeing the number of pregnant women who follow, I suspect it's more of a stupid self-help support group for abandoned women or some shit. She's the one who damn well abandoned me. The whore.

Tonight, I won't follow her. Tonight, I plan on making her realize what a big mistake she has made. It won't be pleasant, but it is necessary. Fear is always a great motivator.

When she's gone, I set out on foot, ambling along as though I'm taking an evening stroll, glancing casually around to make sure no one is watching me.

Getting in proves to be harder than I thought. I hoped to gain entry via the back veranda through where I imagined glass sliding doors would be. But the relic of a building has a solid oak back door. Be it weathered, it still doesn't budge when I shoulder the wood—hard.

Not deterred, I slip on my golf gloves and navigate around to the side of the house I've never been able to see from the road and notice she has left a small window open, most likely the bathroom. Sighing, I take a quick glance around to ensure I'm not seen, then lever it up and struggle through the opening.

I've landed in the bathroom, as thought, and a few steps has me entering the dining area. The house is still lit up, and an aroma I recognize lingers in the air. Coq Au Vin if I'm not mistaken. My mouth salivates from the memory of Paige's good cooking. It will be nice to get her home. Have her back in my kitchen, in my bed, on my arm. A few tried and tested antics should do the trick, and she'll be begging me to take her back. She never was very bright.

The house is warm, which, I discover, is from a wood

heater still aglow in the living area. I go over to it and warm myself for a moment as I take in her habitat. The place is untidy, and it appears she has taken up knitting. It's fascinating looking around at her meager belongings, and I can't help the small, satisfied smirk that twists the corners of my lips.

There is a small two-seater sofa, upholstered in what looks to be cheap fabric. It's sprinkled in animal hair, presumably from her dog, which, until now, I hadn't thought about. A quick look around finds no dog to be concerned about, and I'm wondering now if it had been one she was caring for from work. Picking up some mail left on the kitchen counter, I shuffle through the pile noting they are all addressed to Tammy Anderson. Funny really that she thought changing her name would somehow keep her safe— if anything it's the other way around. She's unwittingly put herself in more danger. Tammy Anderson will never be missed when all along she never existed. Stupid girl. I toss the mail back on the bench, not caring it's not how I found it.

There are a few dishes in the sink, needless to say, unwashed. I screw up my nose. She's become a slob. Doesn't she realize I brought out the best in her?

Two small bowls beside the laundry door explain the animal hair on the couch, and in an instant I'm in her bedroom, discovering a feline curled up in the middle of the bed. It lifts an eyelid when I step closer, pulls back, bristles then sprints from the room. I spin around, trying to see where it ran to, but it's much too quick. Never mind. Next time I'll be faster. I have a right mind to call it Achilles. The stinking thing would most definitely be one of her weak spots. I'm questioning now whether I want the filthy woman back in my life at all. Fancy letting the flea-ridden thing sleep on your bed. The thing is better off dead.

Impulsively, I open drawers and go through her things in

the bedroom, claiming a pair of underwear and bringing them to my nose. Yes, that's her, she's here. Even through the scent of laundry soap, she's there. I pocket the panties and flick through her sparse wardrobe to discover not a tasteful dress in sight. Pitiful.

As I leave the room, I shove the black-and-white photo Sheree removed from my home, leaving it angled and screwed. I should take it back. But then that would be a dead giveaway and defeat the purpose of my visit. Glancing at the clock on the wall, I see I have wasted time looking around when really it doesn't matter. It'll be all gone soon enough, when she's back home with me.

Sucking in a deep breath, I rush around in a flurry. Pull open draws and throw cushions around. Tip over the coffee table. Slap photos face down. Kick the cat bowls across the floor. Push over the standing lamp, casting the room into shadows, then shove all the books from off the shelf and onto the floor. Finally, in a panting rage, I take hold of a kitchen knife and do what I should have done first. Stab at the face in the photo that hangs almost life-size in the hall, then punch it squarely in the center which shatters the glass before the picture flounders, unhooks, and drops to the floor.

Then, and only then, do I feel satisfied. Dusting myself off then unlocking the back door, I leave the place wide open, hoping beyond hope that stinking cat runs off into the night and never returns. Because there's no way that thing is coming home with us.

Angel knows what she needs to do. I'd called and arranged everything from my car. After clearing out the apartment I was staying at, I drove back to the cottage to wait out Gerard's next move.

To my surprise, I catch him walking down the street toward the house. He looks around before ducking underneath the overgrown arbor covered in purple flowers where I lose sight of him. I'd been expecting him to follow the car that should have left minutes before, and now I'm concerned by what he's doing. I needed him to follow that damn blue car. I decide to wait and see what eventuates. If he has any plans of setting fire to the place, at least no one is home. Except—shit—the cat's most likely still inside. I weigh up the ramifications. If I go in after him now, all the planning will have gone to waste. There are people coming, people who I have paid dearly. As much as I want to go in there, to rescue the damn cat, I need to leave it up to fate. If the cat's smart enough, it will get out of the way. I decide it's better to stay put.

Fifteen minutes later, Gerard emerges from the yard. He's hurrying now, his hands stuffed in his pockets, head swiveling from left to right. He breaks into a jog when his car is in his sights, and in seconds, he is driving past me and the street I'm parked on.

I call Angel immediately then peel out of my car and start walking toward the cottage.

"How far out of town are you?" I quiz.

"Only a few miles. Why?"

"Turn around and come back into town slowly. He didn't follow tonight, but I reckon he's on his way there now. Make sure he notices you. Don't speed. I need you to stall him, drive around for a while before heading to the bar. Whatever you do, make sure he's following you."

"Okay. But when I get to the bar, where should I wait?"

"Sit by a window. We need to make sure he can see you. I'll call you to check whether you can see him. Then at 10:15, make a point of talking to some guy. Buy him a drink and make certain to look like you're flirting. That will piss him off and get his attention before you step outside."

"I've got to go outside with some dude?"

"No. Dump him before you go into the parking lot. I've just got to check on something first, but don't worry, I'll be there by then, and then you can go. Just promise me you won't hang around. It could get ugly, and I don't want you anywhere near the place. And remember what we agreed on. You never saw me."

"You sure we can't stay…"

"Angel." I cut her off. Because as much as I'm grateful to her, it's important she understands this was a business transaction, nothing more. "You promised you wouldn't get attached. We can't see each other again. Even if we do, you need to pretend you don't know me. If the police look around, you'll only be jeopardizing yourself."

Angel sighs. "All right, I get it, I get it."

"I couldn't have done this without you," I tell her, my tone softer now. "Really, you have no idea how much I appreciate what you've done. It's almost over. Then everyone can get on with their lives, including you."

"Shit, that was him, he just passed me," she says.

"Is he turning around?"

There's a long pause. I wait patiently by the back door of the cottage until she confirms Gerard is now following her.

"Good. I'll see you soon."

"Okay."

"Oh, and Angel."

"Yeah."

"That name of yours—it suits you to a T."

She disconnects with a giggle. Then I'm getting straight to work to see what might be out of place inside.

∿

"Shit," I swear aloud, when my car flies by Paige's. She's damn well finished early tonight, and I wasn't at all expecting her. Although it's dark, I'm concerned my features may have been momentarily illuminated by the headlights barreling toward me.

The next opportunity I get, I make a U-turn then speed to catch up, glancing repeatedly in my mirror to make sure no police are close behind.

I follow her all the way back into town until she pulls over outside Patties Diner, relieved to see that it's actually her, that I hadn't mistaken the car for someone else's. She meanders her way over to the counter, looking up at the menu for the longest time before ordering. Moments later, she wanders down the side passageway inside the building to use the bathroom, I assume.

I wait with bated breath, counting the seconds, then the minutes, she's gone. After five minutes, I can't sit still for fear she now knows I'm following her and has snuck out the back. Adrenaline is surging through me, and I reach for the ignition. She can't know I'm here. Not yet, I panic. The timing's not right.

Just then, she reemerges, looking down and tucking her shirt in. A horrid one at that, I slump back and draw in a heavy sigh, let my hand fall away from the dashboard before wiping my palms on my jeans. Bitch, testing me like that.

Having her in constant sight, I scroll through my phone, checking emails from work and generally amusing myself and questioning why it's taking her so long to eat her damn food. Food she shouldn't be eating because I notice she's getting fat. Once she's home, we must rectify that. I get a sudden image of locking her in our bedroom. I feel my cock twitch, something that hasn't happened in some time, even when my imagination has gone wild when I observed her as a shadow through the windows. I reach inside my pocket and withdraw her panties, bring them close and inhale. Again, my cock throbs, and I question why I hadn't snuck in earlier to claim a pair. Jacking off, these would have been so much better than the trashy porn I'd been watching.

Lost in my daydream, I only realize she has left the building when she slams her car door.

In a heartbeat, I'm following, leaving at least ten car lengths between us. I'm sure if she weren't a sandwich short of a picnic, she would have realized she was being tailed. But I don't expect she understands too much. How much I love her. How much I need her. And if I can't have her, no one will. Those thoughts put a smile on my face, and I lift what's still clutched in my hand to my nose again. I'm honestly not sure how much longer I can wait before I claim more than just her underwear.

I rearrange myself, try to put my focus on the road, get ready for the action when she gets home. I can almost see the look of distress wash over her face. Taste the tears she will shed. Her home, her sanctuary, her peace of mind destroyed and reminiscent of a time not so long ago, when she was alone and vulnerable. I decide that when I pull up, I'm going to blow my load into her underwear while my mind fills in the blanks. Ahh, sweet victory. I can almost taste it.

Suddenly, she's taking a right turn and heading toward the main center of town. Damn it, what now? Two turns later however, she pulls in the rear parking lot of some bar.

Well, this is new.

I do a drive by to avoid suspicion then double back to park the car opposite the establishment but from where I can see, the large windows out front giving me a clear view. "Just like watching television." I recline my seat a little, curiosity having gotten the better of my desire to know she's flipping out over her ransacked house, which will have to wait.

Watching her from this distance in an iridescent room is

enlightening. Watching the way she moves, her hand gestures and body language seeming elaborate for the Paige I know, which makes me frown. Milling about people she obviously knows, she's being overly chatty and laughing a lot for someone I suspect would be under duress. Maybe those self-help sessions are helping her after all.

I glance up at the neon sign above the front entrance that tells me it's Warren House Bar. Jolting my memory, I realize now it's the place Jamison ventured into, where he discovered the little virgin. Suddenly feeling hot, I wind the window down and let the cool night air rush in. For a moment, when I look back at the bar and see Paige, I get a haunting feeling that Jamison was lying to me. That perhaps he found Paige in there. That his interpretation of the event was him, gloating that he'd secretly taken my wife. *Without me.* I toss the panties I've been clutching in my hand on the car seat and reach for the hip flask. If he touched my wife, so help me, I'll kill the bastard. I'm already on the brink of exposing him and his dirty ways to Casandra.

Just when I'm consoling myself that my paranoia is getting the better of me, I notice something different about Paige. When she lifted herself onto the stool and peeled off her jacket, I caught sight of the markings on her waist. There was no mistaking it. She has a tattoo.

I fling open my door and march across the road, and the closer I get to the windows, the better I see. The shape of her face. The way she fills her jeans. Then when she puts her phone up to her ear, and a hand goes to the back of her head, listening, that's when I understand. She does not have my wife's hands.

When I burst through the door, all eyes find me. I take in a calming breath and unclench my fists, pushing my hands to my side. Forgetting I'm blowing my cover, I pull my jacket up and hunch into it, looking around the room as though curious. When my eyes travel back to the bar, I notice the brunette has risen and is heading toward the far end of the bar. Glancing up, I see the exit sign. Over my dead body.

I march off after her.

"Hey, tall guy. Having a beer?" The bartender sings out, tripping me up. I toss him a look and mumble something about using the restroom first. I'm not sure if the words came out in their right sequence and I don't much care. I need to set proper eyes on the bitch I've been following around for weeks.

I'm so hot on her heels that the self-closing door doesn't even have time to shut. And there she is, standing in the parking lot, rummaging around in her bag until she pulls out a packet of cigarettes. It's definitely not her.

She hasn't noticed me and doesn't even look up when my shoes crunch the asphalt.

"Who are you?" I say, making her spin around, the cigarette poised midway toward her mouth.

"Who are you?"

When I move to approach her, she surprises me by squaring her shoulders and facing me, she draws deeply on her cigarette, one arm tucking under the other, completely at ease. Something is off. A young woman alone in the parking lot with a strange man. Normally someone would make their way back inside.

"I think you know who I am. But I'd like to know what you're doing impersonating my wife."

"Say what? Are you drunk or something? I'm here having a smoke mister, and I wouldn't have a clue who your wife is. Buzz off." She turns her back on me, leaving me momentarily bewildered.

It's only when I move in closer to confront her and she turns that I register the concern in her eyes. Then I notice the hand holding the cigarette is shaking. It makes me smile.

"Look, I don't know what you're thinking, but I haven't done anything to you. And I don't know your wife."

"Ah, that's where I think you're wrong. I know my wife too well…"

From somewhere over in the shadows of the parking lot, I hear several car doors slam. The sudden change in atmosphere silences me. The young lady in front of me turns to look, then comes to stand by my side as if seeking protection.

Together, we watch as four men approach. All of them built for the armed forces, and I would surmise they are, except two of them have man buns and one has left hair on his face instead of his head. He's shaven clean. The fourth man is the warning bell above all else; he's wearing a balaclava. My heart shifts from my chest, making my breathing stilted, and I unconsciously grab the young lady beside me and put her between me and them. The men share a look just as the young lady tilts her head up at me.

"Seriously?" She pulls herself out from my hold and moves not toward the door from which she left through, but toward those four menacing looking men.

I spin on my heel to make a hasty retreat, but in a split second, I have the hooded man's fingers digging into my arm.

"What are you doing? Let me go." I look around for my wife's doppelganger, spot her nearing the door. "Call the police. Tell the bartender I need help," I call out. But the bitch just gives me the finger, then both as the other three men close in around me.

"Do you realize who you're dealing with here? Who sent you, and what do you want? Is it money? Do you need someone to fudge something?" I rant, as they drag me toward the van, I'm gathering they arrived in. "I have friends in high places. I know how to manipulate the law." That statement earns me an elbow to the side of my head, delivered by the hooded man and silencing me into a groan.

Shoving me in the van, two men clamber in behind me. I look around quickly in search of a weapon, anything. A lump of wood, a ratchet, even a screwdriver will do. But the van is bare inside, except for a small cooler and a length of rope. Never have two such simple items struck as much fear in me as those household items. In a stupid panic, I envision my chopped-up body parts stuffed in there, even though the rational part of my mind knows it's an impossibility. Maybe it just for my head. I swivel around and reach for the door just as the van springs to life, and I'm thrust headlong into metal, then recoiling to fall on my ass. Everyone laughs except the man wearing the balaclava who is the one behind the wheel with his eyes on the road.

One man reaches for the rope. When I put up a struggle, I'm pushed to the floor face first and my hands get bound behind my back. Reefing me up together, they thrust me back into a sitting position against the back of the passenger seat and punch me in the solar plexus, making me gasp.

"Where are you taking me? I want to know." My voice comes out as a wheeze.

The men in the back just glare at me.

"Who are you? Did I put one of your friends in prison?" I cough. "I can get them out. What's his name? I'll help him out financially. Does he have a family? Was it one of you? Tell me, tell me how I can fix this."

Again, my rambling is met with violence, a punch straight to my nose this time. I taste the blood as it runs down the back of my throat, and my eyes begin to water. It's enough to successfully subdue me.

It seems we drive for hours when in reality it's perhaps been only minutes, and I don't like the direction we seem to take. It dawns on me that there's been non-stop pines on either side of us and I realize we are going through what I believe to be Ecola State Forest. I don't like how I feel. I'm overwhelmingly nauseous, and there's the real threat I might seriously shit my pants. Maybe if I do, they will throw me out the van, but all too soon, we're pulling up.

"Don't even think about running, rock spider. I know this fucking forest like the back of my fucking hand, and I'm a tad partial to hunting. With a knife," he adds, making my blood run cold. Why is he calling me a rock spider? That term is used to describe pedophiles. He pushes me out of the van but holds tight to my jacket until he and his companions get out. One man reaches back inside to drag the cooler closer and takes hold of a rag.

"Don't make this hard on yourself. It'll be over in seconds," one of the man-bun men says. Looking at him closely and the other with a bun, I swear they are twins. The three unmasked men mill around me, the third being a bald-headed thug with menacing eyes, while the man with his face covered seems to step back and looks around uncomfortably.

"What? What will be over with? Look. I think you've mistaken me for someone else. My name is Gerard Whitmyer. I'm an appointed criminal attorney from LA. I'm not the man you're after. I'm not a child molester."

The three men suddenly stop doing what they're doing, which is positioning the cooler and flipping off the top. They stare at each other and scratch their heads.

Relief floods me. "I'm sorry you wasted your time. Now if you don't mind, can you untie me?" I turn to make it obvious that I mean now.

It starts with one, then another joins in, then the third, and even the fourth one laughs so hard I'm confused.

Suddenly they stop laughing and look at me deadpan. "Nah, we've got the right guy," the bald-headed man says, and in a flash, I'm shoved roughly to the ground, landing face up with them hovering over me, their expression turning so dark, I feel myself leak urine.

When one man sits on my legs, nearly breaking my shin bones, my scream from pain is quickly stifled with a dirty rag shoved in my mouth. Then another man kneels at my head and takes a firm hold under my jaw, gripping my hair in his fist and successfully freezing my flailing head.

I can't move. The weight and strength in them is blinding and forcing my eyes closed, and then it hits me. Something pressing firmly against my forehead. I can't discern whether it's hot or cold, just a searing pain that travels behind my eyes and down my throat. Intense pain shooting straight to my wiggling toes. I scream into the cloth in my mouth, try to use all my strength to shove the men off me as the bald man repeats, "Tick tock," over and over again.

I can't help it. Shit explodes from my body with such force I become deadened from both shock and pain. Never in my life have I felt anything so excruciating while simultaneously feeling ashamed, and above it all, all I can hear is "Tick tock, tick…"

Then the last thing I hear before I black out is, "Fuck, he shit his pants. Now that, is a first, brother."

SIX FEET UNDER

I t's late when I leave the birthing classes Sheree insisted I sign up for, but only because I'd stayed behind to chat with Marlena and Jenny. Two women in their last trimester. I'm desperate for the company because my loneliness has been more profound over the last couple of weeks since Sheree left. And although I've had people around me for the last few hours, traveling home near midnight brings back the empty feeling.

Since leaving Gerard eight weeks ago, life has been like playing skirmish with silver cars and police being the obvious ones to avoid. All interactions with people and any transactions I make need to be conscious. I've been introducing myself and signing as Tammy Anderson from Wisconsin knowing Gerard could have anyone out looking for me, though from what I could gather from Sheree's visit, he hadn't reported me as missing, per se. I can't be too careful because that could easily be a bad thing.

The first few weeks at Cannon Beach before Sheree and her mother had arrived had been an emotional stain. Glancing around at an empty rental cottage, with only basic furnishings provided and not knowing where to start brought me to tears and sent me crawling back into bed. It wasn't just the loss of everything, but because I felt guilty about everything.

After cashing the check Jenna had given me, I'd rented a car, and a short drive later, I was standing in front of Jolene's dilapidated trailer. Even before knocking, I knew something was wrong. I stood there anyway, still hoping she'd answer, before someone startled me.

"She's gone." I looked around the trailer park, then spotted an older woman sitting on her make-shift porch drinking beer. "Jolene. She's gone. Left after that sick kid of hers died," the woman elaborated callously.

"When?" I called back.

"Last week, left with some guy she'd been seeing."

"Oh." I looked at the envelope of money in my hand. "I wanted to give her something. Do you know where she went?"

The lady just waved me away like I was an annoying fly, making my heart sink even further. I had truly wanted to help. To maybe talk with her about Alex. I left wondering if Jolene even knew what happened to him.

I stood there for several minutes, not knowing what to do until I remembered poor little Napoléon in the car. I drove away, never having known her story—what Grace had looked like or why she died.

Cannon Beach turned out to be lovelier than I expected. It was a long drive, especially because every silver car that sped up behind me set my heart racing, my car slowing, me tensing and ducking down. The first opportunity I got, I decided to become the real deal, Tammy Anderson. Ditching the wig I'd been wearing, I then bought hair-coloring and a pair of scissors to chop off my hair.

Jenna had given me a lot of money, but while I was

beyond appreciative, having that much cash on me frayed my nerves every inch of the way. Finally, after two days on the road, Napoléon and I arrived at the beautiful coastal town Alex was so fond of. How it was possible, I don't know, but straightaway, it felt like home. I just prayed Gerard wouldn't come looking for me here.

I think about Napoléon again, concerned that I forgot to let him back in the house before I left? But then I remember seeing him and I left his food in his bowl. I bet he hasn't even dragged himself off my bed. Suddenly, I'm looking forward to getting home, to crawl into bed with a hot chocolate and read until I'm sleepy. I have the morning off, so I can sleep in. If my bladder will let me.

When I pull up outside my ramshackle of a place, the first thing I notice is the lighting inside. It seems duller than usual. Scared of the dark now, I always make certain to keep the place well lit, so by the time I'm standing at the back door, my heart is racing like a track horse.

Turning the key slowly, I push the door open and glance around. I spot Napoléon curled up in front of the heater, which has now died down to embers. Reassured that if my cat is relaxed, it must be a good sign, I enter fully and notice the unlit lamp. Its bulb must have blown. I lock the door behind me.

"Did you eat your dinner?" I ask Napoléon, tossing my bag on the couch before marching to the kitchen and turning on the light. His bowl is still full. "I guess you're not hungry then," I address him again, just to hear my own voice, then pour a cup of milk and turn on the microwave.

Kicking off my shoes, I head toward the bathroom and cry out. I rush toward the frame that's face down on the floor then lift it carefully, groaning because the image of Alex is scratched and torn. "Damn it," I cuss aloud, looking up and down the hall until I find the picture hook lying just a few feet away. Gathering the glass fragments on top, I take the photo and put it in the laundry to deal with another day, relieved I still have the photo on file.

Minutes later, I have slipped into my pajamas and have a hot chocolate in my hand, doing my rounds and turning off lights. I glance around once more to see if everything is where it should be, and then freeze. The books look strange. And then I notice it, there on the bookshelf, right on the middle shelf. Front and center beside hardbacks I've collected from the secondhand bookstore. Right there in plain sight for me to see—lays a single red rose.

I don't get to sleep in, because I didn't get to sleep at all. The rose has haunted me all night, and I've been wracking my brain trying to figure out who could have put it there and how they got in. I locked the door. Everything apart from the photo and the rose were as they should be. There are only two explanations I can think of, and both spook the utter shit out of me. It was either Gerard, or something unearthly.

I keep seeing the photo on the floor and then the rose, making me seriously question the latter. Then I'm thinking of a third, even though it's an absolute long shot. I reach for my phone to call Sheree to ask, then decide against it. I don't want her rushing back here when really, it hardly constitutes a threat. I mean, it's a rose. A nice one at that. I pick it up off the bookshelf and smell its scent, questioning if it's just a peace offering. But still, Gerard must have broken into my house to place it there. Unless… Do I even remember locking it? I know I've been getting forgetful lately—they call it 'pregnancy brain,' apparently.

I shower and dress, then have some breakfast. Next, I sort through my mail. The whole time I keep thinking of the picture frame on the floor. If I don't do something this morning to keep my mind off it, I will go insane. Then I remember what today is.

"Shit." I slap the letters on the bench and snatch up my tea.

With the threat that Gerard could be anywhere around, I pace the house with my tea in my hand, feeling more anxious by the second. There's somewhere I need to be. I've had it arranged weeks ago when I first arrived at Cannon Beach after I'd ventured out to visit Alex's mom's grave, which I found out was located at Evergreen Cemetery back in Seaside.

It took some time to locate her, walking past each plot, glancing at them with pine needles snapped under my shoes. It felt surreal at the time, but also comforting within the peaceful grounds. Studying the graves had me questioning each deceased person's life. How they had lived and loved and who they'd left behind. It reminded me of my own recent loss and cross to bear.

I've been going to the cemetery every week just to talk and straighten the small, dried flower arrangement that seems to always get toppled over by the wind, wondering if it was Alex who had placed it there. The display was old and faded, but I couldn't throw them away. Instead, each week, I paid a visit to bring a fresh arrangement and mumbled on about the son she would have been proud of, and the man I had the privilege to love.

Sitting and talking with Alex's mom, Talia each week brought me as close to saying goodbye to Alex as I could manage without falling apart completely, and strangely, after each visit, I always felt a little lighter. Today was the planned date to erect the monument I'd ordered, using some of the money I had, knowing it would be what Alex wanted.

Beside me, Napoléon twitches his ears. I give him an

absentminded pat. "You know what? I don't care if Gerard's out there, Napoléon. I need to be there. Even if it's the last thing I ever do," I tell him, snatching up my bag and keys.

By the time I get to the cemetery, the contractors are working on lowering the slab of granite onto a concrete slab they must have poured yesterday sometime because it wasn't there in the morning when I came to check.

I greet them briefly then watch with satisfied interest. The new inscription now reads, "Loved and cherished by all, but none more so than her only son, Alexander John Perna." The words bring tears to my eyes. I can't relocate Alex, but I could carry out his wishes for a headstone for his mom. And the little angel on top is reassuring that Alex would always be watching over her.

I might seem strange, but I find it beautiful here. The day is already warm and now that the men have gone, I get the same urge I get every time I come here, to lie down on the lawn and watch the billowy clouds. Usually I get the feeling I'm being watched so I never do. And after discovering the rose last night, it wouldn't surprise me if it's been Gerard who's been watching me. For some unknown reason though, I don't feel a presence today. Maybe I just don't care anymore.

Stepping forward, I caress the large marble marker then run my fingers over Alex's name. The sensation opens a distinct hole in my heart where I feel he should be. A wound so scarred and deep, I'm afraid no one will ever fill it again. Not in this life, anyway.

Stripping off my coat, I spread it out on the ground, then lay down. In the distance, I can hear a lawn mower, making me draw in a breath, wishing I could smell the freshly cut grass. I imagine sitting in the gazebo, watching the love of my life cutting the lawn. The thought sends tears sliding down my temples. I throw an arm over my eyes and reach for my protruding stomach, connecting with Quin to help me survive. The pain of my past and what brought me here makes moving on difficult. But I'm hoping together, Quin and I will be happy.

I have a dream job, and I've even been taking photos again. Mainly of the beach and my cat. I'm sure I'll get more adventurous soon. Lifting Alex's sweater that I wear for this very occasion, I scratch my belly and think about all the photos I'll soon be taking of Quin. I lay there like that for over an hour, then slowly, I get to my feet and head home.

I'm still thinking about the rose when I get back to the cottage. It just feels too strange. Like something doesn't fit. The lamp on its own, sure. But the lamp blowing, the picture breaking. A rose? I've seen movies and what ghosts do to get in contact.

A loud shrill jerks me on the spot, and my hand goes to my heart until I realize it's my phone.

"Morning to you," Sheree says, when I put the phone to my ear. Our daily chats have become the norm now.

"It should be, but I need to ask a ridiculous question."

"Shoot, I'm all ears."

"Would you have any clue how a rose would end up on my bookshelf?"

"That fucking liar. I'm hanging up now to call him."

The phone goes dead.

I stand there, frozen for a moment, no doubt a stunned look on my face before glancing down at Napoléon rubbing up against my leg.

"Well, I guess that answers my question then." I glance at my phone to note the time then put it down to hang washing.

I still have an hour before work, so I plan on doing a few

chores. There are dishes in the sink, and the bin needs emptying. Then my phone rings again.

"He's not there."

My heart skips a beat. "What do you…"

"Sorry. No. I mean, he's not answering so he must be there. Why else wouldn't he answer? It had to be him. He left the rose. Pack some bags and get your ass in the car now," Sheree demands.

Even though my heart is racing, I feel the flight and fight run out of me. I'm so tired.

"I think I need to talk to him, that's all."

"Paige," she yells. "He's playing you again. Do not fall for his shit."

"That's not what I mean. I have no intention of going back to him. Beside I'm sure once he realizes I'm pregnant, he'll run for the hills anyway."

"Why do you sound like that? I know that voice. You're weakening."

"I'm not, I'm just tired, I didn't…" The squeal of tires interrupts me and makes me jolt. "Hang on a minute, someone is pulling up out front." I press the phone to my chest and peer out the kitchen window. A large truck has pulled up at the curb. "What the…?"

I put the phone back to my ear. "Sorry, it's just a truck."

"What is a truck doing outside your place, Paige?"

"I don't know, some people are obviously getting something delivered, I guess. Look, you need to calm down, I can handle Gerard if he turns up. I have 911 on speed dial." I let go of the curtain once I see two men in overalls climb out of the cab looking bewildered and pointing across the street.

"Very funny, Paige. But this is serious. I don't think you understand what men like him are capable of."

Suddenly I have tears in my eyes.

"Maybe not. But right now, I need to get ready for work.

Let me know if you get a hold of him, okay? Tell him if he wants to talk, I will. It might be the only way to get him off my back."

"Hell, no, sister, that ain't ever going to happen, and just so you know, I'm booking a flight as we speak, I'll be there tomorrow."

Before I have time to even dispute, Sheree has hung up. Jesus, Sheree, just because I said I'd talk doesn't mean I need an intervention.

Loading up a basket of washing, I head out the laundry door. I'm just pegging the last work shirt, wishing I had a dryer, when I spot a man in overalls hauling two large rose bushes in pots. Dropping the basket, I come around from the side of the house to investigate.

"Um, excuse me. What are you doing?"

The man jerks around to face me. "Christ. Sorry, love. We were told no one would be home and to just get to work."

"What do you mean, what is all this." I point to the second man carrying pots. "I think you have the wrong address. I didn't order these."

The man places the pots down on the garden bed and pulls out a piece of paper from his shirt pocket. He reads it, then looks at me smiling sheepishly. "Apple Tree Cottage 1605A Lincoln Drive?"

"Yes."

"And you would be..." He smiles again, making his mustache more prominent with his cheekbones flaring. "Princess Paige?" His face falls when I burst into tears, then he looks stunned. He shoots a look to his fellow worker, who is still busy walking back and forth bringing in pot after pot of red roses.

"This is not funny. Who sent these?" I ask knowing damn well it's Gerard. It's one thing to leave a rose but wowing me with pots of them and calling me princess! What sort of sick joke is that?

The man hands me the crumbled piece of paper. "It's got a signature," he offers.

One glance, and all I see is a scribble. Handing it back, I spin around and march off, shouting out over my shoulder how stupid it all is and he needs to take them all away.

When I get home from work that afternoon, I'm both angry and dismayed to find the men have not only ignored my instructions and left all the roses, but they have even planted them. Creating the most magnificent sea of red roses I've ever seen. All gorgeous and in full bloom and without a doubt costing an absolute fortune. The sight wrenches at my heart, and it takes everything in me to tear myself away to let Napoléon out.

Then, against all advice given, I grab the bottle of red wine that Sheree and her mom shared when visiting and pour myself a small glass. I need something to calm the calamity that's raging in me right now. Something to sort the mixture of emotions swirling in my head. When I step down from the back porch and move closer to the display, all I want to do is scream, but instead, tears trickle down my face as I try to sip my wine. My eyes dart to the choppy ocean and setting sun, then back to the roses, the sight saturating me with doubt and fear. Fear of the unknown. Doubt about being a good mother. Fear of the past and doubting I'll ever be able to love again, no matter how elaborate the gesture. I don't know how long I stand there, trapped in a vortex that captures all the crazy sounds around me. Dogs barking, children screaming, cars and motorbikes going by, until I'm so absorbed, it all becomes white noise.

I don't hear anyone approach. Don't sense the pending shock. I don't even hear my name, even if it had been shouted. Because the sound I hear seems to come from somewhere in that void that could be the air itself. But I hear him clear as day.

"Do you know what red roses symbolize?"

I don't turn when I hear the words. Don't move or even breathe. I just let the glass slip from my hand, and freeze. Feeling so weak, I'm unable to stand, like I'm being robbed of my very essence. The pole of energy that runs through my core dissolving, and I'm fading into nothingness. But then he is there, his arms around my waist supporting me, refilling me. My body heaves, desperate to catch a breath. I feel his chest expand and, on his exhale, he is whispering words of reassurance, stroking my hair and shushing me.

I sink to my knees, slip out of his arms because it still feels like a cruel joke. A deceptive twist of fate. Every hair on my arms rises to attention, and I tremble when a large hand rests gently on my head.

"I knew you were a queen all along."

And then—I start wailing.

2 6

LAST DAY ON EARTH

Crumpled on the ground and sobbing, I feel him come down to sit behind me, wrapping his strong arms around and holding tight, trying to comfort me.

"I'm sorry. I'm so sorry. But it's okay now. It's all going to be okay," Alex soothes, trying to turn me to face him. But I don't want to look. I'm scared if I do, I'll find out he's only a figment of my imagination. That I'm sitting on the lawn on my own, looking like a crazed woman rocking and crying. I'm still not daring to believe he is here, in the flesh.

Alex kisses the top of my head and shushes into my hair, murmuring over and over that everything is fine now.

When my crying subsides, I twist in his arms and crawl into him, burying myself in his chest. My jagged inhales take in his familiar scent that's mixed with leather from the jacket he's wearing, smelling masculine and oh so very real.

With my eyes still closed, I press my cheek against his chin, then reach up with my hand to touch his face, to feel his rough stubbled cheek and chiseled jaw. Next my fingers are combing through his hair then gliding around to his neck before I finally look up and open my eyes. I burst into tears again. It's really him.

Rising onto my knees, I throw my arms around his neck then pull back again to search his eyes. Deep sorrowful eyes that search mine.

"It's you. It's really you."

He gives a slight nod, his smile lighting up his eyes before smoothing my hair and frowning.

Instantly, my lips are on his mouth, his cheeks, his chin then I'm burrowing into his neck pressing in as deeply as I can.

"I don't understand," I say, pulling back again.

He rises to his feet then pulls me to mine before taking a step back and glancing down at my stomach.

My elation evaporates quicker than I'm breathing as he stays transfixed on my body and a sinking feeling invades me, causing my flushed body to break out into a cold sweat.

I reach out to grab his forearm and step in.

"Alex."

With both hands, he takes hold of my protruding stomach, then meets with my concerned eyes, his face splitting in to a massive grin before sighing. His eyes glaze over before he's grabbing me by the back of my neck and pulling me in to kiss me passionately, holding firm before realizing there's a bump to be careful of and stepping back again.

"Oh, Princess, God, I've been worried about you," he says, cupping my cheek. I lean into his hand to feel closer to him, to make sure he is real. "Are you all right? Are you managing okay?" He glances toward the house, then back at me. "Please tell me it didn't get too bad before you left him. Jesus." He lets his hand fall away, then reaches for mine, turning us toward the house and walking.

I'm still in shock, but more than that, the sinking feeling

is making me feel nauseous. He didn't seem concerned to know I'm pregnant. It can only mean he's not staying. He's come to see if I'm okay, and then he will leave.

"Everyone believes you're dead, Alex."

He glances at me, wiggles his eyebrows and grins. "That was the plan."

"The plan? What happened? They found a body, Alex." I pull him to a halt.

"Are you happy here? Do you like Cannon Beach?"

"Alex! What happened?"

Twisting me so he can spoon me, he makes us look out toward the ocean and the flaming orange horizon. The beautiful sunset that minutes ago was tormenting me is now casting its last rays over the tops of the rose bushes, highlighting their beauty while Alex holds tight like he is absorbing me. The sensation is pure bliss.

"I had to do things I'm not proud of, Paige," he whispers against my ear, his face pressing against mine. "Things I can't tell you about, but they were just, and necessary."

I nod against his face. "But who did they find in the house? There was a dead body burned to a crisp."

"There are people, Paige. People who hate rapists and pedophiles with a passion. And even though Gerard knows people in high places, I know people who understand justice, and I needed justice for you." Alex clears his throat and lets me go. "You got any beer?"

I turn to face him. "What are you saying?"

Alex presses his finger over my lips and shakes his head. My eyes dart across his. I don't know how I feel. But if it's who I think he's talking about, I think it's *gratitude*. But I'm also scared for Alex. What has he done?

"You know, you left a hose on the other morning when you went off to work." Alex stuffs his hands in his pockets.

"You enjoy wasting water, don't you?" he pulls a cheeky grin, then heads toward the house.

"You've been watching me?"

"Maybe."

"Alex," I squeal, chasing him up the stairs and into the house. "Where have you been, how long have you been here?"

Alex marches down the hall and straight to the kitchen like he knows the place—pulls open the fridge and peers inside. I stand dumbfounded against the island bench.

"Alex." I move closer and brush my hand along his back.

"No beer then?" He pockets his hands again and rocks on his heels. "That chicken you made last week was nice." He smirks.

"Oh my God, that was you? I thought I was going nuts." I push on his chest and laugh, but my confusion returns to cloud my amusement.

Alex snatches hold of my hand and pulls me in, traces a finger along my eyebrow, then flicks me on the nose. "Want to come for a ride on my new bike? I need a beer."

I step back and take him in seriously. "What's going on? Because you're scaring me. How did you get money? And tell me who was in the beach house, Alex?"

"Let's just say I managed…" he holds up both palms at me, "not that I knew at the time. But I killed two birds with one stone. Figuratively."

"That's not an answer. Who was in the house and how did you get so much money? Those rose bushes out there must have cost a fortune."

"No doubt, so did my mom's headstone."

For a moment, we get lost in each other's eyes, then he takes a step closer and lifts my chin when I look to the floor.

"Thank you for doing that. I was going to," he whispers. "But I had some shit to do first." Dropping my chin, he perks up. "Come for a ride with me."

"I'm not sure I should. Sheree thinks… No, wait. Was it—you who put the rose on the bookshelf?"

"It was." He zips up his jacket. "Are you coming? Grab a jacket."

Rushing into my room, I grab a jacket that will fit and follow Alex out the door.

"When I saw the rose, I thought it was either your ghost or Gerard," I tell him, scurrying to keep up.

"You won't have to worry about Gerard, Princess. I doubt he'll be showing his face around anymore."

"How do you know?"

Reaching his bike, Alex hands me a helmet. "You sure ask a lot of questions."

"And I will until you answer them."

Alex pauses at putting his helmet on. "Gerard followed you here."

My blood rushes into a flurry, making me glance around.

"I've been watching him watching you. He's not dead. But he's gone. And he won't be back. I guarantee it."

"You do?"

"I do. Now helmet up, woman, I'm dying of thirst."

When I don't take the helmet from him, Alex sinks onto the bike seat and folds his arms. "I'm not going to give you details, Paige."

"No. It's not that, it's…" I shift around on my feet, reluctant to spoil our reunion but I need to make sure Alex knows about someone so close to him.

"Alex." I step in, pause for a moment to express my seriousness and ready myself to console him. "Do you—Do you know about Grace?"

He nods, but I've made him pensive.

"I'm so sorry. I went to see Jolene. You know, when I left Gerard. I wanted to meet them. I had something to give her, but she was already gone."

Alex rests his hands on his head and draws a deep breath.

"Are you okay? Do you know if Jolene is okay?"

"She'll be fine. I helped her move." He rises off the bike and takes hold of his helmet.

"That was you?"

He nods.

"I wish I'd meet them now, to see what Grace looked like. Was she pretty? Do you still think she was Gerard's?"

Alex shrugs, his breathing notably deeper. After a moment he reaches inside his jacket and produces his phone. He scrolls before handing it to me.

When I see what he is showing me, my heart races.

"Oh my God, is this really her. This is Grace?" I look between him and the phone.

Alex leans forward and checks the screen of his phone. "Yeah, why?"

I can't stop staring, trying to rationalize what I'm seeing. Confused, but also certain. The dark curly hair. The big brown eyes. The heavy-set eyebrows. She's young and she's cute but…

"What is it?"

I reach out for his arm, then look up at him.

"You remember Annabel, don't you?"

Alex nods, his face mapped in curiosity.

"Alex, Grace is the spitting image of Annabel's husband."

Alex flinches. "What do you mean?" Having met Stuart at the Brave Hearts fundraiser, Alex takes the phone from me and studies the image.

"What I mean is… Do you think it's possible Gerard somehow swapped babies? I mean Grace and Katie are the same age. And…Oh my God." I stare at Alex bug-eyed, unsure I want to voice what I'm thinking. "How could I have not seen how much Katie looks like Gerard?" I stumble backward and cover my cheeks. "And Stuart told me himself that he had some bad gene in his family. That's why the DNA sample Gerard had taken came back negative. He must have swapped their babies!"

Alex looks skeptical. When he mulls over the possibilities, he shrugs. "How?"

"Gerard's sister, Casandra. That's how." The triumph of my discovery is laced with contempt.

Still not understanding, Alex shakes his head.

"Alex. She's a neonatal nurse at the children's hospital in LA"

"Well fuck me." Alex hands me a helmet. "Now I really do need a drink."

With an elbow resting on the table, cradling his chin and watching me finish my meal, Alex plays with my feet under the table. Our eyes are locked, and it seems we're both asking question of each other we don't verbalize. We talked over the possibilities of Grace and Katie being swapped drawing the conclusion of a stalemate. Was it fair to take Katie away from Stuart? Would it be right to reunite her with Jolene? There were just too many what ifs to sort through in one night. Instead we put the conversation to rest for the time being so I could cook up a quick meal that Alex devoured and I'm having trouble fitting in.

I pick up a piece of lettuce leaf, pop it into my mouth, and chew it slowly. My eyes are still glued to Alex.

"How you're so fat, I'll never know." He grins.

I kick him under the table.

"Do you like your job?"

"Uh, huh." I nod.

"What's with the cat?" he asks, looking at Napoléon curled up on the couch.

I wave my fork in the air. "He owns the place."

"Does he now?"

"Uh, huh." I nod again and smile, then place my fork down and push my plate away.

Alex sighs and starts picking at the label on his bottle, throwing the shavings onto his empty plate, then looking around the house.

"You seem settled here. Is it home?"

I don't answer right away. Not because I don't know the answer, but because it feels like he's checking off boxes. Even though Alex is alive—my God—he's alive. I revel in the reality and smile. But my thoughts still wander. Is he checking off points so he can comfortably leave? I can't blame him. I'm now free, but I'm carrying another man's child. He didn't want a relationship in the first place, and now there is more of me.

"Are you going away again, Alex?"

He jerks upright. "Do you want me to go?"

"No. Of course not. No way. Are you kidding? I love you, Alex. I've never loved anyone more in my entire life. But…"

Alex flinches. "But what?"

"Come on. You didn't eye off my huge stomach earlier because you were astounded I could swallow a small melon whole and survive. I'm twenty-five weeks pregnant."

"You are?" Pushing out his chair, Alex stands and grabs his jacket as though he's getting ready to leave.

The look of shock on my face makes him laugh, and then he's sitting down again and reaching for my hands. "So, tell me again. What's the 'But?'"

Oh God, I can't believe he's going to make me come out and say it. My face crumbles, and now I can't even look at him. Instead, I mumble into the table. "Do you really want to be a father—to Quin?"

"Is that what you're calling our son?"

My head snaps up. Is he saying what I think he's saying? I'm overwhelmed that he's even prepared to say that. "Really, that's how you'll think of him, as your own son. You're planning on staying. With me—with us?"

Alex pulls back a little, frowning, then scratches his ear. "What do you mean? He is mine, isn't he? Or did you…"

"No. Don't be crazy. You were the only one for me, Alex. But you must realize he's Gerard's."

Alex's face splits into a broad grin, and he huffs. "No fucking way. Have you been thinking it's his kid all this time? Didn't you know? Didn't he tell you? Of course, he wouldn't have told you." Alex answers his own question with venom. "He had a vasectomy fucking years ago. Right after Grace was born. Well maybe Katie. Fuck that's still a head spin."

I'm shocked into silence before I well up in tears, then leap from my chair to sit on his lap and hug him.

"But—there was only the one time without protection. How can that happen?"

Alex scrutinizes me with a funny look on his face like I'm daft. I hit him in the chest.

"Stop it."

"Fuck I love you, my brave queen. Why didn't you tell me?"

"I didn't know for a long time, and then when I knew, well, I assumed it was Gerard's because I kept getting my periods after that one time with you. I'd already laid enough on you." I place a palm over his cheek. God, and to think… I —I almost terminated him, Alex," I groan and rub my belly. When my eyes glaze over, Alex tightens his grip around me. "I was such a blind idiot, Alex."

"Don't go running yourself down. You've been through some heavy shit. And it can't have been easy."

"Do you really want to be a father, Alex? I mean—I love you, and I want you to be a part of Quin's life, but all that stuff you said—about your freedom. This shouldn't change that. I don't want to be the…"

Alex presses a thumb to my lips, shaking his head, then cupping my face, looking me straight in the eye. "I think it's safe to say I feel differently now." He places a hand over my hand, still resting on Quin. "And I didn't mean half that shit. I think I was just playing hard to get, hoping you'd chase me and leave the prick. Seems to work most of the time. But you." He pokes me in the chest. "You're fucking deep. That shit was never going to work on you. Even when I showed up with Genevieve, you played it cool."

When I scowl, he comes closer murmuring against my lips, "I never even slept with her, grumpy." I relax into his neck and plant small kisses there. "Do you know when I fell in love with you?"

I shake my head, still resting it on his shoulder.

"I fell head over heels in love with you that afternoon you came around when Tony was there. It was the first time you were being yourself. Shit, you looked beautiful when I opened the door. Throwing yourself at me like that."

Smiling, I draw in a deep breath. "Seems like we went to a lot of trouble just to get here," I say, rising from his lap.

"Abso-fuckin-lutely. But maybe that's what life's about. If it's gonna last between two people, you've got to go through shit and come out the other end without your baggage."

Looking down at my baby bump, I give Quin another rub. So grateful he's here. I look up at Alex.

"So, ask me again," he says.

"Ask you what?"

"If I'm leaving."

"Well, are you?" I smile, though the answer's written all over his face.

"Not a hope in hell."

Standing, Alex takes me by the hand and leads me toward

the bedroom. I twist my head back at the messy dining table and stretch my hand out. "But, Alex. The dishes," I playfully whine.

"Fuck the dishes, I want dessert."

Pushing me gently against the wall in the bedroom, Alex's hands wander all over me. Kissing me softly then growling when he tries to show some restraint, splaying his hands on the wall over my head and connecting our foreheads.

"Christ, it was hard staying away from you." He sighs. "I was going to. I swear. I thought, shit. She's gone through all that in her life, she needs time and space. I was just going to give you that sea of roses you wanted, to let you know I was still here. But then I saw you in the cemetery laying with my mom, rubbing this." He runs a hand over the belly between us. "I love you enough to set you free, Paige. If that's what you need. But I'll love you even more if you ask me to stay."

"Oh, god, yes. Stay. Please, oh please stay and never leave me again."

We stare at each other, our breathing matched in love and desire. Then slowly, he takes one hand and glides under my top to touch my bare skin, sending waves of pleasure that peak everywhere.

"I see you like my sweater," he whispers against my ear before kissing behind it.

"I haven't washed it since you gave it to me," I whisper back, my mouth finding his again.

"No wonder you smell," he says on top of my lips. "You're such a dirty girl, aren't you?"

I can't help laughing, pulling back to see his sexy eyes. To stare again at his beautiful mouth that spills crude things, but in the most sensuous way.

I love this man. He's everything a woman could want. He is all a woman needs. Someone strong in the bedroom as well as in his own skin. Someone flexible with their morals, but who can take care of your desires. Someone soft when it matters, but tough when it counts. Someone who will love completely without giving away themselves.

Kissing me again, I'm still pressed up against the wall when his hands become urgent and he rips up the sweater. His fingers softly pinch at my nipples, then they're sliding, clawing to get under my bra. I reach behind my back, trying to help by unfastening the clasp. But his lips are on my neck, biting, licking, kissing then giving me a hickey and distracting me. Aborting the task of my bra, I push on his chest. "Alex no, don't mark me."

"If I want to mark you, I will," he growls against my lips, grabbing me under the armpits and walking me back faster than my feet can go. He eases me down gently on the bed. And like a deer trapped in headlights, I watch, mesmerized as he slowly unzips his jeans, his smile so salacious and my need so strong, I think I might climax before he even takes me. Alex is here, and he wants me. He wanted to mark me so he can claim, 'This woman is with me.' I sigh deeply.

He squints his eyes. "I'm going to fuck you hard, Princess. So, if you don't want it, you better say no." His face splits into a big grin and he nudges me down on the bed, crawling over me when I chuckle at him. Straddling me, he looks at the protrusion between us again, then scratches his head and twists his smile.

"Hmm. Not sure how to tackle you with that in the way. Can you take it off for half an hour or so?" he asks, taking the bump in both hands and wiggling gently, then smiles before coming in for another kiss and whispering, "No, I'll be gentle, I promise."

"Do you even know how to do gentle, Alex?" I reply, pulling away and brushing a thumb over his pumped-up lips from all our kissing.

"Do I know how to be gentle?"

Ripping off his sweater and discarding his jeans, he's there between me and finding his way home inside my body. For a moment, he just stays there, both of us absorbing the sublime connection.

"Just warning you, Princess," he says thrusting gently, making love to me. "Once Quin is born, I'm going back to my old ways with you."

"Promise?"

"Promise."

"Good, because for whatever reason, Alex. I still like it when you're just that little bit rough."

ACKNOWLEDGMENTS

I have so many people to thank for helping me get the Bound by Infidelity trilogy published, even those who indulged me without judgment when I began with, "Yeah, so I'm writing a book," and I can assure you, there were plenty of unsuspecting ears, too many to name. But to all those who listened and didn't roll their eyes, thank you. Your interest and encouraging smiles helped me to believe in myself.

Firstly, I'd like to thank my husband Mick. Wow, what a journey you took me on to get me where I am today. Thank you for all your support and encouragement. For believing in my talent regardless of the lack of evidence to support the fact I have any. You have come through for me in so many ways.

Jay-Jay, you brave, patient, indulgent little girl of ours. Thank you for giving me the space to find my writer's voice. Those red flowers truly were a gift from beyond this realm. Without you handing them to me, I wouldn't have persevered to live this, my passion, my dream. A big shout out must also go to you for compiling the playlist. Songs that evoke the true essence of my story. It was a huge task and your selections and ear for music is to be commended. The playlist can be found on Spotify.

Mare, I will never forget you. I dedicated the first book to you because you gave so much to me when I really needed the shove. Not just knowledge, praise, and encouragement but you also shared the pain of real-life tragedies that made me realize these stories need to be told and told in a way that brings empowerment to those who read them. While the topic of my story I know is too close to your bones to read, I hope I have done you proud. I feel honored that you shared so much with me even though we've never met face to face. I love you Mare, for making me forgive myself, for believing in myself, and most of all, for loving myself.

Kira, against your initial reluctance to read your mother's cringe-worthy erotic words, you sucked it up as my first reader. Thank you for being honest and then later, proud. It means so much to now have your admiration and constant encouragement.

To my beta readers that followed. Terrianne, Joy and Timma, thank you. Your feedback gave me more purpose, and my writing got better because I drew from all the experiences we women collectively share.

To developmental editor Cate Hogan. Thank you so much for pointing me in the right direction when assessing my first chapter. Your advice was paramount in crafting this novel to have readers wanting more.

Amber, thank you for beta reading and proofreading draft copies along the way. You did a great job daughter, and thanks for the deadly truth, "No mother. Never, ever use the word moist. EVER!"

To all my family members, thank you for your enthusiasm and undying encouragement. Tyson, my son, for taking me seriously and putting me onto a talented author by the name of Harry Colfer. While Harry's work is not in the same genre as mine, I drew inspiration from his talent then later got to know him which made the world of published authors not so intimidating. Note to mention he also loaned me his grammar guru wife to go over my work.

A massive big thank you to second editor Marni MacRae. Not only is Marni a published author herself, but a fantastic resource who goes above and beyond. I'm so glad I found you Marni. Getting praise and help from another author is truly a gift.

Thank you to those of you who received an ARC and said they loved it. I appreciate your interest and for reading my debut work.

Thank you, author Gerard Byrne for allowing me the use of an excerpt from his novel, © Nemesis Publishing Limited / Gerard Byrne - *No Man's Audience.* You can purchase his interesting and well written book here.

Thank you to all those authors, song writers, bloggers, platforms and writing aids that help writers become published authors. Your advice and online services have been a godsend and truly invaluable.

And finally, the biggest thanks need to go to you, dear reader. Thank you from the bottom of my very humble heart for buying my novel. I hope you enjoyed the fictitious representation of true-life drama as much as I enjoyed bringing it to life.

ABOUT THE AUTHOR

Ariana Keddie is the author of suspenseful, sexy, intriguing fiction. Growing up addicted to romance novels, it seemed a natural progression to hone her passion for writing to become a junkie of the craft. Spending most of her spare time researching the art of storytelling, Ariana hopes to resonate with an audience via her writer's voice. A voice she found while struggling with personal demons which became the inspiration behind her debut work, *Lured - The Unrivaled Serpent.*

In quick succession *Bound - The Catalytic Rose* was published followed by *Free - The Luminous Pearl* to complete the *Bound by Infidelity* trilogy.

A lover of animals, fine wine, and Byron Bay, when Ariana isn't behind her laptop, she spends her time helping her cowboy husband on their Queensland properties and creating memories with their family.

To find out more about Ariana Keddie visit
arianakeddie.com